AN
UNTIMELY
FROST

ALISON MUKHERJEE

authorHOUSE®

AuthorHouse™ UK Ltd.
1663 Liberty Drive
Bloomington, IN 47403 USA
www.authorhouse.co.uk
Phone: 0800.197.4150

Cover design by Pippa Greenwood
The photograph on the cover was taken by Bridget Langford

Published by AuthorHouse   09/13/2013

ISBN: 978-1-4918-7561-2 (sc)
ISBN: 978-1-4918-7562-9 (e)

Coventry City Council		
FML		
3 8002 02137 888 2		
Askews & Holts	Nov-2013	
	£12.95	

For Orpa the Moabite whose story is not
told in the Book of Ruth

GLOSSARY

bauma	daughter-in-law
bindi	coloured dot worn on forehead as decoration
churidar	used by Bengalis to refer to long top and matching trousers (women)
jhol	spicy liquid surrounding pieces of fish, meat or vegetable
kajol	traditional eye cosmetic
karela	bitter gourd
khichuri	a dish of lentils and rice cooked together
khopa	hair styled in a bun
luchi	deep-fried flat bread
lungi	a piece of cloth wrapped round the lower body as a garment (men)
machcher jhol	fish cooked in a spicy liquid
masi	mother's sister
mishti	sweets made from thickened milk or curd
panjabi	long, loose round-necked top (men)
potol	a green vegetable, cylindrical with tapered ends
pujari	Hindu priest
rabindrasangit	songs written by Rabindranath Tagore 1861-1941

ruti	chapatti, flat bread
sak	edible leaves, spinach
shraddh	a Hindu ritual honouring the deceased
tawa	circular metal plate used for cooking ruti
tikka	ornament worn on head

CHAPTER ONE

ONE END OF the room was taken up by a wide bay window and patio doors filled the opposite wall. I loved these large areas of glass and the high ceiling which further increased the sense of space. On sunny days brightness entered and set the place alight while dull days brought their dreariness inside with them. In sunshine you would say the walls were blue—holiday sky above the sea— but when it rained they turned a murky grey. Today the movement was reversed. The mood of desolation emanating from Namita filled the room and spread out across the neglected garden where groundsel choked the borders and tangled grass grew wild.

I visited Namita and Jenny every Sunday and recently I'd taken to dropping in one evening during the week as well. I was Namita's elder daughter-in-law and lived in the south of the city. Jenny, on the other hand, moved into the family home when she married the younger son.

Namita didn't look up when I came into the room or acknowledge my presence in any way. Formerly a proud and upright figure, she now sat slumped forward in her chair, staring at the floor. Although it was late morning she was still wearing her dressing gown which was grubby round the cuffs and stained where she'd spilt coffee down the front. Her hair looked as if she'd pinned it up the previous day then slept on it all night.

I shuffled around trying to get comfortable on the sofa which was one of those you were supposed to sink into. I preferred something firmer and would have sat in Pradip's high-backed chair if Namita hadn't already occupied it by the time I arrived. Pradip's chair was crudely made, legs and arms not smoothly finished, the upholstery rather coarse. He found it going cheap in a small father and son furniture store and insisted on buying it, in spite of Namita's protests that it didn't match her colour scheme. It's comfortable he said, that's what matters. Never mind your colour scheme.

Jenny smiled at me across the room and immediately I was aware of a place inside me I'd forgotten all about until it was warmed by her smile. When Jenny smiled the skin around her eyes crinkled. I read somewhere that was how you could tell if a smile was genuine or just for show. A real smile involved the eyes while a pseudo smile was confined to the curve of the lips and the effect this had on the cheeks. I returned Jenny's smile and wondered whether the skin around my eyes crinkled in the same way.

'How you doing, Ann? Busy?' Fair hair framed Jenny's oval face and hung round her shoulders. Her skin was translucent and delicate as porcelain.

I shook my head. 'Things slow down a bit after Easter. Most of my students are on study leave while they do their exams so there's fewer lessons to prepare and less marking. How about you?'

'I'm okay. Bit tired. Mum isn't too good though, are you?' She reached out and gently rubbed the back of Namita's hand. Namita ignored the gesture. 'We were just going to try some massage. Come on, let's have a go. It'll help you relax then maybe you'll get some sleep.'

Jenny positioned herself behind Namita's chair, loosened the dressing gown then eased the nightdress down to expose bones without a covering of flesh. Resting her fingers lightly on the older woman's shoulders, Jenny moved her thumbs in a circular rhythm from the base of the neck down the valleys on each side of the spine, across shoulder blades and back up to the starting point, then slid them down again in a smooth curve. She stooped slightly, concentrating, making sure she applied pressure evenly as if she expected Namita's bones to yield, her muscles to soften and relax.

'Doesn't change anything,' Namita's voice blew in from frozen Siberia. 'Doesn't make things any better.'

'But I've got to try something, Mum. I can't just sit here and watch you get worse.' Jenny glanced in my direction and, not for the first time, I noted the deep shadows under her eyes. Namita's depression was a dark pit threatening to pull everything into its depths

'You're the one who said we had to go on as normal. Remember?' Jenny's hands continued their fluid movements while she talked. 'Get washed and dressed every day, that's what you said. Eat properly, never skip a meal. Keep yourself busy, don't sit around moping. And that's what we're doing, Ann and me, but you've stopped trying. You can't give up. We won't let you.'

It was true. In the early days, soon after it happened, Namita was the determined one who refused to give in to despair. Her response to the tragedy was to keep moving as if by doing this she could hold the terrible truth at bay. Jenny's reaction was just the opposite; she collapsed completely in a state of shock. Then, as though the sum of available energy was finite, the roles of the two women reversed. Jenny revived and resumed normal life while Namita became increasingly morose. Now it was Jenny's turn to nurse her mother-in-law back into the world of the living. Meanwhile I watched them from the sidelines, persuading myself and others I was independent and strong.

Jenny sucked in her cheeks as she worked. Her hair flopped forward so that she had to pause every now and then to tuck it back behind her ears. Ironic that Jenny should have Anglo-Saxon colouring, pale gold hair, blue eyes, strawberry cheesecake complexion, whereas my hair was only a couple of shades less black than my husband's. And my eyes, according to him, were the colour of treacle. Ironic because Jenny immersed herself in everything Indian following her marriage whereas I remained a visitor, an English guest. I don't mean to imply they treated me unfairly, on the contrary, the choice was mine. I had no intention of being absorbed into the family or of adopting their ways. Damned if I was going to abandon Radio Three in favour of incessant rabindrasangit and eat curry seven days a week.

Jenny made her hands rigid and delivered a series of little chopping blows the length of Namita's shoulders from right to left and back again. It had taken Jenny many months of patient practice to acquire these skills. Chandan teased her at first and told her it was a wife's duty and privilege to massage her husband's feet when he came home tired in the evenings. But Jenny persisted and her dedication bore fruit. When Pradip strained his back as a consequence of over-enthusiastic activity in the vegetable patch, Jenny kneaded away his pain with mustard oil infused with crushed stems of ginger.

No one was foolish enough to suggest I learnt the art of massage, my hands were far too stiff and clumsy. I couldn't squeeze them through the biggest measuring hoop at Akash

Jewellers, even when they were lathered in soap, and the owner claimed the bangles I wore on my wedding day were the largest they'd ever made. I'd never been any good with my hands. At school I hated practical subjects, domestic science was the worst but needlework came a close second, because they provided teachers with an opportunity to humiliate me. Once I spilt a bowl of flour on the cookery room floor and was made to sweep it up while the whole class stood and watched. And when I accidentally cut a jagged hole in the piece of gingham I was embroidering, the teacher held it up for everyone to see. But I was strong and I used this to my advantage. I impressed the other children in the playground by splitting apples clean in two with my bare hands.

My husband Mohan loved my hands. He would grab hold of them, order me to close my eyes and with his forefinger scratch letters on my palms, lightly so it tickled. I had to guess the letters and work out each word until he'd finished the sentence, usually something very rude. As I thought of this my palms began to itch unbearably and I was forced to rub them on my skirt to relieve the yearning for his touch.

Jenny moved her hands up to Namita's face, brought her fingers together at the centre of the narrow forehead and began working outwards, stretching the skin to remove all tension. She stroked her finger tips along the line of

Namita's eyebrows and into the little hollow at the outer corner of each eye.

'Why do I have to keep trying? There's no point.' Namita turned her body towards the fireplace as if to further disengage herself from what was happening in the room. I well understood that state of mind but I also knew the danger of succumbing to it. When you fall in love the whole of creation in vivid clarity rejoices with you, but when the loved one dies the opposite occurs. You can't comprehend how the world continues to exist without the one who is the sum of your existence.

'Have you got a headache, Mum? Shut your eyes, I'll make it better.' Jenny withdrew silver hair pins, placed them in Namita's lap and began to unravel the tangled plait.

'I'm sure Namita's had enough of being pummelled for one day,' I said irritably. 'Come on, you look tired. Sit down for a minute.' I made space for Jenny beside me on the sofa. She looked at me over Namita's head, pleading with me to be patient for a little longer.

'My whole body aches not just my head,' Namita murmured.

'Let me sort your head first then everything else'll get better too. Hang on a minute, I'll fetch some oil.' Jenny brought her lips neatly together in the way she often did at the end of an utterance, as if she was swallowing a final mouthful. As she passed me on her way to the kitchen she whispered, 'Say something, Ann. Please.'

I looked at the figure huddled miserably in Pradip's chair. In the dozen years since my marriage, conversation had never flowed naturally between us. Namita blamed me for stealing her elder son, I was sure of that, and I suppose I'd never been totally convinced Mohan would put me before her if it came to choosing. So I'd done little to endear myself to her. All the same, I did genuinely admire Namita's determination and her many achievements. At least I used to admire them. I wished she would show more of that spirit now.

'I don't think you appreciate how much Jenny does for you, Namita. And Miss Walker from number 47 calls in to see you sometimes, doesn't she? But you've got to make an effort yourself. In the end it's down to you.' Namita shifted her position and I thought I detected a tightening of her jaw.

Jenny came back carrying a little stainless steel dish in which she'd placed a white chunk of solid coconut oil. This quickly melted as she rubbed it into her hands before working her fingers up under the straggle of Namita's hair.

'Miss Walker popped in again to see Mum yesterday. She kept away at first, now she comes round most afternoons.' Jenny's fingers explored every inch of Namita's scalp.

Without warning Namita got to her feet, pushing Jenny's hands away as she did so. Thrown off balance Jenny stumbled sideways against the coffee table. Silver hair pins dropped onto the carpet. Steel dish clattered in the hearth. In the garden startled sparrows flew up sharply from their perches. A cat on the front lawn sped off through the gate.

'Hey, be careful!' I reached out and grabbed Jenny's arm to steady her. 'What's wrong, Namita? What's the matter?'

Namita's thin body shook with rage. Her eyes were round and prominent, black dots inside enormous white rings.

'You talk about Miss Walker! What does she know? Has she got sons, has she got a husband? Miss Walker has no idea. Cleans her windows and polishes her door knob and helps out in the Oxfam shop. She knows nothing. You two, you think you understand because you've lost your husbands. So what? You can marry again. You English always marry again. Tell me, how long have you been married? Six years? Twelve? Pradip Kumar married me more than forty years ago. Think of that! Mohan came first then Chandan and all these years I've loved them with a mother's love. Do you think a wife loves her husband as much as a mother loves her sons? You two, you know nothing.' Namita jabbed her finger in the direction of Miss Walker's house, then at Jenny and me and finally at her own chest.

'Don't I have the right to sit and mourn? Do you think coconut oil on my head and kind words in my ear will make a difference? My life's been cursed from the beginning, since Pradip Kumar took me from my father's house and brought me to this country. Cold and damp and grey. A country of ghosts where you can drive mile after mile and see no-one walking. A country where the prettiest girls dress always in black. My sons stepped in the white man's shit and chose English wives. What good are they to me, these daughters-in-law who don't give me grandchildren? I've lost a husband and two sons and their unborn babies. And you tell me to make an effort?'

Namita hurried over to the desk in the corner by the bay window, pulled out the heavy lower drawer and dragged it to the middle of the room. She tipped the contents onto the carpet and tore open the coloured cardboard files, spilling out wodges of correspondence, bank statements, bills and receipts. Jenny stretched out a hand to rescue the documents but I held her back. I thought it was best to let the frenzy take its course. We stood and watched as Namita stamped on the heap of papers as if she hoped to grind them underfoot. When she saw they couldn't be ground she crouched down and crumpled them by handfuls.

'How dare he leave me, how dare he! What do I care about assets and creditors? He kills my sons and leaves me with a pile of papers, boasts he's left me enough money to live on. I don't want his bloody insurance policies.' She struck her forehead repeatedly with her open palm. 'Why did he have to kill both my children? Couldn't he have left one alive? They went off to buy paving stones for his damn garden. Said they wouldn't be more than an hour and never came back. No warning, no goodbyes. I want a chance to hold them, speak to them one more time. Please, oh please, just once more.' Her voice shrank to a whisper.

As Namita's mania subsided Jenny begged her to come and sit down. Between us we half carried her back to her chair where she slid to one side as if she'd lost the will to hold herself erect. Jenny crouched beside her and stroked her hair. Oil dribbling from the upturned dish deepened the mottled marble patterns on the hearth. In the garden dandelion seeds drifted aimlessly across the unkempt lawn.

For a while no one spoke. I looked at the fireplace and thought of the many disputes it had caused between Pradip and Namita. Was it really carved from stone or a concrete imitation? Namita would argue for its authenticity while Pradip infuriated her by pretending to trace the marks of the mould in which it had been cast. She defended her opinion with conviction and he mocked her for being so easily fooled. Now Pradip was dead and the origins of the fireplace no longer mattered.

'There's nothing left for me in this country. I'm going back where I belong, where I don't need to explain.' Namita's voice was flat, retaining no hint of its former passion.

'You belong here, Mum! Of course you do.' Jenny took Namita's limp hand and held it tight. 'You and Pradip were living in this house before I was born!'

'The myth of return,' I sat back with folded arms. 'It's a well known phenomenon. People think they can go back and pick up where they left off but when they try to do it they find it's impossible to adjust because they've been away too long.'

'And what would happen to me if you went away? I'd have nowhere to live.' Jenny peered into Namita's face.

'You can go your own ways.' Namita looked at each of us in turn. 'I'm giving you my blessing.'

'But I don't want to go my own way!' Jenny protested. 'I want to go with you.'

'Perhaps you could visit your family in Kolkata and stay for a while to see how it works out,' I suggested. 'Then if you do decide to live there permanently, you could come back and sort out your affairs. That would give Jenny time to make her own plans.'

'Perhaps.' Namita sounded unconvinced.

'Mum's not well enough to travel on her own though.' Jenny pulled herself up onto the sofa beside me. 'I'd have to go with her.'

'I can travel by myself,' Namita said. 'I'm not an invalid.'

'Of course you're not, I said. 'And Jenny wouldn't be much help anyway. She's not used to plane journeys. Personally I think you two need to spend some time apart.'

'I'm not trying to take her away from you.' Namita looked at me coldly.

Maybe not, but someone always did. I made my first real friend the day I arrived at university, like me she was more interested in discussing Dostoevsky and Descartes than going to the Freshers' Ball. Our friendship lasted one full term. We would lunch together after lectures then walk over to the library and work side by side, swapping books and reading each other's essays. Then someone warned her she'd never get a boyfriend if she hung out with me and after that she kept her distance. Jenny turned and gave me a reassuring smile.

'Listen Jenny,' Namita said. 'It's very different out there, in Kolkata I mean. You don't know Bengali and you won't understand so many things.'

'I can learn. I know I haven't done much travelling but at least I'd be company for you. I always wanted to go to India. Take me with you, Mum. Please?'

While Namita went upstairs to have her shower and Jenny was busy in the kitchen preparing lunch, I went into the garden in search of fresh air and solitude. Namita's outburst left me feeling nauseous, overt expressions of intense emotion had that effect on me. Out here in the garden I could give myself up to memories of Pradip and the hours he spent working this earth. I wandered along the path noticing the weeds which sprouted between the flagstones, indeed the whole place had a dejected air. The first spring mowing was long overdue and I could see dandelions and docks half hidden in the ragged grass. Pradip would have been horrified, he was obsessive about maintaining this lawn. From spring through to autumn neighbours would visit each other's gardens and argue over whose lawn was the greenest, the flattest, had the least moss. Now as they walked along Queen's Road and peered through the side gate, the neighbours must have felt sad to see its unkempt state.

Pradip's beloved greenhouse stood at the end of the path. His sanctuary, a place of peace. Once when I went to call him in for food I discovered him standing there quietly watching wasps eat greenfly. The greenhouse still harboured last year's plants and white scum covered the surface of dry compost. By now the wooden staging should have been bursting with new green seedlings in little terracotta pots, each bearing its white name tag in a script I couldn't read. Chillies, tomatoes, okra, aubergines, karela, Pradip's personal hybrids created by chance and design, cross-pollinated varieties from around the world.

In the adjourning vegetable patch dried yellow tendrils of last year's runner beans clung to the canes of a misshapen wigwam. A few oversized pods, bulging grossly, dangled from withered stems. I ripped open the tough skin of one and extracted four shiny beans, dappled mauve and black, held them in my palm and studied their unexpected beauty.

Namita was a purist when it came to food. She would use Pradip's home grown vegetables to accompany an English roast but for Bengali dishes she preferred to buy the genuine article from the Asian grocers. She wouldn't even try using trout or salmon in her curries but insisted on dispatching Pradip to the Bangladeshi shop on Sunday mornings to buy ilish and rui before the new delivery was piled into one of the chaotic freezers.

'Keep the two cultures separate,' she said. 'I'll cook cod or plaice with chips but I won't use them for machcher jhol.' Pradip told her cultures evolved, they didn't drop down perfect from on high. He said her beloved harmonium had been introduced to India by Europeans and that tea was not commonly drunk there until the English popularised it.

Jenny stood in the doorway watching as I walked back to the house. Even now, though tired and casually dressed, she looked lovely and I felt plain and ungainly beside her. The feeling was familiar, I towered above most women and certainly couldn't be called beautiful. When I was a child my father forecast, Ann will grow into a fine figure of a woman but she'll never be pretty. And he was right. Individually my features were good, full lips, large eyes set well apart, broad straight nose, but somehow the combined effect was rough and unfinished.

'It's a mess, isn't it?' Jenny indicated the garden. 'I must work out how to use the mower. It was always Pradip who cut the grass, wouldn't let anyone else near it.'

'And the greenhouse, what'll happen to that?'

'Don't know. It's for Mum to decide not me but she doesn't go into the garden much. Only to look at the cherry blossom.' Jenny nodded in the direction of the prunus which was pink and white and sugary like mounds of coconut ice with a sprinkling of crumbs on the lawn beneath.

'Everyone finds it beautiful, petals scattered on grass. Why is that?' I put my head on one side. 'Rather like showering the happy couple with confetti. Autumn leaves falling to the ground are beautiful too but with a hint of sadness. A light covering is most appealing, not too deep.'

'Like in the park after the fair, you mean? Beer cans and litter all over the grass,' Jenny said and we both laughed. It felt good to laugh after Namita's histrionics.

'Ann, will you talk to her? Tell her you went into the garden and noticed it's in a mess.'

I protested, 'Hey, that's not fair! You're the resident daughter-in-law, her favourite. Why don't you say something?'

'I try to but she won't listen. Mum won't make up her mind about anything.'

'That was a clear decision just now, announcing she's going back to India.'

'Bit of a surprise though. Out of the blue. You'd think she'd let me know what she was planning, not just come out with it like that. Mum used to say, individualism is the curse of the West. She said English families break up because they don't have meals together, don't talk to each other enough. And now she doesn't talk to me.' Jenny looked down at the step as she turned to go inside. Her hair fell forward on either side of her neck revealing a vulnerable little triangle of skin.

She went over to the cooker and began stirring the contents of a saucepan. 'D'you want some of our khichuri? I won't have mine yet. I'll wait till Mum's finished her shower. She won't eat properly if I don't eat with her.'

Typical Jenny, putting other people's needs before her own. I'd told her many times she should be more like the students in my class who aspired to be assertive and worshipped ambition and achievement. At twenty four Jenny was closer to their age than mine.

'No thanks,' I said. 'Put the kettle on and I'll make myself some toast.'

I prised frosty slices from a loaf which was stored in the freezer because no one ate much bread in this household.

Pradip used to say he'd have to be starving before he ate bread. Nasty tasteless stuff he called it, clinging to the roof of your mouth in a soggy lump. And Jenny went along with it.

'I've never seen Namita like that before,' I said. 'So much anger! Accusing Pradip of killing her sons. What nonsense! And the bit about grandchildren, very unfair. It's obvious I was never going to produce offspring but I thought you and Chandan wanted to start a family?'

'We did.' Jenny blushed. 'But he said we had to wait till the business was bringing in more money, so as we could pay the school fees. That was his plan, get married, build the business, have babies. Chandan was always making plans.' She stirred in silence for a while.

'You're right. Mum does say some terrible things but you can understand it. What happened was so terrible.' Jenny scooped a little of the yellow mixture onto the spoon and nibbled at it to test the seasoning before adding more salt. She replaced the lid and turned off the hob.

'She's been worse since the inquest. She was coping up till then but now she's lost interest. She won't come food shopping with me, never buys clothes. If we have visitors she won't talk to them. People talk about a broken heart, well maybe Mum's mind has broken as well. Bengalis think their hearts and minds are in the same place anyway.'

Jenny laid her hand across her chest to indicate the general location.

'Namita doesn't have a monopoly on grief,' I said.

Jenny handed me my coffee and sat down opposite. We held each other's gaze for a brief moment, just long enough to acknowledge the unspoken suffering behind each other's eyes.

'Look at you, eating burnt toast when you could've had a hot meal. What's wrong with my cooking anyway?' Jenny frowned and stuck out her bottom lip.

'Nothing's wrong with your cooking. Only I don't like soft and sloppy at lunch time. I prefer a bit of crunch. And, by the way, it's nicely browned not burnt. Look.' I waved my toast under her nose. A dimple appeared in her right cheek and she began to giggle.

Footsteps descended the stairs and we turned as Namita appeared in the doorway. Droplets streaked her face and dark patches were forming as her sweater soaked up the excess water. Her hair hanging loose round her shoulders had the effect of dragging her face down, making it appear even more hollow-cheeked and gaunt. She was dressed carelessly in un-ironed clothes, a shirt half tucked in and then abandoned, one trouser leg partially rolled up. She came and stood awkwardly in the middle of the room.

'I meant it, what I said before. I am going home, going to India I mean. But I've changed my mind about going on my own. You can come with me, Jenny, if you really want to. Think about it, you don't have to say straight off. I won't be upset if you change your mind.' Without waiting for an answer she hurried through the kitchen and out into the garden. We watched her pause for a while to trample fragile blossom into the grass before setting off down the path towards the greenhouse.

Jenny looked thoughtful. 'What Mum said before is true, isn't it? A mother's love is different. Seeing your own child die must be the worst thing ever. My mum says you aren't a real woman till you've had a baby. Well I've heard Asian women, old ones I mean, I've heard them say you don't know what it means to be a mother till you've lost a child. Specially a son. There's something about mothers and sons.'

'The Church certainly thought so,' I said. 'The Mother of God weeping for her son. It used the image to move the faithful to tears. Stabat Mater Dolorosa and all the mournful music that poem has inspired.'

'What?' Jenny made a face. She never feigned knowledge.

'Stood the Mother full of grief, a medieval Latin hymn about Mary watching Christ on the cross.'

'Oh.'

'Woman adoring man or, put another way, emotion worshipping spirit. Emotions are messy so of course they must be female and spirit is pure and rational so it has to be male,' I went on. 'I'm not convinced there's a hierarchy of grief though. Is the death of a child really worse?' Jenny got to her feet.

'It's sad because they've never had the chance to develop their potential. But when you think about it, an older relative or friend dying means you lose someone who's been around while you were growing up. So the loss is greater. And if you lose someone you didn't really love, well that's different again . . . .' Jenny moved over to the sink.

I went and joined her. 'Sorry, I shouldn't have wittered on like that. Why didn't you shut me up?'

We stared through the window in silence. At the far end of the garden a crooked hawthorn, dripping with white icing, snuggled into the armpit of a tall plane tree which swayed gracefully in the breeze. The leaves on the lower branches, trapped in circling currents, fluttered rapidly like moths near a light bulb or the wings of humming birds sucking nectar from a flower. Jenny lightly touched my arm to indicate forgiveness. I retrieved my coffee from the table but it was lukewarm. I preferred to drink it in cautious sips while scalding hot though Mohan insisted taste buds couldn't function at that temperature.

'What did Namita mean about assets and creditors?' I asked. 'Mohan's estate was tied up ages ago.' What a nightmare it had been. Mohan was so disorganised, no proper record of where his money went and no recognisable filing system to help me trace it. I'd made good use of the feelings of frustration this produced in me, converting them into sufficient energy to take me right through to probate. Though I'd been surprised by how little money remained after the process was complete

'Pradip's papers are all sorted. Mum gets muddled, doesn't listen properly when I tell her stuff,' Jenny said.

'And Chandan's business? Pradip's solicitor is dealing with it isn't he? I could find you someone better if you like.' I popped my mug into the microwave and resumed munching toast.

'The solicitor's fine. Everything's okay,' Jenny said with just a hint of impatience. She turned back to the window. Namita hands in pockets was pacing back and forth across the lawn. 'I hope she's right. I hope going to see her family in India will help.'

'Are you quite sure you want to go with her? I think it's a bad idea. You'd be much better staying here, take advantage of her absence and do the things you want to do for a change.'

'I'm sure. I really do want to go with her.' Jenny looked at me earnestly.

'It won't be like a holiday, you know. You'll spend all your time following her around.'

'That's why I'm going, to be with Mum. But that's not the whole reason. I want to go for myself as well. We planned to go to India one day, Chandan and me. He wanted us to see where his family comes from. Now it seems like a good way to get close to him.'

'For God's sake, Jenny! Chandan was born in England and spent his whole life here. He only visited Kolkata once, as a young child. What could you possibly find there that has anything to do with him?'

'It may sound silly to you but it's what I feel,' said Jenny quietly. 'Chandan would've wanted me to go. What about you? Wouldn't you like to see India?'

'I can't be persuaded to go with you if that's what you're asking. If I went to India it certainly wouldn't be to traipse around with my mother-in-law visiting relatives.' I brushed toast crumbs into the bin and rinsed my plate under the tap. 'That didn't come out right. I meant to say I don't think I owe Namita anything. But if you do insist on going I'll help you organise it. And drive you to the airport, of course.'

'Thanks,' said Jenny but her attention was on the figure in the garden. 'I'll just go and see if I can get her to come in for lunch.'

Chapter Two

I FIRST NOTICED Mohan at a staff meeting although he told me later he'd been trying to catch my attention for weeks. We were discussing student recruitment and I'd just spent ten minutes explaining how vital it was, in view of increasingly fierce competition from rival establishments, that we improve on last year's numbers if the college were to survive.

'I've arranged for a group of volunteers to put up posters in the usual places, libraries, schools, community centres, post offices.' I was busy outlining the departmental strategy when Mohan, who'd recently joined the staff, caught the attention of the Chair.

'Don't you find Ann's proposals pretty boring?' he said, jumping to his feet. 'I say forget the traditional venues. Let's be more adventurous! It's the only way we'll beat the opposition.'

He was well built though not particularly tall. The lines of his face with its finely chiselled nose and strong jaw were softened by the curve of his full cheeks. His words vibrated with energy which, at the time, I took to be enthusiasm for his plans but he confessed later was actually enthusiasm for me.

'I thought we'd try a stall in one or two supermarkets as well, just to see how that works,' I continued, determined not to be upstaged by this overconfident upstart.

'How about distributing flyers in fashion boutiques, cinemas, takeaways, pubs, night clubs even?' Mohan piped up again.

'Excuse me?' The Chair gave him a stern look. 'Will you please let Ann finish.'

'Then I've negotiated with the local press to run adverts as usual, full page ones this time, and inserting leaflets in the free paper means we'll reach every household,' I went on.

'Surely the best way to attract new students is to go wherever people are enjoying themselves?' Mohan turned to look straight at me without flinching. His eyes and mouth danced with infectious merriment. People were beginning to react and I was conscious of raised eyebrows and suppressed giggles.

'Mohan! Sit down will you?' The Chair slapped his palm flat on the table in front of him.

'That's when they'll listen to you. Don't underestimate the feel-good factor.' Mohan winked at me. 'Sorry. Nothing personal,' he lied. For of course it was intensely personal. I was tempted to put him in his place by exposing the impracticality of his suggestions one by one but the rippling laughter in his dark eyes flushed my cheeks and quickened my heartbeat. I could live in your smile, I thought. I could happily live forever in your smile.

'The adverts and leaflets contain information on a whole range of courses plus an invitation to our college Open Days,' I continued, trying to recover my composure. 'There are copies of the programme on the table. Please will you each take one and make a note of which days you need to be available to meet the public.'

I sat down and tried to work out how he'd got the better of me. This didn't happen to me. I was always ready with a clearly articulated response which left my opponent feeling embarrassed and their argument in tatters.

'Ann, perhaps you and Mohan could get together on this afterwards? He's obviously very keen,' said the Chair with a touch of mockery. More giggles, louder this time. 'Form a subcommittee. Probably too late for this year but you could put together something exciting for next summer. I'll leave that with you two, okay? Now let's look at item four on the agenda—outings and field trips.' He pressed on with the meeting.

I left the room in a haze and for the next few days the edges of my intellect were soft and blurry. As I read or typed or watched TV, the image of that irreverent, dark-eyed wink came between me and page or screen. At first I wondered if

Mohan had done it for a dare, on behalf of someone who wanted to put me in my place. No doubt there were a few such people amongst the staff. I set myself high standards and was outspoken when others were less principled. Yes, some had reason to resent me.

But I knew that couldn't be his motive because of the effect his laughter had on me. I was surrounded by it, caressed and glowing. His laughter was familiar to me from long ago, it took me back to childhood, to sandcastles and fairgrounds. I recognised it and yearned for more of it and I knew it belonged to me.

I could live in your smile. I could happily live forever in your smile.

I saw him again a few days later in the queue for the photocopier and when he asked me out I said yes even before he'd finished asking. Over the next few weeks we spent a great deal of time together. I took him to the Arts Centre where he sat obediently through concerts from Bach to Philip Glass and he took me to computer fairs to learn about the latest operating software. I invited him round to my flat and cooked for him and he insisted on washing up. When he came next time he brought the ingredients with him and cooked for me because he hadn't much liked my cooking and still insisted on washing up.

One evening as we sat on the settee, my legs stretched out across his lap so he could tickle the soles of my feet, I challenged him to describe what it was about me that had first attracted him. He placed his drink carefully on the carpet and looked at me thoughtfully with pursed lips and a slight frown.

'I'm not interested in glamorous girls with hourglass figures and in having a good time,' he said. 'Well I'm not *only* interested in having a good time. I want something more substantial, and I'm not referring to your figure! I don't have sisters, the woman I know best is my mother and she's a strong person with many layers to her character. That's what I like about you, Annie, you're complicated. Does that make sense?' He stroked the soles of my feet until my toes curled with pleasure. 'Besides, you've got great legs!'

Mohan retrieved his drink and drained it then reached for the bottle and replenished both our glasses. 'Your turn. Tell me what attracted you to me.'

'I would never have noticed you at all if you hadn't made a fool of yourself in that staff meeting. Not in a million years,' I informed him dryly. 'I simply succumbed to your flattery.'

Who could have resisted? He was clever and funny, had the most romantic eyes I'd ever seen, deep set under lids of smoked silk, and most importantly he adored me. They say opposites attract and we were certainly that. In repose Mohan's natural expression was a smile while mine was serious with a hint of irritable. When things went wrong he laughed and quickly forgot whereas I swore and fumed for hours. He fitted work round hobbies and enjoying himself while I managed to squeeze a bit of relaxation into my work schedule. He loved people and sought company while I tolerated colleagues, had no friends to speak of and was mostly content with solitude. He was kind and took pains not to offend while I said what I thought and damn the consequences. Anyone could see the benefit I derived from this relationship but what did he gain? Perhaps he needed someone to add weight to his existence as much as I needed someone to lighten mine.

Mohan understood, as no-one else ever had, that what others took for rudeness in me actually derived from my deep suspicion of the superficial. Brought up in polite society, I rebelled against the demands placed upon me to maintain an outward show of courtesy and good manners. I abhorred hypocrisy and could not ignore what was being said and done behind closed doors, the real thoughts behind masked faces.

At Sunday school my favourite story was the one about the two sons whose father asked them to help him in the vineyard. One said yes but did nothing. For me this represented all those who sucked up to their teachers and flattered their class-mates in order to secure their own popularity. I identified with the other son, the one who told his father to get lost but in the end came up with the goods.

Like him, I could be trusted when it really mattered. Mohan saw through the rough exterior to the honesty and loyalty which formed the centre of my being. He knew my heart was passionate and warm. If the exterior seemed brusque and uncaring this was only because I feared emotions running out of control and despised sentimentality.

My clothes are patterned on the inside.
Spirals and spots, chevrons and dots
hide within, next to my skin.
They see only loose ends and knots.

One day Mohan insisted on taking me home to meet his parents and younger brother. He unlocked the front door of their house in Queen's Road and ushered me inside. Following his example, I removed my shoes.

'Mum, Dad! Come and meet my friend,' he called into the hallway.

A tall, slim woman dressed in loose blue trousers and a white blouse appeared from a doorway on the left. Her hair was loosely tied back from her long, narrow face. She wore glasses and held a magazine in her hand. My immediate impression was of someone capable and confident. She beamed at Mohan, looked puzzled for a moment on seeing me, then corrected herself and smiled in my direction.

'Mum, this is Ann. Annie, meet my Mum. Also known as Mrs Das or Namita.'

Namita said, 'Hello, Ann. Lovely to meet you. Come along, come inside.' We followed her into the front room where I immediately noticed the large bay window and wide patio doors. Namita cleared a space on the sofa. 'Have a seat. Sorry it's so untidy. Mohan didn't tell us you were coming.'

'That's okay,' I said as I sat down. 'No need to apologise.'

'Living with three men! I don't know. Seem to spend half my time clearing up their things. So untidy, all of them,' she said indulgently.

'If it was me, I'd get them to tidy up their own mess,' I said.

Namita gave me a searching look. She abandoned the pile of junk on the floor and came and sat next to me.

'I'm so happy you've come to my house.' She removed her glasses and studied me intently. 'Mohan hasn't told me anything about you. Now you're here you can tell me yourself.'

This inspection at close quarters made me uncomfortable and I looked round for Mohan but he seemed to have disappeared. 'What do you want to know?'

'Where do you work? And where do your parents live? Do you have any brothers and sisters?' She broke into a polite smile. 'Lots of questions. Sorry. Sounds a bit like an examination!'

'Okay,' I said. 'In reverse order. I've got one brother—he's much older than me and I hardly ever see him.'

'That's a pity. Family is very important.'

'My parents live up North in the village where I was born.'

'That's nice,' she nodded. 'So they stayed in the same place. All their friends around them. A long way for you to go to see them though.'

'And finally, I teach English at City College. English language, that is, not literature.'

Namita received this last piece of information with enthusiasm. 'That's a good profession, teaching. That's what I do. Teaching assistant in a school, supporting children whose mother tongue isn't English. I've been doing it for years. Still love it.'

Mohan came back into the room and stood behind his mother, resting his hands affectionately on her shoulders. 'Mum's being modest. She's worked at the school for over twenty years, longer than anyone else on the staff. And she does much more than just support the kids. They made her responsible for training new recruits to the service city-wide. You even did a presentation for a group of head teachers the other day, didn't you?'

'You make it sound like I'm someone important,' Namita smiled up at her son. 'They only asked me because

I've been around so long. I've seen all their ideas come and go and come back again.'

As I turned my head I caught the look of pride on Mohan's face. Fine, I thought, I can live with that. But if I ever thought, even for one second, that your regard for her outweighed your love for me . . . .

Right on queue Mohan grabbed my hands and pulled me off the sofa. 'Come on, Annie. Dad's waiting to show you his garden.' He dragged me through the kitchen and out into the garden then propelled me in front of him along a narrow path running beside a beautifully kept lawn.

'Listen!' Namita called to us from the back door. 'I'm making tea. Don't let your Dad keep you out there too long.'

A crouching figure stood up to greet us as we approached. I recognised an older version of Mohan, the same stocky build, only in his father's case the bulk was more muscle than fat. As we drew nearer I realised Mohan had also inherited his beautiful eyes from his father's side. No wonder Namita had fallen for him. No, I'd got that wrong, their marriage was almost certainly the outcome of careful negotiations between their extended families.

'Hello, Ann.' Grinning widely Mohan's father stuck out his hand and I shook it regardless of the coating of soil. 'Welcome to my garden! You can call me Pradip, no Mr Das business. Come on, I want to show you round.'

Pradip proceeded to conduct me on a guided tour of the neat rows of vegetables, the flower borders and the greenhouse, accompanied by full commentary on each plant and the various techniques he used to cultivate them. We got on like a house on fire. I was able to sustain a lively conversation based on the knowledge I'd gleaned from my father who'd been a keen gardener all his life, although his gardening style was very different. Pradip's plants were evenly spaced in tidy rows, not a weed in sight, whereas my father favoured a casual, cottagey effect. As he showed me round Pradip insisted on giving me samples of every kind of produce so that by the time we eventually came in for tea I was laden with vegetables and fruit.

'I don't know why you're giving all this to Ann,' Mohan said, helping me unload my cargo onto the kitchen table. 'She can't cook.'

Pradip looked up from the kitchen sink where he was busy trying to remove all traces of soil from his finger nails.

'Really? Don't tell your mother that.' He winked at me and laughed. His laughter was loud and unselfconscious and made me want to laugh too.

Namita appeared in the doorway. 'Don't tell your mother what?'

'I was just saying, Dad's given Ann all this stuff but she can't cook.' Mohan pointed at the vegetables piled up on the table.

'She can learn,' said Namita.

'I'm not really interested in learning.' I hooked my arm through Mohan's and planted a light kiss on his cheek. 'I like eating but I'm not in the least bit practical. Mohan cooks well enough for both of us and he enjoys doing it.'

Namita looked displeased but made no further comment

We heard the sound of the front door being unlocked. Mohan called out, 'We're in the kitchen. Come and meet my friend Ann.'

A few moments later a young man dressed in jeans and sweat shirt stuck his head round the door. Tall and skinny and wearing a serious expression he bore more resemblance to his mother than his father.

'This is Chandan, our youngest son,' Namita beamed. 'In his last year at uni. Business studies degree.'

'Going to make the family fortune, aren't you son?' Pradip rolled his sleeves up to the elbow and made a start on his face and neck. 'Going to turn his old man into a millionaire.'

Chandan looked embarrassed. 'Hello,' he said nodding at me. There was an awkward silence.

Namita poured Bombay mix into a bowl. 'We're just going to have tea.'

'Sorry. Got to make some urgent calls.' Chandan disappeared abruptly and we heard him ascend the stairs in leaps and bounds.

'Chandan! Come back here. You can make your phone calls later.' Namita followed him into the hall.

'Let him go!' Pradip shouted after her. Under his breath he added, 'Young people today. Always in a hurry.'

Later Mohan told me how difficult it had been for his mother when she arrived in Britain. Perhaps he sensed a hint of animosity between us and hoped these insights would win my sympathy. Namita had come as a new bride, Mohan said. At first she wore saris and put vermilion in the parting in her hair. She would go out in search of familiar vegetables and spices and come home with tears trickling down her cheeks because of the rude stares and unkind comments she attracted. At sunset and sunrise she opened her windows, hoping to catch the sound of the conch being blown in one of the nearby Hindu households.

She didn't feel at home with other Bengali wives, Mohan explained, because although she and Pradip were from East Pakistan, as it was then, unlike most other East Pakistanis they were not Muslim. No one was openly hostile but differences in diet and family traditions left Namita feeling isolated. Some of the men from West Bengal secretly despised Pradip because he'd never been to medical college and was their social inferior by many degrees. In the early days Pradip would go along to join in the winter celebrations organised in honour of Saraswati, goddess of music and the arts, but he always finished up in the kitchen scraping khichuri off plates or collecting discarded paper cups from under the tables. 'Ask Pradip bhai to do it, he won't mind.' Slowly Pradip withdrew from Bengali society, turning to fellow workers in the factory for friendship and spending hours engrossed in rambling conversations with his neighbours in the pub. And, of course, he took up gardening.

Namita soon realised she must create a network for herself so she enrolled for English classes and picked up enough Punjabi and Gujarati to allow her to widen her range of friends and contacts. Then, when Chandan started school, she took a part-time job supporting immigrant children in the classroom. Mohan saw this as the turning point. Receiving a salary increased his mother's self-confidence, he said, and gave her a measure of financial independence. Namita's colleagues paid regular visits to their families in India and she longed to do likewise. Mohan remembered overhearing the same conversation year after year.

'Are you never going to take us back?' Namita began. 'The boys should get to know their relatives. I want my sons to be proud of where they come from.'

'Use your brain, woman! They come from this city. This is where they're growing up,' Pradip replied.

'You know what I mean. I want my boys to be proud of the blood in their veins.'

'Their blood is made from the food they eat here,' Pradip pointed out. 'There's nothing of Bengal in their veins. Especially Chandan, he's entirely made in England.'

'But *I'm* not! I want to see my brothers' children? Won't you let me see my mother before she dies?' Namita persisted.

'Go by yourself if you want to. Don't ask me to come.'

'Shameful! You think I'd go home leaving my husband here to look after himself? What would people say?'

'None of our relatives live in Dhaka any more, they've all escaped to West Bengal so you wouldn't really be going home at all.'

'Home is where the heart is,' said Namita grandly.

'Well my heart is here. Anyway I can't go in the summer. Don't even suggest it. My plants need watering twice a day.'

'You could ask someone to do it for you. You've got plenty of friends.'

'No one would do it properly. A quick wave of the watering can, you can't expect a neighbour to do more than that.' Pradip was growing impatient.

'We could eat fresh mangoes, langra, phajli, himsagar,' she tempted him.

'I can buy you boxes and boxes of delicious mangoes from Pal Brothers.'

'Will you take us at Christmas then? Nothing happening in the garden in the winter.'

'Woman, leave me alone. Can't you see I don't want to go? They charge twice as much at Christmas anyway.'

'What about Easter? Will you take us then?' Namita was desperate.

'Too hot. The boys couldn't stand it.'

They only went together once. Mohan remembered how much he loved it. Freedom to play where he wished without being told off for dirtying his clothes or messing up the house. But Chandan found it confusing. He mooched around clutching a cuddly bear as if he was clinging on to a symbol of normal life. One morning he wondered aloud whether the other Chandan, the one back in England, was eating his breakfast cereal. Namita thought his infant brain just couldn't cope with the adjustment.

Pradip never took them again. He believed in putting down roots, he said, in being content with where he lived and with being the thing he had become. He didn't see himself as a displaced person, an economic migrant, an exiled minority. He was simply Pradip Kumar Das, take it or leave it. By the time I arrived on the scene, he was able to expound his philosophy with some fluency.

'Listen to me, I'll explain. We're individuals in our own right. We're not like pieces of a jigsaw that only make sense when you put them together. We don't need to be fitted into a religion or class or colour to be understood. I won't say, he does this because he was born in Pakistan or he says that because his father is an aristocrat or is a Roman Catholic or whatever. Be colour-blind and blind to religion and culture and class like me, then people will take you for what you are.'

This never failed to provoke an impassioned response from Chandan who poured scorn on his father's political naivety. 'If you refuse to notice someone's race, how will you overcome racism? If you don't notice some people are in wheelchairs and can't get up the stairs, why would you put in ramps and a lift? You can only bring about social justice after you've exposed the injustices.'

And Namita, citing examples from her school, would pitch in on the side of her younger son while Mohan and I laughed aloud at the predictability of the argument. I laughed but actually I agreed with Pradip. Why do you need to know what my job is, who my parents are, what school I attended, who I married? I once heard a colleague welcoming a new member of staff.

'Ah so you're Mandy. Is that short for Mandira or Mandeep or Amanda?' It was obvious he wanted to establish whether the name was abbreviated Sikh or Hindu, or if her parents were aspiring to be English.

'No, my name's Mandy. Just Mandy,' the young woman replied.

Good for you, I thought. Keep him guessing.

One day, as Mohan and I were driving through an area of the city popular with professional couples, we noticed a For Sale board in the garden of an attractive terraced house. Mohan braked and reversed the car so we could have a better look.

'What d'you think?' he asked.

'Let's do it,' I said.

'We'll put in an offer . . . .' he smiled.

'. . . and move in together.'

He became serious. 'You do realise we'll have to get married first? For my parents' sake.'

'Call that a proposal?'

Mohan reached out, drew me to him and pressed his lips to mine. His mouth was warm and moist and I didn't want him to stop.

'All right,' I said when he eventually released me. 'I give in. I'll marry you.'

Pradip greeted the news of our forthcoming marriage with delight. He tousled Mohan's hair and gave him a congratulatory hug.

'Fantastic news! I was hoping you'd settle on Ann. She'll make an excellent wife. And bring in some useful money.' He winked in my direction. 'Tell you what, let's all go for a drink to celebrate.' And he insisted on dragging Chandan and Namita away from their video to share in a round at his local.

Namita on the other hand was much more circumspect. Her lips smiled but her eyes were uncommitted and I knew her expression hid a tangle of conflicting thoughts which she needed time to unravel. She placed her relationship with her sons at the very centre of her life and wouldn't allow herself to say anything which might jeopardise this, especially as Pradip had welcomed Mohan's news so unreservedly.

But in fact Namita was horrified to think of her eldest son tied to an English wife. Keep them separate like vegetables, either Bengali or English, side by side maybe but not mixed up. No way, not Benglish. She couldn't make her objections known and risk losing her elder son's devotion, but if she trod carefully she might in due course be able to exert her influence and get him to reconsider. So she took my hand and smiled and nodded then waited till they were alone before pursuing the matter further.

Chandan had just graduated and was contemplating setting up his own business.

'What are you thinking of?' he asked his brother scornfully. 'Are you really going to marry someone three years older than you and at least a couple of inches taller?'

'So what's it to you?' Mohan retorted. 'She's a good investment. I'm getting more for my money!'

Mohan eventually convinced Namita he wasn't going to change his mind then tactfully declined her invitation for us both to move into the family home. 'The house is plenty big enough,' she argued. 'But if you like, your father could build an extension.'

Pradip and Namita wanted us to do the thing properly with a Hindu priest and all the trimmings, vermillion in my parting, his dhoti knotted to my sari, seven times around the sacred fire. But I refused. Mohan tried to persuade me for his parents' sake, after all he was their first born son, and Pradip tried on Namita's behalf but I was adamant. I didn't object to the rituals per se, no doubt they were right for some couples, but they had nothing whatever to do with me. However I did agree to wear gold bangles with my wedding outfit and spent an enjoyable hour at the jewellers selecting the design.

We invited only immediate family to the registry office. My parents came but not my brother who pleaded a long standing commitment to an international symposium. To compensate for Namita's disappointment over the ceremony, Mohan suggested we ask her to organise the reception which suited me just fine. I was only too happy to delegate responsibility and gave her carte blanche, so long as she wasn't too extravagant. I puzzled her. What kind of daughter-in-law was this who didn't want to be involved in drawing up a guest list, choosing table decorations and deciding on a menu for her own wedding feast? No hope of female bonding there.

Afterwards we moved into our own house, replaced the kitchen units, put in a new bathroom and decorated throughout. I chose bright colours, lotus pink, Jamaican bronze and peacock green, overruling Mohan who preferred wishy washy mushroom and magnolia. And I can honestly say that in the main we were happy. It caught me unawares when I came upon him humming in the kitchen or woke to see the morning sun illuminate last night's wine glasses together on the carpet or glimpsed our joint reflection in a shop window. That sudden red gold blaze which confirmed our happiness.

Of course we quarrelled at intervals over the usual things like sex, I favoured afternoons while Mohan became amorous only after sundown; and money, he bought what he wanted and then calculated whether he could afford it while I saved up before making a purchase; and in-laws, he went round to Queen's Road for a meal with his parents most Sundays and occasionally I let him drag me along too. And in the still hours of the night I sweated over who he would save first from a hypothetical inferno, Namita or me. This maggot of doubt wriggled away in the dark, hidden like the princess's pea beneath layer upon layer of feather mattresses. Midweek we phoned my parents and every so often drove up the motorway to spend a few days with them.

For our tenth anniversary Mohan gave me, amongst my other presents, a jar of pickle.

'Mango and lime, extra hot, for a wedding anniversary?' I was incredulous.

'With good reason', he said. 'It's symbolic. Two different fruits immersed together for so long in the same oils and spices they've begun to look and taste alike.'

'Not really,' I pointed out. 'They keep their original shape and texture.'

'Precisely! We're still individuals but the marital juices unite us.'

'Ugh!' I put the jar down and kissed his eyelids. 'Since when have you started using metaphor? It's not a bit like you.'

'Proof positive of the pickle theory. Like I said, we're absorbing bits of each other's personalities. I soak up your creativity and you're steeped in my technical know how . . . though I have to admit that bit seems to be taking rather longer.'

I rolled the jar at his bare feet. 'Hey, that hurt!' he complained. While he was busy inspecting his injured toes I came up behind and put my arms around him, pinning his arms to his sides. I locked my hands together across his stomach, a stomach which bore witness to the fact Mohan enjoyed eating as much as he enjoyed cooking. He tried to weaken my grip by attacking each finger in turn, starting like a coward with the little fingers. I trusted the strength of my hands and my hold remained secure.

'What's this in aid of?' he muttered as we struggled, neither of us willing to surrender. I could feel the solid warmth of his back against my breasts and his bristly hair pressing into my cheek. I tried to bring my teeth close enough to his ear to bite it playfully.

'Shall we go up and finish this in the bedroom?' Mohan asked, making his voice deep and sensuous.

'What, in broad daylight?' I relaxed my grip and stared in disbelief. He took advantage of this lapse in concentration, forced my hands apart and turned round grinning.

'See, Annie, even in that department I'm absorbing your tastes! The proof of the pickle is in the eating.' Grabbing my hands he pushed and pulled me, wobbly with laughter, up the stairs.

One afternoon, four years after our marriage, Chandan turned up on our doorstep hand in hand with a pretty, fair haired girl. I showed the two of them into the sitting room, where they huddled together giggling and cooing on the settee, while I went to fetch Mohan. Chandan rarely graced our home with his presence, only when specifically invited for birthdays and special occasions, and I'd certainly never seen him behave like this with a girl before.

When Mohan came into the room Chandan quickly put some distance between himself and his girlfriend.

'What's up?' Mohan looked at his brother sternly. 'We don't see you round here very often. You in some kind of trouble?'

'Why would I be?' Chandan was defensive. 'We came round because I wanted to introduce you to my girlfriend. Jenny and me have been together for six months.'

Mohan plonked himself down in a chair and turned on the television. There was a long silence while he flipped between channels.

'Thing is we've got a bit of a problem,' Chandan addressed the back of Mohan's head.

'Thought so,' Mohan said without looking round.

Chandan shuffled restlessly and shot a furious look in my direction. Jenny's eyes flitted between the two men. I noticed her eyes were a startling blue and her skin as fine and pale as porcelain.

'Stop it, Mohan.' I snatched the zapper out of his hand. 'Stop messing about. Jenny thinks you're serious.'

Mohan turned round grinning, then jumped up and went over to shake Jenny's hand.

'Hello, Jenny. Just showing this little brother of mine who's boss. Welcome to our home. Can I get you something to drink?' Then he yanked Chandan off the settee and steered him towards the kitchen, leaving me alone with Jenny.

I took the opportunity to find out more. Jenny told me she lived on one of the new estates on the edge of town, that she'd left school as soon as she could and now worked behind the counter in a high street store. She said she met Chandan at a friend's party. She kept tucking her hair back behind her ears as she talked. She seemed very young and a little in awe of me but she handled herself well, responding to my questions with quiet confidence. She would be the kind of student who paid attention in the classroom and always submitted her assignments on time.

Mohan and Chandan came back into the room.

'Jenny's looking for somewhere to live,' Mohan announced as he handed round the mugs. 'Her father doesn't approve of my brother.'

'My Dad likes Chandan. He just doesn't like the idea of us getting married,' Jenny explained. Chandan sat down and she slid her hand through his arm.

'Married!' I looked at her doubtfully. 'How old are you?'

'That's the problem,' said Chandan. 'Jenny's not eighteen till October. After that we can get married without her parents' permission. She needs somewhere to live for the next few months.'

'Dad'll be fine once he gets his head round it. Only it's better if I'm out of the way, else he and my mum row about me.'

'Couldn't you move in with friends?' I suggested.

Jenny shrugged. 'My friends all live at home still. It wouldn't be fair to drag their families into it. My Dad might go round and make trouble.'

'What about Namita? Have you told her? Couldn't Jenny stay there?'

'No,' said Mohan firmly. 'Not before they're married.'

'Then she'll have to come here.' I made the offer somewhat reluctantly but I was growing impatient. If my parents had even hinted disapproval when I introduced them to Mohan, I would have walked out in disgust.

'What did you say?' Mohan stared at me open-mouthed.

'Well why not? She can have the spare room. What's the matter, Mohan? You look as if you've seen a ghost!'

So it was settled and Jenny moved in the very next day. She added a new dimension to our lives. If we were diamonds, sharp and clear, emitting sparks of brilliant colour then Jenny was a pearl, round and warm and softly opalescent. I came home of an evening railing against the inflexibility of senior management or complaining of interminable traffic queues. Mohan bounced enthusiastically around the house outlining the properties of some new anti-virus software. In the midst of it all Jenny remained tranquil. She tempered her words and weighed her responses with a wisdom of which neither Mohan nor I was capable despite our seniority in years. And yet her self control seemed to me unnatural. I longed to hear her shout for joy and yell in anger. I wanted to warn her life didn't come in manageable parcels, neatly wrapped. One day she would need to explode and she wouldn't be able to unless she'd put in a bit of practice first.

Chandan wanted them to live with his parents in Queen's Road after their marriage and Jenny seemed keen on the idea. I didn't think she'd fully considered the implications so I tackled her about it one day as we sat in the kitchen surrounded by the remains of the evening meal.

'Try to imagine it,' I began. 'They'll expect you to eat together every day. That means Namita decides what you eat. What if you fancy something different, or if the two of you want to eat alone? They'll accuse you of being selfish.'

'But I'm looking forward to cooking with Mum, learning how to make curry.' Jenny stood up and made a start on clearing the table.

'Leave those, we'll do them in a minute.' She sat down again and I continued. 'I'm serious, you'll have no privacy. Namita and Pradip will be there all the time, watching everything you do.'

'Bugging all your conversations, secretly filming your every move,' Mohan shouted through from the front room. 'Don't be ridiculous, Ann!'

'Shut up Mohan! Let me talk to her. It's for her own good.'

'But that's why I want to live with them,' Jenny said. 'I'm happiest with other people around. Maybe because I'm from a big family. I don't like being alone in the house. Actually, I'm not sure I've ever been alone.' She got to her feet again and began scraping bay leaves, burnt sticks of cinnamon and half chewed chicken bones into the bin.

'Really? I adore being alone. Absolutely alone in silence, or with music. So I can think without distraction, follow my thoughts as they weave in and out.' I cleared a space for my elbows and rested my chin on my hands. 'That's the one reservation I had about getting married, not being alone in my own house.'

Jenny leant thoughtfully against the worktop. 'I like the house full of people and untidy. If a room's too tidy it's sort of dead.'

'Untidiness saps my energy. I get mentally tangled with the mess and all I can think of is restoring order.' I paused and looked at her suspiciously. 'Are you trying to change the subject?' She knew very well I was obsessively tidy. Jenny giggled and turned back to the sink.

'Namita has rules about everything. She'll even tell you the proper way to stack your shopping trolley!' I tried again.

'Hey! That's my mother you're talking about,' Mohan called out.

'You keep out of this! I'll let you know when we've finished.' I slammed the kitchen door and wedged it with a chair. I ignored the sound of Mohan hammering on the door and got on with clearing the table. The bowls which still had food in them I crammed into the fridge, balancing them precariously on top of other dishes until the shelves sagged. Jenny squeezed washing up liquid into the stream of hot water and methodically rubbed the dishcloth over the oily curry coloured plates. A shadow passed the window and we heard a key turning in the lock. Mohan burst in through the back door letting in a swirl of cool air.

'Annie, stop bullying my little brother's future wife!' He wagged a finger at me. 'Poor girl, you'll scare her off completely. Jenny, I want you to know I'm delighted you're going to marry Chandan and if you really want to live with my parents, well then that's what you should do.' He scowled in my direction, reached for a tea towel and began drying the dishes as Jenny placed them on the drainer. I left them to get on with it and retreated to my study.

Jenny entered into the spirit of things and was pleased when Chandan opted for a traditional wedding. She sat patiently while Namita's friends hung garlands round her neck, smeared turmeric on her body to brighten her complexion and fed her Indian sweets. Personally I thought she resembled a goldsmith's advertisement on the day itself, with a ring on each finger, bangles up to her elbows, a broad filigree necklace with dangly earrings and tikka to match. Her sequined sari came from an exclusive Asian boutique and every inch of Chandan's panjabi was covered with embroidery.

The reception was equally lavish. Each table was furnished with two bottles of the best whiskey and the starters would have constituted a feast on their own. Jenny's parents came but neither of them seemed to enjoy the occasion much. Her father was a restless man, constantly anxious about whatever it was he needed to do the following day, but her mother made more of an effort. She quizzed Namita about various items on the menu and engaged in conversation with the other guests. Pradip did his best to make them welcome and introduced them to a friend of his, well-versed in Hindu rituals, who supplied them with a running commentary on the ceremony.

After the wedding Jenny moved into Queen's Road as planned thereby providing Namita with the daughter-in-law of her dreams. It no longer mattered that Jenny was English. Namita was too relieved to find her younger son had chosen a girl who wanted to learn to cook Bengali food and in general follow her husband's way of life, to complain about her ethnic roots. Conversations now focussed on what Jenny could do rather than on what I couldn't, on how wonderful she was rather than on my shortcomings. Jenny rarely went to see her family and they rarely came to visit her. Like a true Hindu bride she seemed to regard herself as the property of the family into which she'd married.

Seven years down the line and Pradip was enjoying his retirement. Namita had two more years to go, that is if she decided to go at sixty. Personally I thought she'd be miserable sitting around at home. My fortieth birthday came and went and I was quite content to enter the ranks of the middle aged. Mohan was waiting to hear whether he'd been short-listed for a senior post in a rival company and Chandan's picture framing business was doing well. He'd started with a single shop and rapidly expanded into a number of new outlets across the region.

That's when it happened.

CHAPTER THREE

S ATURDAY MORNING. I woke late and lay in bed squinting at the light as it shone through the curtains. Folds in the cloth varied the intensity of colour and distorted the patterns. Sleep was rinsed out of my body except for a delicious tingle where it still clung to the bends and corners—knuckles, elbows, knees.

I could hear Mohan in the kitchen. The gurgle and throb of the boiler as he ran hot water to wash up last night's dishes, the banging of cupboard doors and pulling and pushing of drawers as he put away plates and cutlery. Fledglings in the nest under the eaves squeaked madly, begging their parents to bring worms and insects. I listened to the scrabbling of adult birds as they landed for a moment to stuff food down their babies' throats before flying off in search of further supplies.

I stretched my limbs to summon life back into them, climbed out of bed and crossed the landing to the bathroom. On my way back a few minutes later I was amused to see Mohan descending the stairs at great speed.

'Breakfast in bed, Madam,' he called over his shoulder. 'Hope it's to your satisfaction. If you need anything else you'll have to fetch it yourself. I'm going over to Queen's Road to help Dad with the patio. Remember?'

I stood for a moment or two and watched him disappear rapidly from view. Beside the bed he'd placed a tray bearing poached eggs on toast, salt and pepper. He asked no questions, offered no suggestions as to how I should spend my day, content that I should do whatever made me happy.

When I replayed this scene to myself later I always edited the sequence, played about with the timing, included some extra shots. In the revised version I emerged from the bathroom a few moments later so that the two of us made eye contact and shared a brief cuddle on the landing before he went pounding off down the stairs.

'Excellent room service!' I called back as I snuggled down under the covers and began reading while I ate.

I heard Mohan shout goodbye and slam the front door. I heard the familiar sound of his car as he started the engine and drove off, hesitantly at first and then picking up speed as he got underway. I continued reading, on and on until I realised it was almost lunch time so I decided to call it a lazy day and not bother getting dressed at all. I drew back the curtains, fetched coffee and a sandwich and returned to bed and book. Lying in bed during the day when you should be up and doing reminded me of school days when I pretended to have a stomach ache so I could steal time alone to dream. My mother left me to my own devices because, according to her rules, if you were ill you shouldn't be entertained or made a fuss of.

I remember noticing the mug, a perfect circle, hard and shiny, sunk in soft billows of duvet. I heard the drone of an aeroplane drifting down through the clear sunshine and watched lines of white exhaust grow fuzzy against the blue. I remember every detail of that day because I've been over it a million times meticulously, to fix the precise order of events in my head.

The doorbell rang and I decided to ignore it but the caller persisted so eventually I went to the window to see who it could be. I noticed the police car parked at the other end of the block and vaguely wondered which of our neighbours had got themselves into what kind of trouble. The bell rang once more and this time I went down and opened the door.

'Is this the home of Mohan Das?' The officer's face was carefully composed to express deep sympathy. On seeing me his expression changed to register surprise and then uncertainty, clearly I didn't look to him like Mrs Das. But it was too late for caution, I had seen his original expression.

'That's right,' I said. 'I'm his wife.'

'Can I come in?' I stepped aside and the policeman entered, closing the door behind him. He was stout and red-haired and there were little purple veins on the side of his fleshy nose.

'I think you should sit down. I expect you've guessed I'm bringing bad news.' I noticed the freckles on the back of his hand as he gestured towards a chair.

'I'm fine,' I said. 'Just tell me what's happened.'

'Your husband's been involved in a road traffic accident.' He paused. It would make his job easier if, fearing the worst, I broke down in tears. But my eyes remained dry. 'Mr Das was fatally injured. I'm very sorry.'

My brain was perfectly clear. I remembered Mohan had a new jacket hanging in his wardrobe with the shop tags still attached. I could get a refund if I returned it immediately.

'And what about the others, Mohan's father and brother? Were they injured?' I asked, my voice as calm and steady as the officer's.

'I shouldn't really tell you,' he hesitated. 'But you'll find out soon enough. I'm sorry to say there were no survivors.'

Something exploded in my head and from that moment on events became thinner. I could still hear and see of course, but everything was reduced to a single dimension. Sounds all shared one pitch and volume, words conveyed only a brittle surface meaning, objects drained of colour turned a monotonous grey, nothing possessed weight or substance. All in cruel contrast to the vivid sensations of the morning.

'Is there anyone I can contact to come and sit with you?' The officer's voice reached my ears from a great distance. I shook my head. 'I can't leave you here alone,' he persisted. 'Will you let me take you over to Queen's Road? I was there earlier. They know already.'

So I went upstairs to dress although I haven't a clue what I put on. I recall nothing of the journey except that it was chilly. I know we arrived to find Jenny curled up on the sofa while Namita rubbed her hands and feet. Namita looked up when I entered.

'Jenny fainted when he told us,' she said. 'Just trying to get her circulation back.'

I stood and watched as Namita continued to massage Jenny's limbs. Jenny didn't move or speak but every now and then I heard her moan. Their house struck me as cold and I wondered why Pradip hadn't turned up the central heating as winter approached.

The officer went out into the hall to check with the mortician if the bodies were ready to be identified. I heard him mumble into his radio,

'Crushed but not minced? I get the picture.'

When he came back into the room Namita said, 'I'll go with you and identify them. I need to see for myself. You know, be sure it isn't a mistake.'

God only knows what it cost her to obtain that terrible certainty. I volunteered to stay with Jenny. I had no wish to see my husband dead when I knew him to be warm and vital.

The policeman looked at Namita doubtfully. 'Can you find someone else to go with you for support? A neighbour or a friend?'

'I'll be okay.' Namita buttoned up her coat.

'Then I'll get a female constable to meet us at the mortuary.' As they left he was making the arrangements via his radio.

I went over and tried to comfort Jenny but she kept her eyes closed and didn't reply so I sat down near her on the sofa and waited I've no idea how long. Eventually I heard Namita's key in the front door and then I heard the officer telling her he was going back to the station. Namita came into the room and sat stiffly in Pradip's chair without taking off her coat.

'He said they died straight away. Wouldn't have felt any pain. They can tell from the injuries and the damage to the car. Lorry driver's in shock but he's not hurt. They'll interview him later. It's too early to say how it happened, that's what the inquest's for.' Her words slid coldly to the floor where they formed a pool of mercury. 'Post-mortem on Tuesday. He said they always do post-mortems when someone's killed in a car crash. After that the coroner will give us a certificate and the funeral people can take the bodies away.'

Who closed his eyes
and pulled the rings from his dead finger?
Who removed his clothes
and placed them, folded, in a carrier bag?
Who washed him down
and slid his body onto the cold shelf?

We sat there a long while in silence except for Jenny who whimpered at intervals. Then Namita went to make sweet tea and urged us both to drink. I refused but she persuaded Jenny to swallow a few mouthfuls. Eventually I stood up to go. I'd noticed our car parked by the front gate when I arrived with the policeman and for one unguarded moment I expected Mohan to appear and offer to take me home.

'Better call a taxi,' said Namita, looking me up and down with a hint of contempt. 'You're shaking. You shouldn't drive.'

I was beyond exhaustion but couldn't go to our bedroom because I knew Mohan's smell was on the pillows. So I lay down in the spare room and remained there rigid with shock until the early hours when I crept into the bathroom and heaved and retched till my guts ached. Then I lost consciousness. The phone woke me and when I opened my eyes I saw it was late morning. I couldn't stand because the powerful throbbing in my head unbalanced me so I crawled into our room to pick up the receiver.

'Ann? You took a long time to answer,' my mother said cheerfully. 'Just phoning for a chat.' On hearing her voice my tears began to flow.

'What's the matter, darling? Are you crying?'

'Accident,' I gasped between sobs.

'What accident? Who's had an accident?'

'Mohan,' I whispered. There was a short pause.

'Is he hurt?'

'Dead.' My voice was barely audible.

'We're coming down.'

'No. I'm okay,' I said.

'For God's sake, Ann. Of course you're not okay!' She was shouting now. 'What are parents for? We'll come straightaway.' They arrived three hours later.

I let my mother make a fuss and nurse me because I hadn't the energy to resist. She contacted the college where I worked, explained what had happened and informed them I was taking compassionate leave. She insisted I stay in bed, arranged for the doctor to call, ran hot scented baths and cooked me simple food. Before long I began to rally and as strength returned to my body so the sharpness of my pain increased and I longed for weakness and oblivion again.

One day, having reassured herself I was well enough to be left in the care of my father, my mother decided it was her duty to drive over to Queen's Road to convey her condolences to Namita and Jenny. On her return she described the scene.

'They've taken all the furniture out of the front room. The women were sitting on the floor, even the older ones. How do they keep so supple?' She patted her own arthritic hips. 'Some of them had brought food for Namita and Jenny, you know, so they didn't need to cook for themselves. And the men were hanging around outside. Lots of them. You wouldn't get that number of people coming to call on an English family! It must be gratifying to know so many people care. Exhausting though. How long does it go on?' She turned and directed the question at me. 'Can Namita tell them when she's had enough or would that be considered rude?'

But I refused to be either interpreter or apologist for my husband's family. If you wanted to learn about their customs you had to go straight to the horse's mouth. Mohan was second generation and would have commented from that perspective, very differently from the way Namita would explain things. Or you could consult a book. I've heard of students telling their parents the 'true' meaning of their own customs on the basis of having read a text book.

My father said, 'They do it publicly while we keep it hidden. We do now at least, gone are the days of wakes and funeral feasts. The theory's obvious. Gets it out of the system. Less danger of it festering away, becoming a problem later. Unlike the constipated Brits who like to keep everything under control. Though that is changing I admit.' My mother smiled wryly. She knew my father would be the last one to lose control, the most constipated of the Brits.

But it was my father who sensed when it was time to leave. One morning he wandered into the kitchen where I sat nursing a hot drink and wondering how long it would be before I slept normally again. Each morning my body ached as if I'd been jolted and thrown about by an express train and my head buzzed as the engine roared through a night tunnel. My father propped himself up against the worktop while he flipped through the pages of a cookery book.

'I'm planning to take your mother home tomorrow. She's getting bored. Her own house has never been this clean! Your bathroom smells like an operating theatre and she's emptied your ironing basket.' He paused because we both remembered that while sorting through the ironing she'd come across Mohan's crumpled clothes along with mine and had been unsure what to do with them. Iron them, I said, and I'll donate them to Oxfam.

'If she stays any longer she'll start cleaning out your study and reorganising the kitchen cupboards. Anyway you'll have to get used to . . . .' His voice faltered.

'. . . . to being on my own. Yes, I know, and I'm not begging you to stay. Go home whenever you're ready. In fact go today,' I snapped. 'I appreciate you giving up the time to come down but you're right, it's time you left me to my own devices.'

'That's a good sign. You're getting stroppy with me. Now I know you're on the mend!' He reached up to replace the cookery book on its shelf. 'I hope you'll come and see us before too long. Give yourself a change of scenery, a rest cure in the midst of the English countryside.'

'Later maybe. I need to stay here till the inquest. They say it can take months to arrange. There's lots to sort out and I don't intend to be off work for long. Perhaps we'll . . . I'll come up in the summer.' I kept my back towards him as I plunged my mug into soapy water. That treacherous pronoun, beware the royal 'we'.

I had no stomach for the comings and goings of Queen's Road but I couldn't stay away because I needed to find out how Jenny was. The scene my mother described earlier was very familiar to me, roads clogged with cars double parked or left inconsiderately across accesses, the ebb and flow of pale shrouded figures stretching in tangled lines the length of the street.

For Pradip and his sons things were on a more modest scale than usual because Pradip had stayed on the outskirts of Asian society, rarely attending the temple or taking part in cultural events. Like his vegetables his friends belonged as much to England as to Bengal. Pradip had little time for the mythical Asian community and its patriarchal leaders, outdated and hypocritical he called them. Conning the Council into providing grants for ill-conceived projects no one wanted and then failing to implement them. In any case the tragedy was so terrible no one would think of coming out of idle curiosity. You only visited a woman widowed and bereft of both sons at a single stroke if you absolutely had to, unless you were a trauma junkie

At first Jenny said she wasn't well enough to leave her bedroom but Namita quickly put a stop to that and insisted she get dressed and come downstairs. When Jenny obeyed but said she couldn't face the endless stream of visitors, Namita stationed her in the kitchen and made her responsible for refreshments. That's where I found her, slumped over the table with her face in her hands. When she looked up I saw how dreadfully pale she was, her eyes dull and heavy with the sorrow of centuries.

'Did you sleep any better last night?' I sat down opposite.

'I was still awake at three. My pillow was soaked. I had to get up and change it. What about you, Ann? Did you sleep?'

'Not too bad,' I lied. The cheese wire slicing through my skull had kept me awake most of the night.

The doorbell rang and Jenny got slowly to her feet, making a half-hearted attempt to straighten her uncombed hair.

'I can't let them see me like this. I must look awful.'

'It doesn't matter how you look. They know what's happened. They'll expect you to look rough.'

'Will you go, Ann? Please?'

'Okay, I'll go and take their orders,' I said and Jenny managed a grateful smile.

Between us we kept a succession of visitors supplied with refreshments. It felt good working alongside Jenny, having something to do, but I noticed how the cups and glasses trembled in her hands as she placed them on the tray.

At midday Namita came into the kitchen. Her hair was neatly tied, her clothes clean and ironed but she wore a grim expression and there were massive shadows under her eyes.

'Time for lunch,' she said briskly. 'What shall we have?'

Jenny said. 'I'm not really hungry, Mum. I think I'll go and lie down.'

'Come on, you can manage a little bit.' Namita peered into the fridge and checked through the assorted offerings from thoughtful friends and neighbours. 'Must be something here you like.' She selected a number of dishes and proceeded to heat them by turn in the microwave. She looked over at me. 'Are you going to eat with us, Ann?'

'No thanks. I'll have mine at home.'

I dragged myself away and spent a wretched afternoon alone. I found it impossible to remain in one place for more than a few minutes, it didn't matter whether I sat or stood or lay down nothing gave me any relief. So I paced back and forth and back again through every room in my house, upstairs and down.

Why had Mohan done this to me? I was whole and complete, an impenetrable sphere, until he broke me open with the brilliance of his smile. Then, just as abruptly, he disappeared and I was left with a jagged, gaping wound which felt as though it would never heal.

He gave me rubies and emeralds,
Sapphires set in gold.
Now he's dead I wear lead
Inlaid with coloured glass.

I went into our bedroom, pulled one of Mohan's T shirts from his drawer and wound it round my neck like a scarf, tight against my skin. By then I was sobbing so violently I had to steady myself on the walls and furniture as I stumbled from room to room.

The day after she identified the bodies Namita telephoned Pradip's cousin's son who lived in London, the only adult male relative she had in Britain. He came immediately to assist with arrangements. Apparently male relatives took the lead role in funeral and cremation rites as they took the lead role in most other rites of passage. The cousin's son expressed his disappointment on hearing the bodies had been subjected to post-mortems and warned Namita orthodox Hindus would disapprove. Furthermore, he said, from the Hindu perspective the manner of their death was absolutely the worst possible. Pradip's eldest son should have led the mourning, failing that his youngest. The case was even worse for Mohan and Chandan who had not a single son between them. It was unlikely they were spiritually prepared for death, he pointed out, and goodness knows what filled their final thoughts. Unfortunately they departed this life separated from wives and mother but no doubt they would derive some benefit from the fact they died together.

The cousin's son consulted widely to determine who should conduct the ceremonies and find out exactly what needed to be done. He was rewarded with as many opinions as he had friends and acquaintances, depending upon the part of India from which they originated. I overheard some of the debate.

'We must wash the bodies in diluted yoghurt, in milk at least.'

'No need to make a fuss, water will do just as well.'

'Remember to tell the undertakers when they bring the boxes to the house. They must line them up heads towards the south.'

'What are you saying? They have to lie east west!'

'I suppose we'll need a pandit to do everything properly?'

'Not necessary. We can do it ourselves so long as we can get hold of some tulsi leaves and sandalwood.'

'And Ganges water. Where'll we get that? If we ask the pujari for a bottle he'll be offended we're not inviting him to lead the ceremony.'

'He won't mind. He'd rather not do things with the dead. Contaminates him.'

'No one else can read Sanskrit well enough.'

'And gold, a small piece of new gold, we must have that. Akash Jewellers might let us have a piece. I'll go and ask.'

And Namita was right there in the midst of it all having her say, recalling the deaths of her grandparents and how the funerals of neighbours in England had been ordered, arguing each detail to its hair-splitting conclusion. Her fingers were entwined in the entrails of this world so that in spite of her great loss she was driven to oversee the final departure and be fully involved in its planning and execution.

It would have made no difference to me if the discussions had revolved round whether it was better to accept flowers or ask for donations to a favourite charity, what music to play during the service and which hymns to sing. It didn't matter whether the traditions were from west or east, I had no interest in either. I did not have my fingers entangled in the entrails of this material world and was interested only in my beloved who I carried within my heart.

I wrestled for a day or two with the question, but in the end Jenny's pleading won me over and I gave permission for Mohan's body to be included in the ceremonies alongside his father and younger brother's. Namita didn't say a word to me on the subject but I knew she dreaded the consequences if I chose to be awkward. I gave my consent not out of deference or pity for her, Mohan was my husband and I had the right to dispose of his body in whatever manner I saw fit, but because ultimately I was not interested in what was done to the corpse.

No invitations were issued for the day of the funeral, instead the date and time were conveyed informally by word of mouth. I arrived to find the cousin's son on the doorstep busy welcoming mourners and directing them inside the already crowded house.

'Ann, can you stay here and give me a hand? Help greet people when they arrive.' Namita accosted me as soon as I entered. She wore a light beige sari with a wide border of deep blue. According to tradition she should have worn white but Pradip had disliked the custom.

'I'd rather not. Can't you get someone else to do it?' I said. 'Where's Jenny?'

Namita nodded towards the front room.

'I'm going through to sit with her.'

'Go on then. I'll manage.' Namita turned to the next visitor. She let them peck her on the cheeks but fended off more heartfelt expressions of sympathy.

I moved on to the front room and immediately spotted Jenny sitting head bowed in front of the patio doors. She was wrapped in a sari of blue silk, the end piece carefully draped so that it partially hid her face. I recognised the sari, Chandan chose it for their first wedding anniversary because the colour matched her eyes. I went over and stood beside her.

'Are you all right?' I asked in a low voice.

'I'm okay,' she lifted her eyes to meet mine. 'I can't believe it. So many people!'

Glancing round I saw men from Pradip's work place and teachers from Namita's school, also some self-conscious lads from the boys' club where Chandan helped out as a volunteer. A contingent from Pradip's local and a couple of fellow gardeners from the neighbourhood occupied one corner. Jenny's parents and two of her sisters formed a little group and I noticed a few of Mohan's friends. I hadn't invited them and I deliberately avoided meeting their gaze. New arrivals made their way over to embrace Jenny and were themselves comforted even as she drew comfort from them. Although I was standing next to her no one attempted to touch me, instead they nodded or inclined their heads in my direction. As usual they mistook my courage for coldness.

When the hearses drew up outside a hush fell upon the assembly, except for two girls who didn't notice and continued their whispered story telling until an older woman nudged them sharply from behind.

'Shut up you two. Can't you see the boxes coming in?' she hissed down their necks. The girls exchanged embarrassed glances and hid their blushes in silence.

The cousin's son and friends of the deceased carried the trio of coffins one by one into the house. People pressed back against the walls and into the bay window as the front room grew more congested. Someone suggested the last coffin should be left in the hall but Namita insisted all three were lined up together which meant some people were pushed back outside the door. Others sat in rows right up the stairs.

Three coffins, an appalling sight. When the lids were removed, as directed by the priest, the atmosphere grew opaque with sorrow. I refused to look and kept my eyes fixed upon the apple tree which I could see through the patio doors, illuminated by the autumn sun. Its top was flattened as if by some giant hand and its upper surface was outlined in red. Red apples flecked the green of its mass and hung down below. A circle of fallen fruit lay on the grass beneath, reflecting the shape of the outspread branches.

One of Pradip's English friends wept quietly into his handkerchief. An older woman nearby rocked to and fro and struck her chest repeatedly. When I looked again, I saw the apple tree was drenched in globules of blood which oozed from wounds all over its body and coagulated in a bloody pool on the lawn beneath.

Fortunately the priest knew Pradip's views on religion and kept the rituals brief. 'Swami Vivekananda said, Work is your Worship. That's good enough for me,' Pradip would excuse himself when Namita begged him to accompany her to the temple during Durga Puja. 'I'm busy in the factory all week and with my plants at weekends. That's what I believe in. That's my religion.'

Garlands were placed on the bodies and the priest sprinkled them with holy water as he chanted verses from sacred texts. At this point many of those gathered in the room folded their hands and saluted whatever spirit it was they believed in. Then Namita marked her husband's forehead with red paste and beckoned to Jenny and me to do likewise.

'Come on, Ann,' Jenny whispered getting to her feet. 'It's our turn.' I shook my head. Jenny hesitated then sat down again. 'We're not going to do it,' she mouthed to the cousin's son. Namita covered her face with her hands and her body was wracked by dry, shuddering sobs.

When it was finished the coffins were carried, one by one, back to their vehicles and we three sat together in a black limousine as the slow procession moved onwards to the crematorium. Jenny climbed out of the car and immediately fainted. She sat on the gravel in front of the chapel with her head between her knees while Namita ordered them to fetch a wheelchair. I couldn't do any more to help so I walked briskly on into the lobby, through the glass doors and up the aisle to the front seats, all the while keeping my eyes on the ceiling. You're less likely to cry or vomit if your head is held high.

Namita came slowly, leaning on the cousin's son, and sat down next to me. They parked Jenny's wheelchair in line with the front row and I reached out and covered her hand with mine. And so we three sat side by side at the funeral of our husbands. I didn't listen to the recitation of poems or to what the various speakers said in praise of those who had died. Nor did I watch as the curtains opened but I did hear Namita groan as the coffins finally disappeared. My eyes remained fixed on the ceiling and inside my head I chanted over and over

My name is Ann and my husband's dead.
That's what I said, he's dead.
My name is Ann and my husband's dead.

as if each line of this crude little ditty was a thorn which firmly pinned me to the fabric of reality.

After everyone had dispersed the priest instructed Namita to arrange a shraddh in ten days' time. She informed him she had no intention of doing so because that was another custom Pradip had disliked. Then the cousin's son offered to take Pradip's ashes back to India so his relatives could scatter his remains on the waters of Mother Ganga. Namita should have taken them but she excused herself, claiming she didn't want to be parted from her youngest daughter-in-law who needed her care and attention. I allowed Jenny to persuade me to have Mohan's ashes put in the ground along with Chandan's in the tawdry crematorium grounds.

I went back to work pretty quickly as that seemed to be the best way of surviving. I tried to keep the surface, the daily routine and duties, ticking over and left the deeper, churned up layers to settle as they would. It was a miserable business, for weeks I felt numb and hollow and couldn't respond to anything. I taught my classes and did what was required of me without any sense of being there in person. But I clung on grimly for I had to believe it would get better.

CHAPTER FOUR

THE INQUEST WAS held early the following year. Namita had coaxed Jenny through her grief with just the right balance of chivvying and indulgence, and dealt with the solicitor who was handling Pradip's affairs. But all the while her attention was focussed on the forthcoming inquest, as though she drew her strength from the anticipated outcome and expected the toxic fallout from the accident to be neutralised by the investigation into it.

I, on the other hand, decided to approach the inquest in the spirit of an academic exercise, a matter of logic, an impartial investigation which, after all, is what it claimed to be. This was the only way I could shield myself from emotional contamination as I sat through hour upon hour of detailed evidence relating to the accident in which my husband died. So long as I succeeded in keeping it cerebral and didn't engage my feelings or imagination, I would come through unscathed.

I arrived at the magistrates court to find Jenny and Namita sitting in the lobby on plum upholstered chairs.

Jenny smiled at me, Namita frowned and checked her watch. The three of us waited in silence surrounded by a milling crowd. Suited men with clutches of files shoved into their armpits consulted together in confidential huddles. Their clients, the troubled and the truculent, paced up and down or stood, hands in pockets, shifting nervously from foot to foot. I wondered whether the row of green and white ambulance men were there to give evidence or to administer first aid. Individuals were summoned by name over the Tannoy while ushers in black gowns moved from group to group inquiring hopefully,

'Anybody for court three, please?'

'Anyone waiting for court two?'

'Are you here for an inquest, at all?' asked a dark-suited gentleman in a subdued voice, bending sympathetically over Jenny.

'Yes,' I intervened. 'We're family.'

'I'm Mrs Das,' said Namita importantly. 'And these two are my daughters-in-law.'

'Won't be long,' he said. 'Just waiting for the investigating officer.' He returned five minutes later. 'We're ready for you now. Please follow me.' He led us down a short flight of stairs into a room lit solely by artificial light. At the far end a silver-haired gentleman, the coroner I assumed, was already ensconced behind the bench. We were directed to sit in the middle of the room alongside a table bearing a carafe of water and some plastic glasses. An assortment of uniformed personnel filed in and occupied the chairs arranged around the edges of the room. The coroner came down to shake hands with each of us in turn. He was extremely thin and moved very slowly. A reverential hush fell as he climbed back behind the bench and shuffled through his papers.

'I'll begin by making clear the purpose of this inquest.' The coroner's voice was feeble, his delivery painfully slow. 'Our task is to unearth the facts. We are here to establish the time and place and circumstances of the deaths, not to apportion blame.'

Namita was called first as she was the one who had identified the bodies. She declined to swear on the New Testament and there was some urgent whispering as they settled on an acceptable alternative. She sat up straight and gave her evidence in a strong, clear voice. When she'd finished, the coroner advised us we could ask questions at any time during the proceedings. Namita rummaged in her bag and extracted a notebook and pen.

One of the policemen who had responded to the 999 call came forward. Out of the corner of my eye I could see the neat line of hair curving round his ear, the bulging flesh trapped by his tight collar, the cloth of his shirt straining to contain his broad shoulders. I raised my hand to block him from view. If I allowed myself to imagine this man, sirens wailing, hurrying to the scene, I would be lost. He gave his evidence with unnatural fluency as if he'd spent hours rehearsing it.

Next came an ambulance service technician (the job title was met by a derisory snort from the coroner). Jenny fidgeted in her chair as the paramedic described his actions on discovering the bodies. An officer from the investigation unit told us how he had preserved the scene and how later a meticulous survey was carried out, including the measurement of skid marks as a means of calculating speed. The vehicle examiner had ordered the removal of both vehicles to a secure compound where he studied them with equal rigour. As I anticipated, hearing the case discussed like this, with liberal use of jargon, had the effect of distancing the events and giving them an objectivity which helped preclude close emotional involvement.

Then a scale reconstruction was carried in and set before the coroner and various witnesses used the model to track the paths of the two vehicles. We sat patiently through argument and counter argument yet no credible reason for the accident emerged. Why had the car not given way to the lorry but instead joined the roundabout directly in its path? Even though he'd immediately applied the brakes, the lorry driver had no chance of avoiding the car. The coroner announced a lunch recess. We went back upstairs and found a snack bar opening off the lobby.

'It's just like what you see on tele.' Jenny bit into her sandwich. 'Only much worse, of course, because it's happening to us.'

'Except that on television they find out exactly what went wrong,' I said. 'We don't seem to be getting anywhere. No closer to an explanation.'

Namita stopped sipping her coffee and looked up sharply. 'But it's obvious, isn't it? It was the lorry driver's fault.'

'You don't know that,' I objected. 'We may never have a satisfactory explanation. It could simply have been a unique and random combination of circumstances.'

'Of course they'll find out why it happened! That's what we're here for.' Namita was scornful. 'It was his fault, the lorry driver's. Wait till you hear his evidence.' I was on the point of introducing her to the basic principles of chaos theory when Jenny's eyes begged me to let it go.

Only a few of us reassembled after lunch to hear the coroner read out the statements made by those not able to be present. Contrary to Namita's expectations, the lorry driver's account gave no fresh insight into the sequence of events. The coroner skimmed through the post-mortem reports. The injuries were particularly severe, he said, because cars do not have the strength to withstand a sideways impact. Had the collision been head-on there would have been some chance of survival. Then the pathologist confirmed what we already knew, the lorry driver's breathalyser proved negative and no trace of alcohol or drugs was found in the blood or urine of any of those involved. The coroner brought the proceedings to a close.

'We've heard a great deal of evidence today. Now it's time for me to make my concluding remarks. I find the cause of death in all three cases to be multiple injuries. My conclusion is that the cause of the accident lies in the hands of the driver of the car, and I'm delivering a verdict of accidental death.'

Namita gasped and clapped her hands to her cheeks. 'What d'you mean? Are you saying it was my husband's fault? You've spent the whole day trying to find the reason for the accident and you couldn't find anything. Now suddenly you're saying it was the car driver's fault! I don't understand.'

'It's a form of words,' the coroner said patiently. 'I'm not saying it's anyone's fault. Remember, I gave a verdict of accidental death. As I said at the beginning, Mrs Das, it's not the purpose of an inquest to apportion blame. Nevertheless the cause has to be placed somewhere so I say the cause lies in the hands of the driver of the car.'

Flushed and bewildered, Namita continued to stare at him as he packed away his papers. Jenny coaxed Namita into her coat then steered her through the lobby and out into the fresh air. We stood for a while adjusting to the daylight and the noise of passing traffic.

'I need to get Mum home quickly.'

'I'll give you a lift,' I offered. 'I'm parked at the bottom of the street.'

Jenny shook her head. 'I don't think she can walk that far. Wait here with her a minute, will you, and I'll get a taxi.' She reappeared within a few minutes. The two of them climbed into the cab and drove off leaving me to battle rising nausea as I walked back to my car alone.

That night I was plagued by nightmares. I stood beside the road and stared in terror at the face of the driver high up in his cab. As he came nearer I could see the whites of his eyes discoloured by blood. His fingers gripped the wheel and his thundering lorry bore down upon me. I tried to step forward to bar his way but my feet stuck fast to the pavement. I tried to lift a hand to warn him but my arms wouldn't leave my sides. I tried to shout at him to stop but my lips refused to part. When the lorry ploughed on past me I could feel its hot under belly and smell the choking diesel fumes.

Now that the inquest was over I decided I must try to avoid thinking about Mohan altogether. Remembering brought no benefit, on the contrary it was destructive and could destabilise me in an instant. I started by removing from my home, as far as possible, all visual traces which might trigger memories. I'd long ago removed the photographs but some of the pictures still in evidence we had bought together or were linked to him in some obvious way. Like the Heaton Cooper we brought back from the Lakes after sheltering in a gallery to escape a downpour, or the Pollock print he gave me to hang in my study. So out they went. Then I rummaged through bookshelves and desk drawers and kitchen cupboards and the garage, throwing out everything with Mohan's name on it, however faint the writing. The process was heart-rending but then strong medicine was called for.

I soon realised this was not enough. I could still *hear* Mohan, especially when my sleep encrusted mind hovered on the margins of consciousness. On waking early, my ear caught the high-pitched buzzing of his shaver and strained to pick up the monotonous vibrato as he hummed an accompaniment. Reaching out at midnight to bunch the duvet more snugly round me I heard the floorboards creak as he crossed the landing and braced myself for the jolt as he flopped back onto the mattress. Or dozing over late night television, tired but reluctant to climb the stairs alone, I was startled by the slamming of his car door and waited, breathless, for his footsteps beneath the window.

These experiences were intimately connected to the home we'd shared and couldn't be contained. So it was for these audible reasons that I finally decided to put my house on the market and spend the summer with my parents in the place where I belonged before I met Mohan. I needed to rediscover that younger Ann, the very essence of myself.

CHAPTER FIVE

J ENNY THREW HERSELF wholeheartedly into preparing
for their India trip. I trawled through all available flights
and selected the most suitable, though not necessarily the
cheapest, and went with her to buy the tickets. I guided her
through the process of acquiring a passport and helped her
navigate the eccentricities of the Indian Consulate to obtain
a visa, but I left her to consult the local surgery about pills
and injections on her own. At first Namita refused to take
precautions saying she was immune to the diseases of her
own country but she gave in when Jenny pointed out she
hadn't lived there for so long her immunity would have
lapsed. Jenny made repeated expeditions to the shops in
search of suitable shoes and clothes and presents to take
with them. Namita dug out a few faded photos of her
parents and brothers and told us how happy they had all
been as children. I doubted the idyllic picture she presented
was entirely true.

I drove over to Queen's Road on the day of their
departure and arrived an hour before we were due to set off

for the airport. I reversed into the driveway and parked in front of the garage, it would be easier to load their suitcases this way. A bike skidded to a standstill in front of the little wooden gate which barred the path to the front door. The boy stood on the pavement, one foot resting on his pedal ready for a quick get away. His hair glistened with gel and his forehead with perspiration.

'Hello Miss.'

'Mrs,' I corrected.

'Hello Mrs,' he grinned.

'Do you want something?'

'They going away today?' He nodded towards the house.

'Why do you ask?'

'My mum says they won't be back.' He turned down the corners of his mouth.

'And who told your mum that?'

'She says they won't stay here after what happened. She says it's not right for anyone to live in this house. There must be a curse on it.' He unclipped a plastic water bottle and sucked on the tube for a while before re-attaching it to the cycle frame. 'See yer!' Leaning forward over the handlebars he sped off down the pavement.

I passed the dining room window on my way to the front door. The sill was rotten where the paint had blistered and the metal frame was beginning to corrode. I glanced up at the weathered shingles covering the upper wall of the house. Two or three of the tiles hung crookedly from single nails, and a few roof slates were missing altogether. Although internally the house was in reasonable condition, from the outside it looked jaded. I wondered whether Namita could afford to maintain a property this size on her own modest pension and the widow's portion of Pradip's.

Jenny was surprised to see me. 'You're early!'

'No harm in that.'

Her hair was fastened back so more of her face was visible than usual and I detected a flush of excitement on her cheeks. Over the past six months anxiety had slowly established itself in Jenny's face but, since deciding to go to India with Namita some of her natural cheerfulness had reappeared and today she looked positively radiant. I wished she wasn't going away.

'Don't worry, we won't be gone for long,' she said, sensitive as ever to my mood. 'And I'll write to you.'

I raised my eyebrows. 'We'll see.'

'Honestly, I will. I'll write and let you know how we're getting on.'

I looked her up and down. 'Jeans? You're travelling to India in jeans? I expected to see you in something special, a sari, churidar at least.'

Jenny laughed. 'Mum said we'd be more comfortable travelling like this. Our Indian clothes are in the hand luggage. We get changed at Bombay airport, in the ladies loo!' She gestured towards the collection of matching bags and suitcases which occupied the centre of the hall. 'Almost ready.'

'No hurry. We've plenty of time.' I skirted round the baggage. 'Some lad on a bike was asking questions. I didn't tell him anything, probably safer if people don't realise the house is going to be standing empty.'

'Too late, they know already. Mrs Hussain from over the road has been round to wish us a safe journey. And this morning Mrs Nagra came. You know, from the broken down house next door but one?' Jenny busied herself with her hand luggage. 'My mum and dad are coming to the airport to see us off.'

Namita came slowly down the stairs, two feet on each step like a child, straining to control the weight of a large suitcase which threatened to pull away from her and bump down the stairs on its own. I took the case from her and placed it with ease on the floor beside the others. Namita clung onto the banisters still puffing from her exertions.

'Let's have coffee,' Jenny said. 'You've been on the go all morning, Mum. Time to sit down. Can you make it, Ann? I just want to do one more check upstairs.'

I carried the drinks through to the front room where Namita was sitting on the sofa checking their documents. When I entered she replaced the papers hurriedly in her handbag. Jenny ran down the stairs, took her coffee and went over to perch on the window sill, betraying her excitement. Jenny didn't run, she walked calmly and she didn't perch, she sat serenely. We sipped in silence. This was the moment when somebody should start crying or trawling through past conflicts or confess to some ghastly misdemeanour.

'We never did find out the truth about the fireplace.' Namita was staring at the dead grate. 'If it's really stone or just a fake. Made from a mould, I mean.'

'I'm sure it's stone. Pradip pretended it wasn't just to wind you up,' Jenny reassured her.

'Does it matter?' I asked irritably.

'It would be good to know,' Namita said. 'It would be good to know for certain I was right and he was wrong.'

I loaded their luggage into the boot while Namita climbed into the front. Jenny all too eagerly locked the door and we were off. As the car pulled away the three of us looked back, half expecting to see a ghostly figure waving Hollywood-style from each window. We saw only sightless glass eyes.

We waited at the entrance to the airport for Jenny's parents to arrive, which they eventually did, bringing with them an ill-disciplined assortment of children. Jenny entertained the young ones while her mother made polite conversation with Namita and her father studied his watch. They couldn't stay long, he told me, he had another appointment which he couldn't miss. After a while they shook hands with Namita, kissed Jenny goodbye and left.

Jenny came over and stood close. 'If I get any letters can you put them in my bedroom?'

'I will if I'm back before you are.' I lowered my voice, 'You don't have to stay for long. If you're not enjoying it just come home. And don't do too much for her. She'll wear you out.'

Jenny put an arm around me. 'Don't worry. I'm going to have a great time!'

I hung about till they'd checked in safely and watched as they made their way with their fellow passengers towards the departure lounge. Namita walked with determination while Jenny almost bounced along. As they turned to give a final wave then disappeared from sight, I was surprised to find my misery was tempered with relief.

I didn't wait for their flight to leave but drove straight back home. I took the CD player into the garden and balanced it on the bird table and sang along to arias and danced myself back and forth across the lawn and round the shrubs. I felt the cool shiny grass under my feet and the soil from the flower beds crumble between my toes. My performance was punctuated with repeated sorties into the house to prepare it for the eyes of prospective purchasers.

Later that evening I phoned my mother. 'I'll be with you in roughly a couple of hours.'

'Good, you can join us for supper.'

'No, don't wait for me. I'll eat at a service station on the way.' I hung up before she could denounce the extortionate prices and dubious standards of hygiene prevalent in motorway cafes.

For the second time that day I loaded suitcases into the boot. I paused briefly to post my house keys through the estate agent's door then set off northwards, driving up the motorway excited as a child on Christmas Eve. As I travelled further from the city and its suburbs, past undulating fields dissected by crooked hedges and speckled with the occasional coppice, I realised how hungry I was for all things rural. I wound down the window to catch the smells and sounds of my childhood but was rewarded with diesel fumes and the churning of HGVs.

I stopped briefly to use the service station loo and grab a sandwich which I ate as I drove because I was eager to be there as soon as I could. Eventually hedgerows gave way to dry stone walls and sheep were substituted for cattle. My excitement increased as I drew closer to the village where I'd grown up and finally arrived at my parents' home. I crunched up the drive and came to a halt in front of the house. My father, a giant in checked shirt and baggy cords, come into the glass panelled porch and peered out. He recognised my car and came down the steps in the half light to greet me.

'Good to see you! We weren't expecting you for another half hour at least. Hope you haven't been speeding?'

'Of course I've been speeding! Never dropped below ninety the entire journey,' I said keeping a straight face.

He insisted on struggling with my cases even though they were too heavy for him, so I let him get on with it and went inside. My mother was in the kitchen boiling the kettle.

'Hello darling. Good journey?'

I felt the softness of her cheek as she tried to hug me, before I wriggled free. Her hair, once as dark as mine but now silver grey, waved across her forehead and nestled in little curls around her ears. She covered the pot with the tea cosy I remembered her buying years ago at a WI sale. My mother mixed her own blend of tea leaves, no teabags permitted in her home. Sweepings from the warehouse floor, she declared.

'Fine. Not too much traffic. I enjoyed the drive.' I stretched my arms and arched my back. 'It's far too long since I was last here. Feels really good to be back. I need a change of scenery and different company.' I beamed her a wide smile. She looked surprised and gratified.

I discovered a dusty bottle of Amontillado hidden behind a bowl of fruit on the sideboard and poured myself a glass.

'But I'm making tea!' she protested.

'No problem. I can manage both.'

I watched her lay the breakfast table while the tea was brewing, to save time in the morning, a custom she hadn't dropped even after my father retired. Everything was positioned with precision on the checked table cloth; marmalade pot and silver marmalade spoon, toast rack on its own special plate to catch the crumbs, butter dish and baby butter knife, sugar bowl with sugar spoon shaped like a miniature shovel, bone china cups placed upside down on their saucers, handles aligned. All the social niceties I scorned but which reassured me I was home.

'How was Namita when she left?'

'Okay.' I wasn't going to be drawn. She'd taken me to task often enough for lack of warmth towards my mother-in-law.

'Any idea how long they'll be away?' She laid knives and spoons carefully along the lines of little puckered squares.

'No idea. At least a month, maybe three. My guess is Jenny will be homesick.'

My father came and stood in the middle of the dining room, arms folded across his massive chest. 'I've put your cases in your room. Hope that was right? Pressure's a bit low in the front offside tyre. I'll take a look at it for you tomorrow. While I'm at it, I'll check the oil.'

'No need. I took it in for a service last week.' I finished my sherry and took the glass through to the kitchen. 'I'm forty one for God's sake, not fourteen. I can take care of my own car,' I shouted through the serving hatch.

My mother followed me. 'He was only trying to help. You didn't have to speak to him like that.'

'Like what for goodness sake? I only said there's no need for him to do anything to my car.'

'Well you could have said it nicely,' she muttered.

'I believe in open communication.'

She frowned. 'You believe in being rude.'

Here we go again, I thought. 'I'm only following the rules. Do as you would be done by. I want people to be forthright when they speak to me.'

My father poked his head through the hatch. 'You don't really think the way Ann talks is going to upset me, do you? Come on, let's have this cup of tea and talk about what she plans to do with her holiday.'

I carried the tea things into the sitting room, poured the dark aromatic liquid through a strainer, which needless to say came with its own little dish to catch the drips, and handed round the cups. They raked over village gossip, telling me about the newly arrived couple who wanted to extend their property.

'Why on earth do they need two bathrooms and a second lounge?' said my father. 'An ostentatious building, quite out of keeping with its surroundings. They'll never get planning permission. And if they'd only bothered to talk to the locals they'd have discovered there's a preservation order on those beeches.'

They told me about the old man in the house at the far end of the lane who'd been put in a nursing home after suffering yet another stroke, and speculated whether his son would sell the house as it was, pretty run down by all accounts, or renovate it first and make himself a tidy profit. And then I told them I'd put my house on the market.

'Have you now? How interesting! Have you seen a property you want to buy?' This was something my father could get his teeth into. He saw it as his duty to provide advice thereby helping to safeguard my investment. 'You'll need to act pretty sharpish. Houses don't stay on the market long these days.'

'True, especially in my road,' I said. 'Very popular with young families. The local secondary school has an excellent reputation. I haven't decided yet but I've an idea I might move to a small town, possibly a village.' This was another reason for my visit. I wanted to test out how I felt about being in the countryside, whether I could survive for any length of time away from the conveniences of the city.

'But you couldn't wait to get away from village life!' exclaimed my mother. 'You wanted to live amongst theatres and art galleries and concert halls and eat food from around the world. You said villages were all right for holidays but not for living in.'

'That was then, mother. I am allowed to change, you know,' I said with laboured sarcasm.

'Now your brother was different. He spent all his time outdoors. You wouldn't catch him living in a city.'

My mother's face assumed that particular tender but proud expression she reserved for conversations about her son who was something high up in Forestry and, unlike me, had not betrayed his rural roots. My brother and I had little to do with each other as I was growing up, older than me by eleven years he was entering sixth form by the time I started school, yet all my life I had walked in his shadow. He was good looking and well behaved, even as a child. He excelled at all types of sport and had a flair for science which made my parents very, very proud.

I couldn't compete on the rugby or cricket pitch, or in the laboratory, but I did write poems and stories and articles for the school magazine. My mother read most of what I wrote but my father didn't and he was the one I really wanted to impress. The only time my father paid me any attention was when I was contrary or answered back.

'Come to her senses at last,' he murmured. 'It's no life at all being surrounded by concrete and tarmac and seeing nothing of Nature except the sky. Even that's polluted by chemicals and street lights.'

'Oh for goodness sake! What about the gardens and parks and tree lined avenues and urban foxes?' I was tired and had no patience for this. 'And anyway, what makes you think everyone in cities chooses to live there?'

'You two . . . . !' My mother shook her head in exasperation and looked from one to the other. Then she began to giggle. For a moment I was annoyed, then I joined in. My father, looking offended, stood up and collected the empty cups thus signalling he was ready for bed.

'What time will you be getting up tomorrow, Ann?' he asked.

I shrugged. 'Haven't a clue. I'm on holiday, I'll get up when I feel like it. Why?'

'It's the farmers' market. I wondered if you'd be interested in coming. We try not to miss it.' He paused in the middle of the room. 'Your mother buys cheeses, sausages too if we're lucky. We aim to leave around half nine.'

'Maybe,' I said. 'If I'm up in time.'

But I wasn't up in time. I was woken in the night by the sound of my father crossing the landing on his way to the spare room to escape my mother's snores. I lay sweating as Mohan filled the darkness. I was furious. He'd left me to face this terrible sorrow all alone, how dare he now sabotage my attempts at recovery? But I couldn't stay angry for long. I took his dear face in my hands and held it close, kissing his eyelids and stroking his cheeks until he faded with the dawn. When I finally came downstairs a chainsaw was tearing through my skull and the house was empty.

I took in the familiar objects, the piano hidden beneath piles of magazines, obviously no one had lifted the lid for a long while. When I was a child I practised nightly with ferocious self discipline and trudged to my music teacher's house after school on Thursdays. She exhorted me to touch the keys lightly, to pretend I was a gazelle not a herd of elephants. But my fingers, so plump they often depressed two keys together, simply wouldn't do gazelles however hard I tried. One afternoon my teacher clapped her hands to her ears, threw the music book across the room and shouted at me to 'go away, just go away *now*'. I remember being impressed by this display of temper from an adult. Later she phoned my mother and advised her not to waste any more of her money, so I was forced to give it up.

I stroked the pale oatmeal surface of my mother's sewing box which stood in the corner, rediscovering the waxy sheen. I remembered picking out the finest needles and using them to lance my teenage spots, face pressed up close against the oval mirror which still hung above the fireplace. And borrowing a pair of pinking scissors to nibble at my fringe.

I carried my cup of fair trade coffee back upstairs and ran a bath. There was a shower of course, and in my own house I always showered, but lying in a bath until the water grew lukewarm and my skin wrinkled was part of the ritual of being a child in my parents' home again. How easily I slipped back into the role, insolent and irresponsible. I stepped in, dropped a battered plastic duck into the water and watched as it floated in lazy circles above my stomach.

You saw your body from a different angle in the bath, spread out in front of your eyes. In the shower all was fore-shortened when viewed from above. I stared, fascinated, at the silver outline of my submerged legs, a coating of tiny bubbles which I could erase by running my finger along the curve of my calf. The steam relaxed and cleansed me and diffused the pain in my head. But I didn't linger because I could hear birdsong through the open window and as soon as I was dressed I went outside to make the most of the sunshine and clear air.

I followed the road which led out of the village between fields, glad to leave pavements behind and walk along grass verges. In the summer I used to walk home from school along this route, lost in daydreams as I walked. The day was warm with a light breeze and at first I forged ahead, cutting through the wind so my thoughts streamed out on either side in my wake. I kept this speed up for a while then reminded myself I was on holiday and didn't have to hurry to attend a meeting or teach a class, so I slowed to a gentler pace and let memories gather and settle around me.

The roadside plants alone were enough to stir memories, especially the long grasses. Some you could pull through thumb and forefinger, for others you had to use your first and second fingers side by side. Sorrel was easily the most satisfying, yielding a palm full of rusty fairy pennies. Delicate pink plumes, floppy foxtails and coarse clumps on wiry stems needed more persuading. I pulled meadow grasses from their tough outer sheaths and stuck the succulent new growth between my teeth. I placed a foxglove bonnet on each finger and draped skeins of sticky goose grass, dotted with little hairy globules, round my shoulders.

I wondered why I hadn't done this before on the many occasions when Mohan and I visited. Then I remembered, Mohan was not one for walking. We would drive my parents to a beauty spot and treat them to a leisurely lunch but we never walked. Once we had invited Jenny and Chandan to come north with us for a few days. Chandan was planning an adventure weekend for members of his boys' club and wanted to explore the area. He volunteered to accompany me on a hike and we made good walking partners so long as we kept conversation to a minimum. Jenny, who loved the views but hadn't brought suitable footwear, preferred to stay home and help my mother bake scones to eat later with clotted cream and jam.

My father kept Mohan busy at the sawhorse cutting branches into logs which he did so vigorously that sawdust went everywhere, even in his hair. Then my father handed Mohan a pair of overalls and put him to work in the garage. Chandan and I found him there on our return, flat out under a car and wielding a spanner.

I came to a halt as my nostrils filled with the smells of fresh sawdust and engine oil. No, no. That way madness lay. I breathed deeply and took in the smell of cattle. Behind a nearby gate stood a bevy of brainless beauties, black and white with grubby knees. Their tranquil eyes weighed me up as clouds of tiny flies encircled their heads.

When I arrived home my parents were just finishing their meal so I fetched myself a bowl and joined them at the table. My mother looked up reproachfully.

'You didn't leave a note to say where you were. We were worried.'

'The great out doors beckoned and I obeyed.' I helped myself to some soup. Whatever the weather, at midday they had soup.

She studied my hands suspiciously. 'Aren't you going to wash your hands?'

'Yes, all right, I'll wash my hands. They need washing. I've spent the morning playing with grass.' I laughed at her puzzled expression.

'You look happy,' my father said, putting down his crossword. 'Healthy, contented. Where d'you get to?'

'Oh just wandering about, you know, revisiting old haunts. How was the market?' I went back to the kitchen to wash and noticed a collection of cellophane wrapped wedges on the worktop. One was pale cream laced with blue, another had a dark green rind bearing the imprint of muslin, a third was mottled with random maroon blotches.

'I'm saving those for dinner tonight,' my mother called out, afraid I might insist on having a tasting session right away. But I was in a good mood and didn't want to pick a fight with anyone.

'D'you have any plans while you're here?' my father asked when I came back to the table. 'If you like we could invite some of your old classmates round for a meal. A few of them still live in the area. You know, so you can catch up and compare notes.' My mother gasped.

'Sure. I can explain how my husband was killed in a car crash last year, along with his father and brother, and how I'm selling up because I can't bear living in the same house without him. And my old classmates can offer their profound sympathies. Should make for a jolly evening.' I chucked a handful of croutons into my soup. My father's ears turned red as he bent over his crossword. My mother swept invisible crumbs into her hand.

'It's alright,' I said. 'I don't want to talk about Mohan but that doesn't mean I'm made of porcelain. I'm not going to seek out company but if I do bump into someone who knows me, well then, I'll handle it. Just don't go arranging anything. Leave me to drift. Okay?' They glanced at each other in evident relief.

'Okay,' my mother said and went into the kitchen to make coffee and consume a bar of fair trade chocolate.

And drift I did, frequently arriving home beyond rational conversation. My parents found this odd but dare not criticise and in general respected my wish to be left alone. I spent part of the day on college work, preparing materials for the new syllabus, and the rest of my time aimlessly wandering, getting back in touch with a younger version of myself. The wandering triggered the memories and then the memories took over and became more real than the things I saw before me.

I walked along the path beside the stream as I'd done so often as a child. When I came to the little bridge I peered underneath to see how many trolls were hiding in the shadows. I played the detective game where broken twigs and displaced stones became vital clues in a murder hunt and dark patches on the path were pools of the victim's blood. As I walked I breathed in the spirit of this child who created the world according to her own imagination, hoping her imagination would bring meaning to my world which was utterly without meaning.

One day I found myself on the pavement in front of the village school so I came to a halt and stared through the railings. I'd always disliked the playground not because it was scary, I could easily hold my own if a fight broke out, but because I found it boring. I couldn't see the point of skipping ropes or games involving balls. In any case I didn't have friends to play with but that didn't bother me, I was content with the conversations which played continuously inside my head. Rainy days when we were allowed to stay inside suited me much better. I remembered the thrill of sitting in the library corner working on my first ever project, Scott's expedition to the Antarctic, a tale which fired my imagination.

I was engrossed in the pursuit of my childhood but that didn't stop me thinking about Jenny and I longed to hear how she and Namita were getting on. When, about a fortnight into my holiday, my mother handed me an airmail envelope at the breakfast table, I recognised the handwriting and my heartbeat quickened.

CHAPTER SIX

I SLIT OPEN THE envelope with my father's silver letter knife, a family heirloom, then slid the blade back into its red leather sheath. Jenny's handwriting, immature and backward sloping, was easy to read. She left school as soon as she could so her writing had never degenerated into the scrawl of someone who'd spent hours scribbling lecture notes. I scanned the contents quickly then took the letter into the living room where I could read it through more carefully.

> Dear Ann,
>
> How are you? How are your Mum and Dad? Hope you're enjoying your holiday. The journey went fine, Mum was brilliant on the plane, no trouble. We got through the passport check's and custom's okay, just followed everyone else. There was a big crowd of Mum's relation's waiting for us at the airport, they hugged us and cried but I think it was

too much for Mum she was very quiet. She hardly talked to anyone.

We stayed with Boro Uncle the first few days, that's Mum's oldest brother. He lives in a town on the edge of Kolkata, Boro Aunty says he's an important person but I don't think he has much money looking at his house. Now we are with Choto Uncle (youngest brother), he has three son's and they all live with him, it's a busy house with lots of children so I'm happy!! Choto Uncle is more fun than Boro Uncle and the house is much cleaner. One little girl has the job to wipe dirt off the window grills, that's all she does all day!! She's so sweet, I've made friends with her and her brother, he washes the floor's.

It's the rainy season (monsoon) very hot and sticky. I get really sweaty so I keep going for a shower. I've got prickly heat, it looks like frog spawn under my skin!! I can't stop scratching, they got me some powder to put on it.

They are looking after me very well. They worry about me getting a bad stomach so they make me drink boiled water and to start with they didn't put chilli in my food so I told them at home I eat everything Mum eats. The food is really great, they have their own cook!!! The women measure out rice and dal and give him fish and vegetable's and spice's and he cooks them. Mum said she was looking forward to fresh spice's instead of the powdered stuff in packet's, but now she isn't much interested in food, I'm worried she's losing weight. They bought cereal and cake specially for me, the cornflakes are soft and the cake is dry but it was kind of them. They buy Indian sweets for visitors, the best one is called shondesh and it's out of this world nothing like the barfi you get at Royal Sweet Centre. I eat LOADS which makes them happy.

Mum thought coming here would help but I can't see it has. She sits by herself most of the time or wanders around the house looking for something, I don't know what but she never finds it. I wish I could help but when I speak to her she doesn't answer, it's like she doesn't want anything to do with me. Hope I haven't done anything to upset her.

Choto Uncle's son's wife took me out shopping for present's. In the tourist shop everything is fixed price and dead expensive but you can bargain in ordinary shops, I had to hide when she bought something in the market cos they think all foreigners have lots of money!! I got a lovely shawl for you.

One day we took a picnic and drove out beside the river Ganges to cool down. We had loochi and *meat (goat!!) curry and mango's. I haven't told you about the mango's they're much nicer than the ones we get at home cos they get ripe on the tree. One of Mum's nephews (sort of) sang for us, he's got a lovely voice. Absolutely BRILLIANT day!!*

Look after yourself Ann, at least let your Mum look after you. I'll write again soon. Lots and lots of love

Jenny X X X

How happy and relaxed she sounded. She was making the most of the experience and I was delighted for her. Jenny had only been out of England twice before, with her school on both occasions. This trip was very different, living with the locals, a chance to see Kolkata from the inside. I tried to picture her playing with the children, eating Indian sweets, tucking into curry while enjoying the breeze on the banks of the Ganges.

But I was puzzled by Namita's treatment of her. She'd agreed to take Jenny as her companion, why ignore her once they'd arrived? As usual Jenny didn't complain but she was clearly hurt. Of course there were some advantages, Jenny was free to do the things she wanted without always having to consider her mother-in-law.

I folded the thin sheets, pushed them back into the envelope and gazed out at the garden. Encountering Jenny through her prose seemed to open up a gap between us. The punctuation was poor, a dearth of full stops, an excess of apostrophes and exclamation marks, the vocabulary somewhat limited. The letter highlighted the contrast between Jenny's education and mine and I began to wonder what she really thought of my intellectual ramblings. She never appeared intimidated or unduly impressed, most probably she dismissed my book learning as irrelevant. For all her lack of formal education, Jenny negotiated life more successfully than either Namita or me. Hadn't someone defined intelligence as the ability to adapt to changing situations? Well Jenny did that admirably. I knew she'd get on fine in Kolkata whether Namita spoke to her or not and it was clear she'd already won over Namita's relatives. I wrote back immediately and before too long I heard from her again.

> *Dear Ann*
>
> *I got your letter thanks for writing. What do you mean you didn't know I minded about a little bit of dirt, what a cheek!! You wouldn't believe how filthy the other house was.*
>
> *I really really LOVE it here. It was so quiet with just me and Mum at Queen's Road but there's always something happening here. They have lots of visitors then we go and visit back. And every*

week there's some kind of festival. Remember I said part of the reason for me coming was to get closer to Chandan and you said RUBBISH? Well you were right I'm not closer to him here, in fact I hardly think of him at all. His cousin's look a bit like him but they don't remind me of him cos their lives are so different. I'm enjoying myself but that's got nothing to do with Chandan.

They took me to see Raj Bari yesterday. Raj Bari means king's house only it isn't a huge posh building like you imagine a palace, there were lots of small king's in the old days. What an AMAZING place!!! There's a big hall where the king had feasts for hundreds of priest's. The god's and goddesses on the walls look like flesh and blood human's. There are stone steps going down to the river for the men to wash themselves. The women lived in rooms with tiny window's, I wonder where they had their bath? I bet they weren't allowed near the river in case the men saw them. No one looks after it so it's falling down, the army holds training camp's in it.

One night the Rani (queen) had a dream about a new goddess and she told the Rajah (king) so he told all the statue maker's to try and make a statue like the goddess in the Rani's dream. One man got it just right and the Rajah was so pleased he gave

him some land and made him the royal statue maker.
That man's family still live in the town and still
make clay things. They sell huge statues of famous
people to America and Japan and places like that. I
bought some clay biscuits and butterflies and lizard's
for present's, hope they don't get broken.

Poor Mum. She's not happy here. She's going
back to Boro Uncle's house tomorrow, maybe Choto
Aunty is finding it too much or Choto Uncle has had
enough. They asked if I wanted to go with Mum and
I said NO, I'm happy here. I couldn't do anything
for her if I did go cos she won't let me.

Lots of love and take care,

Jenny X X X

A lovely letter, so full of life. I particularly liked the
description of the rajah's palace. Being exposed to another
culture seemed to have unlocked Jenny's creativity. Bengalis
are the poets and musicians of India, Pradip would often
boast.

So they'd split up and were staying in different houses.
The thought of Jenny liberated from her role as dutiful
daughter-in-law gave me some satisfaction. Long may it last!
Well not too long actually, I was looking forward to seeing
her again. I'd talked more to Jenny than to anyone else since
Mohan died and, what's more, she was the only person who

touched me. I mean physically touched me. Gently chaffing the back of my hand when she wanted to calm me down, resting her hand lightly on my arm to coax me towards her point of view. No one else dared touch me, though my mother attempted to.

Oh God, how I ached for his lips warm on my palm, a string of little kisses tracing the blue veins up the inside of my arm until he reached the bend of elbow, pausing there before continuing upwards to the armpit. Skin on skin, flesh on flesh. In bed I missed the solid weight of his body next to mine. Sometimes I gathered up all the cushions I could find, heaped them beside me and draped an arm over them while I slept.

I must concentrate on the here and now and, as it happened, I was faced with a practical problem. I'd accepted an offer for my house and, although I knew it might take some time to conclude the sale, I wanted to move my furniture into Queen's Road straightaway and stay there until I found a suitable property. I planned to do this before the start of the academic year so I sent off a letter to Namita and while I waited impatiently for her reply something unexpected happened.

CHAPTER SEVEN

I T WAS A hot and breathless afternoon. I heard a pheasant bark from inside a little wood where I remembered playing at weekends so I struck out across the rough ground to investigate. I climbed the wooden style and began to explore the shady world inside the boundary.

'Ann, isn't it?' The voice startled me. I turned my head and scowled at the tall, round-shouldered figure emerging from the gloom. As he approached I realised I'd passed him a few times while out walking. Each time I thought him vaguely familiar but we hadn't spoken.

'Yes, I'm Ann. Why d'you ask?' I was annoyed at the intrusion.

He peered at me and came closer. 'I thought it was you. I've seen you round and about but I wasn't quite sure. I'm Colin. Your brother's friend, Colin. Remember?' He raised his tangled eyebrows expectantly.

I studied his long, narrow face for anything that might provide me with a clue. His features were surprisingly delicate for a man but it was his eyes, pale grey with tiny pupils, which finally jogged my memory. I could smell coffee, stale beer, cigarette smoke. It was late and my brother and his friends were huddled in our kitchen comparing notes on the girls they'd danced with that night.

'D'you recognise me? I knew you as a kid but I've seen you a few times since then.' He inclined his head hopefully. 'I've been to your house many times. Don't you remember, I'm the one who passed out in your bathroom with the tap running . . . .'

'. . . . and the basin full of regurgitated take-away,' I said. 'Yes, I remember. How could I forget?'

'By the time your brother found me . . .'

'. . . the bathroom was flooded,' I interrupted again. 'Water collected under the bathroom floor and poured out through the hole round the light fitting downstairs if I remember correctly. We were without electricity for ages. My father was livid. The ceiling was ruined. We had to put in a new one.'

'Your father demanded my parents pay for it. In the end I think they agreed to go halves. No pocket money for months.' Colin grimaced. 'I've a feeling that was the last time your brother invited me home. Not surprising really.'

I recalled the incident clearly because it was one of the rare occasions when my brother was in trouble. Being in trouble was usually my prerogative. I studied this man with interest, intrigued by what the years had done to his appearance. Those pathetic grey wisps trailing down his neck were presumably an attempt to compensate for the loss of a full head of hair. What colour had it been? Dull and mousy probably, nothing distinctive or I would have remembered.

'What's your brother doing now? We've lost touch unfortunately.' He leant against a tree, pulled a pipe from his jacket pocket and knocked it on the heel of his shoe dislodging the burnt tobacco. He refilled the bowl from a leather pouch.

'Pursuing a career in Forestry. Doing very well for himself or so my mother tells me. He and I don't keep in touch either, as it happens. We've nothing much in common. He's Science, I'm Arts.'

I had no wish to prolong the conversation. Indeed I hoped that if I ignored Colin he might go away. I stretched out my hand to retrieve a ball of yellowing sheep's wool caught on the barbed wire running along the top of the wall and rubbed the greasy fibre between my fingers. The field on this side was dotted with sheep. If you listened carefully you could hear the rasping of their teeth as they single-mindedly grazed their way forward.

Colin tried again. 'I've passed you a few times when I've been out. Are you up visiting your parents?'

'Sort of. I've become too much a city girl of late, thought it would do me good to get back in touch with my rural roots. A bit of solitude, peace and quiet. Escape the masses.' He didn't take the hint.

'Couldn't live in a city myself. Don't mind the odd visit, but live in one? No thank you.'

'Things here aren't so different,' I said, drawn into the conversation in spite of myself. 'Yesterday I was listening to a bull roar. Put me in mind of drunks at closing time! And take these trees, I can go to the park and walk through trees just like these.'

'Not the same thing at all.' Colin waved his pipe to take in a broad sweep of the wood. 'These trees are in control of their own territory, city trees are merely invited guests.'

I looked at the massed ranks towering above us, dipping and nodding in the breeze, each tree moving in a different pattern according to the shape of leaf and length of branch. When I first left home I'd tried to convince myself I only needed a single tree to gaze on from my city window, a soloist, a principal ballerina. But in the face of this orchestra, this chorus, I couldn't maintain the deception. Perhaps my father was right, a life composed of tarmac and concrete diminished one's soul.

'I heard about your husband. Killed in a road accident, wasn't he?'

I glared at him. 'Well good for you, come right out with it why don't you? Please don't worry about upsetting me.'

'Sorry.' He looked away not knowing what to say next.

'Sorry for what? For the accident? Well that was hardly your fault, was it? Or sorry for speaking out? Please, don't apologise. It's so refreshing. Most people can't bring themselves to mention the fact I'm a widow.'

'Look, Ann, I'm disturbing you. Would you rather I left you alone?' He bent forward, tapped his pipe against a fallen trunk and stuffed it back into his pocket.

'Yes, actually, I would.' I turned away and tried to focus on the sheep which continued to graze, oblivious to our presence.

'Before I go I'd like to explain.' He hesitated. 'Is that all right?'

I didn't answer.

'Fact is, things aren't going too well for me either. I needed to get some perspective on things. Take myself out of the situation. So I came back to my parents for a while to see if that helped me understand what was going on.' He sighed and kicked at the dark leaf mould covering the ground. 'I don't even know what I want out of life. It's not as clear as it was when we were younger.'

'Why are you telling me, for God's sake?' I was genuinely puzzled. I barely knew this man and within five minutes of striking up a conversation he was threatening to unburden himself of heaven knows what intimacies. A typical man, he assumed every female he met was willing to provide a listening ear.

'Sorry,' he said. 'But it's not as if you're a stranger. I suppose the real reason I'm talking to you is because I thought we were treading similar paths. You know what I mean. I've seen you tramping the lanes deep in thought and I'm doing the same. I've got things to ponder and sort out in my head too.'

He was looking at me earnestly, waiting for me to acknowledge we were kindred spirits. His expression made me want to laugh. But after all, I thought, he might have a point. He belonged to the time before Mohan, exactly what I needed. It would do me good to reminisce.

'I used to come to this wood at weekends. A group of boys played here and sometimes they let me join in. They pretended those were bones picked clean by vultures.' I pointed to a spot where the dead white stems of bluebells streaked the bare earth. 'Climbing trees, that was my speciality. I always managed to go higher than any of them. I was tall so I could reach further but I was heavy which was a handicap.' I remembered the sense of danger as I worked my way upwards, testing each hold, easing my body higher and higher until the swaying branches were too thin to bear my weight. 'I was something of a tomboy.'

'I can believe it.' Colin's eyes were dull as unpolished slate.

'They hung a rope from one of the branches.' I scanned the surrounding trees looking for clues. 'I think it was on this side, can't be sure. The canopy's so dense, not enough light for anything to grow here now. Anyway, you had to swing out on the rope and let go just when you were above a patch of nettles. Landing in those nettles, they were so deep they covered you completely, well it was an initiation rite of sorts. If you weren't brave enough to drop into those nettles you couldn't join their gang.' I smiled as I brought the long forgotten image to mind.

'I guess jumping into a nettle bath would seem pretty pointless to today's lot. What would the equivalent be? Shop-lifting, covering your school in graffiti?'

'What about you? Did you ever come here with my brother?' I was determined to draw him back into the 'I remember' game.

'We did, but not together, and you wouldn't want to hear the details! For us it was more a place to bring your girlfriend. Wouldn't put up with the discomfort now-a-days, would they?' He was smiling now.

'I think my lot made the best of the back row at the Plaza. Not me though, I was always glued to the screen.' I had no regrets on that score. I wasn't interested in the opposite sex until I was much older.

Colin grew serious again. 'Thanks for talking to me, Ann. And I'm sorry I was a bit tactless earlier. If you're going to be around for a while shall we meet up for a drink? A meal if you prefer?' He spoke tentatively, unsure of my response. In fact his overall demeanour struck me as apologetic and uncertain.

'Okay, why not? Call me at my parents'. Their number's in the book.'

Instead of going for a drink we went to a concert. It was my idea but Colin agreed immediately. Like me he enjoyed going to concerts but classed himself a musical amateur. The performance was given by a touring national orchestra and staged in the town hall ten miles away. This was a regular event organised by the local Arts Committee whose raison d'être was to introduce young people in particular to the playing of first rate musicians who could usually be heard only in large cities. In other words to bring high culture to the peasants.

I offered to pick Colin up. I stopped in front of his parents' house and hooted but when no one emerged I walked down the uneven path and pressed the bell. An elderly gentleman, who I presumed was Colin's father, opened the door and leant for a while against the door frame struggling to catch his breath. I followed as he shuffled slowly down the dark and narrow hallway into a small sitting room where he showed me to a chair. The experience was like passing through a tunnel in the rock before entering Aladdin's cave. Photos smothered the walls, stood in lines on shelves and mantelpiece and balanced on the tops of cupboards so that the place resembled an over-crowded portrait gallery. As Colin's father shuffled off again to fetch his son I heard him mutter, 'dreadful business, dreadful business'. I wasn't sure if he was referring to the idea of Colin and me going to a concert together or expressing sympathy at Mohan's death. In either case I didn't think he was expecting a response.

A quick glance at the chair warned me it was probably too spongy for comfort, so I moved about the room inspecting the numerous photographs. They depicted a boy at various stages of development; a baby in christening robe, a toddler paddling in the sea, a whole series of class photographs taken with teacher at the end of successive school years. I examined them closely but couldn't pick out Colin from amongst the other children. However, I did recognise the face of the young graduate sporting gown and mortar board. Then came wedding pictures and pictures of the happy couple on holiday, followed by family groups when babies started to arrive and themselves moved through childhood. The most recent photograph showed Colin shaking hands with a suited official as he accepted an award of some kind. In each and every picture Colin wore a cautious expression as if he were uncertain why he was there and hoped someone would soon arrive to tell him what he should do next.

I could hear noises off, the bubbling, sizzling and clattering produced when someone's busy in the kitchen. Colin's father returned to inform me his son had gone on an errand but would I please wait as he would be back soon and would I like a cup of tea? I declined the tea but decided after all to risk the chair. We sat in silence until we heard a door opening at the back of the house and Colin came into the room.

'Sorry about that, Ann. Had to pop out for a minute.' He looked flustered.

'No problem. Your father's taking good care of me.' I smiled at the old man who nodded graciously.

'Hope you've introduced yourselves. Ann's brother came here once or twice but you don't remember him, do you Pop?' Colin tugged at his collar and tie before putting on his jacket. 'Shall we go?'

An elderly woman bustled into the room. She wiped her hands on a towel then flung it over her shoulder as she stretched up on tiptoe to peck Colin's cheek. He stooped to receive her kiss. So that's why he's round shouldered, I thought, all those years of bending to his mother's lips.

'Bye, Ma. Don't wait up.'

His mother smiled at me mischievously. 'You'll look after him, Ann, won't you?'

She followed us down the hall and stood in the doorway watching as we walked along the path towards my car. Her hair, shining white and smooth, framed her maternal smile. As we drove off I noticed Colin's father had joined her, one hand gripping her shoulder for support as he raised the other to wave goodbye. They continued waving until we were out of sight.

'Don't wait up. Look after him, Ann,' I mimicked. 'How old do they think you are!'

'It's what we do, it doesn't mean anything.' Colin was defensive. 'Yes, they treat me as if I was still a child. So what? It costs me nothing to play along. There's no harm in it.'

'If you say so.' I was surprised by his touchiness. 'At least it's an improvement on the way I am with my parents. When I'm at home I revert to stroppy teenager.'

'I can believe it.'

'Your father's very breathless.'

'His chest's been bad for years. Sometimes doesn't even have the puff to talk. Ma copes pretty well but I've noticed they've started to depend more and more on me for help,'

Colin said. I dreaded the thought of my parents becoming dependent on me.

Colin was a poor passenger. He pressed his foot onto an imaginary brake when we encountered traffic lights, craned his neck to look to the right every time we approached a roundabout and made disapproving noises when I changed gear. I suggested he shut his eyes. If he couldn't see what was happening, I explained, he wouldn't be so nervous.

'Sorry. No offence intended. I've always been a hopeless passenger. Susan, that's my wife, refuses to let me into her car. Just ignore me. We're almost there anyway.'

Once inside the hall Colin was a very attentive companion in an old-fashioned sort of way. He helped me off with my jacket, made sure I could see without obstruction and during the interval insisted on buying me a drink. We spoke little, both absorbed in the music and our own thoughts.

The first part of the programme was lightweight, designed to appeal to a younger audience. The second half was devoted to Rachmaninov's second symphony, a lyrical work with which I was fairly familiar. The audience listened entranced as the subdued and wistful opening passage developed into menacing brass crescendos, haunting and mysterious motifs, and swathes of passionate melody. According to the blurb on the back page of the programme the *Dies irae* from the Latin requiem mass, a musical allusion to death, underlay the piece. No wonder, then, I felt immediately in tune with it.

For the most part the music engaged my mind as well as my emotions, demanding intelligent involvement. But I had no defence against the little moan which came near the beginning and again at the close of the first movement. In its elemental form, before it was extended and elaborated upon, that feeble scrap of sound bypassed my head and pierced directly to my soul. It came only a handful of times but it continued to moan and echo within me long after the brass and strings had faded.

We emerged from the town hall into the warmth of a summer evening and together descended the pretentious flight of steps. We stood for a while watching the other concert goers as they said their farewells and moved off towards their cars. Colin took out his pipe, knocked it against his shoe, refilled it from his tobacco pouch and lit up.

'Let's go for a drink,' he suggested.

'Okay.' I was in no hurry to break the symphonic spell. 'What about your folks? Won't they wonder where you are?'

'Ma will be sound asleep by now, and Pop, well he hardly gets any sleep at the best of times. Spends the night propped up in bed and dozes off when he can.' Colin's eyes begged me not to resume my teasing. 'The fuss they made about seeing us off. They worry about me, especially at the moment. Same way I worry about my kids who aren't actually kids any more.'

'So where d'you suggest?' If he was going to unburden himself I'd rather he did it while I was comfortably seated.

'There's a decent little pub near here. Walking distance.'

'Lead the way,' I said.

We walked a little way down the hill, passing the well lit scenery in shop windows. He stopped in front of a stone archway and led me through it and across a dim cobbled yard to an entrance set back behind the main street. Inside everywhere was dark wood panelling, there were stags' heads all over the walls and the lighting was too dim. A few patrons sat chatting quietly in one corner. Colin bought the drinks, mine a bitter lemon with ice, and carried them over to the table I'd chosen.

'My father-in-law used to say it shouldn't be called bitter lemon,' I said. 'He said lemons aren't bitter, they're sour. He maintained the English palate wasn't capable of distinguishing bitter from sour. Coffee powder and paracetamol are bitter, limes and lemons are sour.' I could hear Pradip voicing his complaint. He would repeat it whenever he overheard a customer ordering a bitter lemon.

Colin said, 'Lemon rind can be bitter. It's the pith actually. That's why you have to be careful when you're grating lemons, not to grate too deep.' After a brief pause he continued, 'When I spoke to you in the wood that day, I told you I'd come back here to think. Well, I expect you've guessed. My marriage is in trouble.'

I looked at this person sitting opposite me. I saw a lanky climbing plant, tendrils quivering, exploring, reaching out for a firm structure to twine around, buds searching this way and that for the sun's warmth to coax them into flower. Whatever made him think I could supply what he needed?

'For God's sake, Colin. Why are you telling me? We've only just met!'

'No we haven't,' he protested. 'You're my school friend's sister. I've known you since you were a little girl. Anyway, listening to music always loosens my tongue.'

'You might have warned me.'

'Susan and me, we're having marital difficulties,' he went on undeterred. 'If that's how to describe it. In fact it's more a lack of anything remotely marital. Since the children left home we don't have a shared focus. Known as empty nest syndrome, I believe. Why maintain the nest once the fledglings have flown?'

It's me not you, I thought bitterly, who has an extreme absence of everything marital.

'We both work, you see.' Colin leant forward, removed the beer mats from under our glasses and placed them far apart. 'All our energies go into our jobs, so we also get our rewards from work.' He spun the mats around in little circles, maintaining their distance from each other.

'We have more in common with our colleagues than we do with each other. They share our frustrations and successes first hand. Susan and me, well we don't talk, we don't argue. Sometimes I wish we did. More a case of long range hostility.' He moved the mats right to the edges of the table. His hands were pale, his fingers long and delicate with red wrinkles around the knuckles.

'What do I know? I don't have children, let alone an empty nest.' I stared unblinking into his grey eyes. 'Try talking to someone who understands what you're going through.'

'I'm not looking for advice, just thought I should explain my situation.' He lowered his eyes. 'Though it would be good to discuss things with an outsider, someone who could be objective I mean.'

'Alright. So now I know why you're here. I hope you and your wife sort things out, come to an agreement and do whatever seems best.' I retrieved the beer mats and replaced them under our glasses. 'Meanwhile I'd like to discuss the concert, if that's okay with you? I thoroughly enjoyed it. The Rachmaninov was especially good . . . .'

'There's a short wail,' he interrupted. 'A little half-formed curling motif, at the start and end of the first movement. Did you notice it? Cuts straight to the heart every time.'

'A moan,' I whispered. 'It's a moan not a wail. A feeble scrap of sound. Pierces the soul more powerfully than all the sweeping emotion of the violins that follow.' I sipped my bitter lemon to moisten the dryness in my throat, shaken by Colin's reference to the very sound which had so affected me. This echo of my own emotions was uncanny and left me feeling, quite illogically, that I was somehow betraying Mohan who had no time for my kind of music.

'Come on, that's an exaggeration. The passion of the third movement is superb, equal to anything Tchaikovsky produced.' Colin swirled his hands gracefully to press home the point.

'I've a feeling most critics would say that too was an exaggeration!' I laughed.

We continued to discuss the concert, commenting on the programme, the orchestra and the audience. We shared the same opinion on most things; the acoustics could have been better but the atmosphere created by the crowd of hungry concert goers was terrific. We disagreed on other counts; the conductor's exuberant showmanship appealed to me whereas Colin condemned him for being flowery and playing too much to the gallery.

But as soon as the opportunity arose Colin reverted to what was obviously his favourite topic, himself. He insisted on recounting the course of his life since he left the village which had been his home and mine. He told me how he'd stayed on in the university town where he was a student because he wanted to be near his girlfriend. By the time she graduated he'd been lucky enough to find a job working for the local Council and had worked there ever since. He married his girlfriend and they bought a house, the house in which they still lived. He'd lived in the same house and worked in the same office for over thirty years! No wonder his life was stale.

'Susan didn't go back to work until the kids were well into secondary school but she quickly made up for lost time. Studied alongside the job, gained all the qualifications, shot up the ladder and now she earns more than I do. Like a hare released for the greyhounds, let them give chase but they'll never catch her! What's she running from? I never realised she was so unhappy.'

'To, not from,' I suggested. 'Perhaps she's running towards, rather than away from.' Then, determined not to let him dominate the conversation, I told him my story. How I couldn't wait to leave home and the narrowness of village life. How, after university, I'd done a variety of jobs in different cities, studied some more, and finally settled in the Midlands where I was pursuing a career in further education. I told him I waited until I was thirty before marrying and that I was widowed soon after I turned forty. I said I'd been working at my present college far too long and was planning to change direction, maybe go self employed. Colin listened intently, his thatched brows drawn into a slight frown, but made no comment.

We finished our drinks and went out into the cooling air. Our footsteps echoed as we walked back towards the car park along deserted streets.

'I love being outside at night. When I was a child I used to creep downstairs after the grown ups were in bed and unlock the back door,' I said. 'I'd pretend to see ghosts and murderers lurking in the shadows. Then I'd dare myself to go outside and run right round the house. I remember once when my cousin came to stay, to make it even more scary, I shut the door before he got back inside. He nearly died of fright!'

We reached the car park where my car was waiting faithfully and drove home in satisfying silence, in contrast to the fraught outward journey. I glanced at Colin to see if he'd taken my advice and closed his eyes but it was too dark to be certain and in any case the roads were almost empty. We drew up in front of his parents' gate.

'Thank you, Ann. I enjoyed the concert, and your company. Most grateful to you for suggesting it.'

'The pleasure's mine.'

He unfastened his seat belt then turned to look at me before opening the door. 'I want to ask you one question. Why don't you talk about your husband?'

'Why the hell should I?' I gripped the steering wheel. 'What precisely is it you want to know?'

'What he was like. Whether you were happy.' Colin frowned like a child who knows he's done something wrong but stubbornly refuses to say sorry.

'What's the point? It's not as if you're ever going to meet him. He's dead.'

'I'd like to be able to form a mental picture, that's all.'

'Listen, Colin. Mohan's no longer around and I have no intention of talking about him just to indulge your curiosity. I refuse to be a weeping widow. I came here to forget all that. I have no wish to talk about the past. Now would you please get out of my car so I can go home?'

Reluctantly he climbed out. 'Goodbye then. See you again soon.' He shut the door.

For a few moments I sat with my forehead pressed against the steering wheel then I reached over and wound down the window. 'If you really want to know, Mohan was three years younger and at least a couple of inches shorter than me. Yes, we were happy. Extremely happy. Satisfied?' I wound the window back up and started the engine.

Colin stood and watched as my car disappeared from view and I was reminded of his parents waving us off earlier that evening. My stomach heaved as I drove through the silent village and the crematorium ditty began to circle mournfully in my head.

My name is Ann and my husband's dead.
That's what I said, he's dead.
My name is Ann and my husband's dead.

A few days later I heard from Namita's elder brother. Namita wasn't well enough to write in person, he said, but she gave me permission to store my furniture in her house and stay there for as long as I needed to. So when later that afternoon Colin phoned to invite me out for an evening drink, I said sorry, no, that wouldn't be possible. I needed to spend the evening packing as I was leaving the next day.

My parents wanted to come down and give me a hand but I pointed out their days of furniture moving were long gone. Then my mother became maternal and piled a load of food into a cardboard box in case I was too busy to go shopping. My father offered, rather sheepishly, to wash my car and remove all traces of the countryside from it, no doubt expecting me to decline. Instead I thanked him and wondered aloud if he had the energy to polish it as well.

'When are we likely to see you again?' my mother asked. The three of us were standing in the porch looking out at the garden because at that moment, pregnant with emotion, this was preferable to looking at each other.

'Can't say. I might come up for Christmas.'

'That would be nice. Your brother's planning to come for Christmas. We could make it a family gathering.' She glanced up at me hopefully.

'On the other hand I might leave it till next spring,' I added hurriedly.

'I have to say, Ann, you look much better than you did when you arrived,' my father said. 'Colour in your cheeks, altogether more relaxed. It's the country air what does it. Let us know when you've found something you like and I'll come down and give it the once over. Always good to have a second opinion. I know a thing or two about property.'

'Isn't it time you two thought of moving? You could do with being closer to shops and a bus route. You don't need four bedrooms at your stage in life and there's way too much land.' I spoke without conviction for I didn't really want to see any changes. I'd be happy for them to remain where they were forever.

'You see!' my mother pounced on my words. 'I've been telling your father for years we need a gardener. Does he listen? Oh no! Too stubborn to take any notice of me.'

'Just a minute, wifey. Let's get the facts straight. What I actually said was I would appoint a gardener when you employed someone to do the housework. You complain of arthritis but flatly refuse to get in any help.'

'I don't need help. The best thing for arthritis is to keep the joints moving.' Their bickering reassured me, so long as they competed in this way there was no chance either of them would give in to old age. I watched as they trundled off round the corner arguing about whose responsibility it was to weed the borders and whose to prune the shrubs.

Then off I went, dragged back down the motorway like the weight on the end of a fishing line which, having been cast abroad, is reeled in once more.

CHAPTER EIGHT

I ENTERED MY HOUSE through the back door as if slipping in this way would wake it gently from its reverie. Shafts of sunlight flecked with dust fanned out across the kitchen. The rays passed through purple stains on a glass standing in the sink and I remembered drinking claret as I danced over the lawn the evening I left to go up north. I'd deliberately placed the glass alongside a pile of cups and plates from lunch and breakfast. 'Leave a few dirty dishes in the sink,' my mother advised. 'A burglar peering in will think you're coming home soon.' As if all burglars shared her intolerance of unwashed dishes! I ran water to soak the plates and soften weeks' of hardened residue.

As I'd driven down the motorway imagining this moment, the picture of the house which formed in my head was drab and grey with blurred edges. Now I'd arrived I was relieved to find the room appeared clear and bright. But there was an unpleasant smell and I sniffed anxiously to see whether I could detect the sickly sweet stench of death. No, it was only stagnant air so I threw open the kitchen window then moved rapidly from room to room opening windows and ushering the outside indoors. I went back to the car to collect the rest of my bags and finally dumped my mother's box of provisions on the table.

Saying goodbye to this house would not be easy. I must view it purely as an asset, a possession I'd just sold for a good price. I must forget it was the home I shared with Mohan, the setting for the life we wove together and embroidered. Forget this landing was the vantage point from which I stood and watched the top of Mohan's head disappearing as he rapidly descended the stairs in a hurry to fulfil his promise to help his father lay a patio. Forget I lay reading and snacking in this bedroom, revelling in my laziness, at the very moment when a lorry ploughed through Pradip's car transforming it into a mangled mess of metal. Forget Mohan sat and ate his farewell meal in this kitchen before his body, crushed but not minced, was cut from the wreckage.

No, this was a desirable property located in a much sought after residential area, a deceptively spacious 'halls together' terraced house boasting three bedrooms and a garage. Benefiting from gas central heating and double glazed throughout, and incorporating some period features, the property was well cared for and in good decorative order. Located within the catchment area of a highly popular secondary school, it was equally suited to the first time buyer or to a young couple with children.

I was already deciding what to transport to Queen's Road for temporary storage. I would keep the best pieces, the valuable and well made furniture which would serve me for many years to come, but anything flimsy or flat pack must go. I began taking pictures off walls and books off shelves, emptying drawers and wardrobes, filling black plastic bags with assorted rubbish, too purposeful and focussed on the task to allow emotion to slip in. I didn't allow myself time to finger crumpled scraps of paper, shopping lists, scribbled notes, till receipts discarded at the back of drawers or inserted between the pages of a book, and recall the events and incidents which gave rise to them. I resisted the temptation to stare at patches on the walls where the paint had been shielded from daylight and ponder the passage of time. I went into the kitchen and raided my mother's box of provisions, consumed a tin of farmhouse soup, extra thick, and two crusty rolls generously spread with soft cheese from the farmers' market and was back to work again.

I didn't stop till it was dark, exhausted but satisfied at what I'd achieved. My plan was to hire a van and ask one or two acquaintances to help. I worked through a list of individuals I might approach, most of them Mohan's friends or colleagues. But when I imagined them actually doing the job, my stomach curdled and bile rose in my throat. I knew for sure that every one of them would ask questions, indulge in reminiscences and offer sympathy. I may have banished emotion from the operation but it would creep back via the reactions of those who understood the significance of what I was doing.

No, I had to find someone neutral who'd never seen Mohan and me together in this house. Of course I could always pay total strangers but the job was hardly big enough to interest a removal company. I spent a restless night. The first anniversary of the accident was fast approaching and I was determined to move out before that day arrived. In the early hours of the morning I made my decision.

Colin's mother answered the phone and said she was sorry but her son was no longer staying with them. She chatted cheerfully for a while then, before I asked for it, gave me his office number. He answered immediately.

'Hello?'

'Hello, Colin. Ann speaking.'

'Ann?'

'Ann of the bluebell wood and Rachmaninov Two,' I said.

'Oh that Ann.' He sounded cautious. 'Hope you're well?'

'Your mother gave me this number,' I said. 'I assume you don't object?'

'Never heard of the Data Protection Act, my mother. No secret's safe with her. Don't be silly, of course I don't object.'

'She told me you left a few days ago,' I said.

'Had to come back home. Used up my annual leave.'

'I see.'

'I don't think you do.' A short silence followed then he asked, 'What can I do for you anyway?'

'There is something you could do.'

'I guessed there might be.'

'I need someone to help me move my furniture. No distance, just south to north across the city. I was wondering if you could spare me a few hours?' I hated having to beg in this way. 'There's not a lot of stuff, not enough to justify getting in a removal firm. I'm going to hire a van and do it myself.'

'Well that's a first! I'd hardly call myself the weight lifting type. Can't you find someone more suitable? I mean someone with a bit more muscle.'

'None of it's very heavy, just awkward,' I said. 'I can shift it around by myself once it's inside but it needs two people to get it in and out of a van.'

'To tell the truth, Ann, I'm not keen. I don't exactly live on your doorstep. It would take me at least an hour to drive down. There must be someone closer.'

I said, 'As it happens, there isn't.'

'I find that hard to believe.'

'Well, all right,' I said. 'Of course I know people here but I can't ask any of them.'

'Why not? What makes me different?' he persisted. 'If you can't ask them how come you're asking me?'

'I can ask you because you never met Mohan.' I resented having to spell it out. 'Because you never saw us together in this house. Because for you it'll be a simple question of logistics. With you there'll be no, I remember when . . . . , and that's the bit I really dread.'

'Right, now I understand. Okay, I'll do it. How soon do you want the stuff moved?'

'Yesterday. Just as soon as you can get here.'

'How about this weekend?'

'This weekend will be fine.'

'I'll give you my email and you can send directions. Detailed instructions, mind. I have an annoying habit of getting lost. See you around nine on Saturday.'

'I'm most grateful,' I said. 'Thank you.'

'Don't mention it. We aim to please.'

The following morning I drove over to Queen's Road. A September chill sharpened the air and set me shivering as I stepped out of the car onto the toasted, crunchy leaves which speckled the hard standing in front of the garage. The front gate was missing leaving a gaping hole in the hedge like the smile of a child who's lost her first milk tooth, and someone had dumped a pink tricycle minus one wheel beside the main entrance. This was serious, the dumping of a single item could encourage others and the place would quickly become a communal tip. To complete my inspection I made my way down the narrow passage between house and garage. Dry yellowing leaves swirled idly in the confined currents but when it rained they would turn soggy and clog the gutters and gullies.

Autumn confronted me as I rounded the corner to the back garden. Rowan trees bounded the lawn on one side, chevrons of burnished leaves interspersed with clusters of brilliant red. At the far end of the garden a sturdy holly boasted a crop of waxy berries, each clump surrounded by dark, oily leaves. Pradip had tried repeatedly to get rid of this tree because it cast a shadow over his greenhouse and Namita fought with equal determination for its survival. Every Christmas she would cut a heap of sprigs and take them into school as her contribution to the seasonal decorations. Through gaps in the rusty corrugated fence which ran along the other side of the lawn, I could see bald patches in next door's lawn where the family had kicked a ball around all summer. I glanced instinctively at the greenhouse and was relieved to see there were no broken panes. A prunus stood near the house, its leaves a robust red in stark contrast to the delicate pink and white of its spring blossom.

I branched off across the dew damp lawn where scarlet apples lay scattered on the grass. I nudged one of the windfalls with my toe, rolling it over to reveal a pale underbelly riddled with little tunnels where slug and grub had guzzled the rotting flesh. There were still some apples on the tree so I twisted one from its twig, wiped it on my jacket and took a bite as I walked back along the path.

The front door jammed on a pile of accumulated mail and it took some effort to force it open. I held the apple between my teeth, scooped up an armful of post and carried it into the front room. The house exhaled contentment and didn't seem at all disturbed by my entrance. I sniffed the air but it wasn't musty. Poorly fitting sash windows (Pradip refused to install double glazing) meant the building was well ventilated. I put the papers on top of the desk in the corner of the room and continued to munch as I sorted junk from genuine letters.

A brown envelope addressed to Jenny drew my attention. On the reverse there was a PO Box number but no clue as to the nature of the correspondence. Also a letter from Pradip's solicitor, again with Jenny's name on it, and I wondered if there was some problem with Chandan's estate. No, I was sure Jenny had said everything was going smoothly. She'd have told me if it wasn't. I continued leafing through introductory offers, menus for local takeaways, charity appeals. I slipped a couple of electricity bills, one a final demand in red, into my pocket with the intention of contacting the suppliers and settling the account. Namita would reimburse me later.

A determined tapping broke my concentration, Miss Walker was mouthing at me through the window. She gesticulated towards the front door indicating I should let her in. I'd been on site for less than fifteen minutes and already she was investigating my presence!

'Oh it *is* you, Ann. I thought I recognised your car. Can I come in just for a moment? For a chat, you know, to catch up with the news. Will that be alright? Quite sure I'm not disturbing you? I'll take off my shoes, of course. I know Mrs Das is very particular about people taking off their shoes.' Miss Walker made a big fuss of stooping to unlace her shoes and ease them from her feet.

'They do it in their temple, you see, as a mark of respect to their gods. Though I still don't understand how on earth they find their own shoes afterwards. I'm quite sure I'd lose mine. In the house it's more a way of keeping the carpet clean, isn't it?' She came into the hall and shut the door behind her. 'I always make sure I'm wearing a decent pair of tights when I come here, don't want Mrs Das seeing my toes poking through!' Her eyes focussed on my shoes which remained firmly on my feet. 'Oh! I see you haven't taken yours off. And look, they're covered in grass.'

'A bit of wet grass never hurt anyone.' I said brusquely. 'How are you, Miss Walker? Anything to report?' She followed me back into the front room.

'Well, let's see. Obviously you noticed the gate's missing. Two boys walked off with it a few days after Mrs Das went away. I shouted at them to bring it back but they ignored me of course. I can't for the life of me think what they want with a gate. In my day we might have played with a gate like that, made a den or used it to build a tree house. Not now-a-days. Children don't use their imaginations any more. Everything's provided for them on a plate. Wouldn't know what a tree house was, or see the point of it. May I?' I nodded and she lowered herself onto the sofa.

'There's a tricycle . . .' I began.

'I was coming to that,' Miss Walker hurried on. 'It's been there since last Wednesday. I've asked around but, surprise surprise, no one saw anything. No sense of community. In the old days we looked out for one another. I was brought home more than once when I stepped out of line. And I used to go on messages for people in the street. "An ounce of help is worth a tonne of sympathy," Mother used to say. A lot of good it did us! I have to pay from my own pocket if I want anything done.'

'You lived here with your mother? Were you born in this road then?' I came and sat in Pradip's chair, in the mood for listening. 'You must have seen lots of changes.'

'My parents moved here a few years after they got married. Mother saved up to buy the house, Father hadn't a clue about money. They lived with his parents at first but

Mother couldn't wait to move out. They bought number 47 and then a year later I arrived.'

'I expect you knew who lived in every house in the street.'

'That's right. You know Mrs Hussain's opposite? Well, I watched that being built. Dr Bell built it for his daughter. Mrs Bell persuaded him to put the kitchen at the front so she could wave to her daughter doing the washing up. The big house next door but one, where the Nagras live, that was Dr Bell's. The likes of us never got invited in except when we went carol singing, and even then we never got beyond the hall. Just look at the state it's in today!' Miss Walker paused as if expecting me to express my disgust at the deterioration in the condition of Dr Bell's former dwelling.

'The house doesn't belong to Mr Nagra you know, he's only a tenant, so you can't blame him for the condition it's in. The landlord's a rogue. Asian. He wants them out so he can put up the rent but Mrs Nagra won't budge.'

'How long have they been there? When did Asian families start to move into Queen's Road?' I asked.

'Enough of that. Don't get me started!' Then leaning forward, eager and attentive, she said, 'Tell me about Mrs Das. How's she doing? Is she feeling any better?'

'Namita's staying with one of her brothers but it doesn't sound as if she's any better, in fact she's pretty miserable according to Jenny. She's not eating much and doesn't talk to anyone. They're quite worried about her. And of course the heat makes it worse.' Miss Walker's shoulders collapsed in consternation. I could hear my mother telling me I should be sparing with the truth and keep from saying things, however true, which might cause worry or offence.

'By the way, I've sold my house,' I announced. 'I'm going to be staying here for a few months, just until I find something suitable to buy. I'll store what I can in the house and the rest of my stuff can go in the garage. I've cleared it with Namita.'

'Do you know when they're coming back? Oh dear, I wonder how they're going to manage.' Miss Walker sounded troubled. 'Wait a moment, I've an idea. I'll pop home and fetch some teabags and milk and we can have a brew. I'll bring the biscuit tin. Is that okay?" Her face recovered its former cheerfulness.

'Not really. I need to get away as soon as possible.' I wasn't prepared to waste a whole morning. 'You've done a good job keeping an eye on the house. Thank you. But I'll be taking care of things myself from now on.' I moved towards the door and Miss Walker followed me reluctantly into the hall. She crouched awkwardly to tie her laces then pulled herself upright with the help of the door frame.

'One more thing, Ann, before I go. It's been plaguing me and I need to tell someone. Immediately after the accident . . . . well I didn't call and tell Mrs Das how sorry I was. I tried to avoid her and I'm ashamed of it. It brought back memories of when Mother died, you see, and I was afraid it might start me off crying again. Mrs Das probably thought I didn't care but that wasn't the reason. Just the opposite, I was terribly upset for her.'

'I'm sure she understood. Now if you don't mind I must get on.'

I ushered Miss Walker out of the front door then went back inside to consider where I would store my furniture. The dining room could take a couple of large items and most of the boxes, I wouldn't be eating in there anyway, and my bookcase would fit nicely into the front room. All I needed now was a place to sleep so I went upstairs to investigate the options.

The front bedroom belonged to Namita and, filled with curiosity, I stepped inside. The carpet showed signs of wear and its bold pattern quarrelled with the vivid swirling of the curtains. The furniture too was homely, wardrobe, bed and chest of drawers didn't belong together, but the room was tidy and well ordered. Like the living room below, the deep bay window gave this bedroom a light and airy feel. Looking round I picked up signs of Pradip. An assortment of gardening books ranged along a shelf, on the dressing table a framed photo of him enjoying a work's Christmas party and on the window sill, silhouetted against the light, a trophy awarded for his vegetables. I could easily imagine Pradip opening the wardrobe and complaining that his shirts weren't properly ironed or rifling through a drawer in search of an elusive sock.

The room next door was the one Mohan had occupied before he married me. I hesitated for a moment before entering. I'd never lived in this house, I reasoned, indeed I'd only come upstairs on a few occasions, so there was no fear of emotional fall out. I pushed open the door to reveal a room freshly decorated and furnished in a simple manner, probably with the idea of using it for guests. I sat on the bed for a while to gauge the atmosphere and quickly decided I could sleep there happily. The drawers and wardrobe were empty which was an added bonus.

I moved over to the window and looked across the road at the Hussain's house to check the accuracy of Miss Walker's account. The window to the left of the front door was exceptionally wide and higher than its partner on the right. Sure enough the window was shaded by horizontal blinds pulled up just far enough to reveal Mrs Hussain's rubber gloves busy at the sink. I thought of Mrs Bell and glanced instinctively down at the Nagras' house. No sign of movement, only a couple of rusty cars slowly decaying in the front yard and an unruly tangle of weeds bursting through the rotting fence.

Passing the door of the little room Chandan had used as an office I proceeded to Jenny's room at the back of the house, overlooking the garden. The bedroom suite was gold and white, the carpet a delicate shade of pink and fussy lace curtains tied in loops with pretty bows hung at the window. The room was warmed by a personal presence as if it had just then been vacated and instinctively I glanced behind me, convinced someone would emerge at any moment from the bathroom. Skirts, towels, trousers, handbags, tops, underwear and toiletries were strewn over every available surface as if a typhoon had passed by. I remembered Jenny telling me years ago she disliked tidiness but I never imagined this! My hands longed to place shoes together in pairs, fold garments and restore them to their proper place.

Pictures covered the walls, soft focus photographs of Chandan and Jenny framed in a variety of mounts and ornate mouldings. The happy couple smiling at the camera had no premonition of what lay ahead. Above the bed Jenny had placed a line drawing of her husband, executed by a grateful client, a local artist for whom Chandan imported unique trademark frames from Spain and Italy. The picture presented Chandan as thoughtful and caring, the way Jenny chose to remember him. Chandan was thoughtful about his business and caring towards the members of his boys club but so far as I could tell he hadn't paid Jenny much attention.

Jenny's letters were still clutched in my hand. She would tell me, wouldn't she, if anything was wrong? I went over to the window and placed the envelopes in the top drawer of her dressing table. From here I could see into the gardens of the surrounding houses and I stood for a while studying the scene. Tree surgeons were busy attending to a neighbour's tree. Already they'd removed the horizontal branches and were left with a few giant fingers pointing forlornly skywards. A noose around one digit provided a swinging support for the workmen as they sawed away at its companions. What an undignified way to go! Not the spectacular demise of a great tree crashing to its death, more like rats gnawing away at a leper's toes and fingers. The scene depressed me and I hurried downstairs again.

I peered into number 47 as I drove past. There were no obvious signs of life but I was certain Miss Walker was spying on me from behind her net curtains. No doubt she checked her watch and felt aggrieved that, although I said I couldn't spare the time to drink a cup of tea, I was content to linger on alone.

That night I was visited once more by the dreaded nightmare. This time I stared into the cavernous black eyes of a leprous ghost sitting high above me in the cab, and I noted with horror that the driver had no fingers with which to grip the wheel of his thundering lorry. When I tried to step forward to bar its way the vehicle ploughed straight through me as though I didn't exist.

Colin arrived punctually and congratulated me on the excellent directions I'd provided. I was surprised by the sense of relief I felt on seeing him and I ushered him inside with genuine warmth. While we sat in the kitchen eating toast with heather honey he quizzed me on the plan of action. He asked to see a list of the furniture to be transported so he could decide how to load the van. He was organised and earnest and I was taken aback because his approach was so different from the haphazard way Mohan would have approached it. Mohan didn't plan; he worked intuitively, responding flexibly to unexpected obstacles as they arose.

Colin and I made a good team. We proceeded with caution which prolonged the task but meant we neither damaged the walls nor scuffed the furniture. He needed frequent breaks so he could light up his ubiquitous pipe, while I tried to control my impatience to get on and finish the job. By midday the van was loaded and I was eager to set off but Colin insisted on having yet another rest, this time in the form of a meal break.

'I'm shattered.' He leant against the worktop and watched me heat up a carton of soup while rolls warmed in the microwave. 'I spend all day sitting at a desk. Hopelessly out of condition.'

'Come on, that's no excuse. I'm not a bit tired and I spend most of my time standing in front of students.'

'Just wait till you're my age!' He smiled and the eyes which could be steel or slate, suddenly softened. But you couldn't lose yourself in pale eyes, not in the same way you could drown in the depths of dark ones. Pale eyes kept you on the surface, projected you back again at a tangent.

'I'm impressed,' I said. 'You managed everything most efficiently.'

'It's what I do. For thirty years I've sat in the town hall doing just that, managing operations. Don't usually get to carry them out first hand though.'

I poured soup into bowls and placed them on the kitchen table. 'Sorry this is pretty basic.' I sat down. 'Thanks for coming, by the way.'

'As it happens I'm quite pleased you asked me to help out this weekend. Gave me a reason to get away. Things are pretty strained at home. Our cold war is definitely hotting up.' Colin carried over the plate of hot rolls in one hand and a cellophane wrapped block of mousetrap in the other

Here we go, I thought. So long as we'd been busy our conversation was confined to discussion of the task in hand but this lull in activity gave him the chance to introduce more personal, and to me unwelcome, topics.

'Colin, as I explained when we met before, I don't do agony aunt.' I stared him full in the face and shook my head firmly to drive home my point.

'And I told you I don't do labourer. Be fair, Ann, we're in the same predicament, you and me. You needed someone neutral, an outsider, to move your furniture and here I am. Well I need a neutral ear, an outsider who doesn't know Susan, and there isn't anyone. So I'm talking to you.'

'Oh God, is there no escape? Do I really have to listen?' I clasped my head in an exaggerated gesture of despair. If I was obliged to hear him out he should at least allow me to inject a little humour. His eyes became cloudy skies.

'Oh for goodness sake, Colin, don't take yourself so seriously! I'll listen for as long as it takes us to finish this food. After that it's back to work, and moving furniture is the only legitimate topic for debate. Okay?'

'Okay,' he smiled and tore open a roll. 'I told you we were living separate lives, remember? When the children moved out we began sleeping in separate rooms, must be nearly two years since we shared a bed. We didn't row or argue, no chance to, we rarely saw each other. Now it's different. I think Susan wants to take it to the next level. You know, make a clean break, declare the marriage officially defunct.' As he bent his head to spoon liquid into his mouth, the bones of his skull were clearly visible through the threadbare patch on top.

'You need to build up some momentum, work up the energy, to do a thing like that. She's trying to goad me into action. Stoking up the passions so we actually do something about it. God, I can't face the thought of it. Such an upheaval! Dividing our possessions, selling the house, buying something smaller.'

I said, 'She's right, of course, you can't perpetuate a lie. You're lazy, that's your problem. Be honest, face up to the truth.'

'For someone who teaches great literature you have very little heart,' Colin complained.

'Language,' I corrected. 'I teach English language, not literature. You want metaphor? Okay, I'll give you metaphor. You're a self-satisfied old cat who's unwilling to leave his snug little spot in front of the fire. Take a good look at the grate, Mr Cat. The fire's gone out!'

'Oh very clever,' he said. 'It's still warm, I don't feel cold. How d'you explain that?'

'Habit, memories, self-deception,' I replied. 'There's no logical reason for you to curl up in that spot any longer. She wants to block up the chimney and you're in the way.'

'But the hearth rug's still soft and cosy.'

'Open your eyes and look,' I said. 'Nothing but charred logs and ashes.'

'If I shut my eyes I can see the flicker of flames on my eyelids. I can still feel the warmth. I remember what it was like to purr.' He spoke quietly, more to himself than to me.

We finished our meal and I began to clear away. 'Coffee?'

'Only if it's the real thing.' Colin went over to the sink and prepared to wash up. 'Don't drink the instant stuff any more. I've been spoilt.'

'The real thing?' I said ruefully. 'It's a long time since I had the real thing.' And we both laughed.

The afternoon session went much as the morning had done except that the angle between porch and hall presented us with a challenge. In the end Colin decided the only solution was to take off the internal door. I searched in vain for a screwdriver but salvation arrived in the form of Miss Walker. She scuttled off and returned triumphantly with her father's bag of antique tools. Afterwards she proposed tea and shortbread, homemade with butter and rice flour, an offer Colin accepted before I had the chance to intervene.

I left them to it and went upstairs to try to impose order on the chaos in Jenny's room, a satisfying task with instant results. Glancing through the window I noticed the mutilated tree had vanished entirely, allowing air and light to enter the adjacent gardens. There was a moral in there somewhere about the benefits to be derived from change and loss. I must remember to pass this piece of wisdom on to Colin.

Tea break over, we finished emptying the van, re-hung the door and locked up. Colin insisted on stopping outside number 47 to return the screwdriver. He stood so long chatting on the doorstep I became impatient and sounded the horn.

'You're very rude,' he said as he climbed back into the passenger seat.

'Not rude, just businesslike.' I signalled and pulled away. 'I need to return this van tonight and we're already late.'

'It is possible to be businesslike without being rude,' he grumbled.

By the time we finally reached home we were both exhausted and I suggested a takeaway which Colin dismissed as wasteful and unhealthy. Apparently Susan always cooked him meat and two veg, or the equivalent, even though they never ate together.

'You'll soon be catching your own mice,' I warned.

'But I enjoy my saucer of cream!'

'I suppose I could throw something together,' I relented. 'I'm trying to use up whatever's left in the freezer before I move out.'

'Does that also apply to your wine cellar?' he enquired.

We sat a long while over the meal talking mainly about our respective jobs, comparing colleagues, management structures and the impact of government initiatives on our workload. We identified a surprising degree of correspondence despite the difference in our professions. It was a long time since I'd so enjoyed an evening, the company and conversation.

Eventually I stood up. 'Past my bed time. You'd better be on your way. Leave the dishes, I'll see to them in the morning.'

'Sorry, Ann, I don't think I'm safe to drive.' Colin wore the embarrassed and apologetic look with which I was now familiar. 'Tired and tipsy. It'd be irresponsible of me to get behind the wheel in this state. Can I stay over and leave first thing in the morning?'

I looked at him in dismay. At that moment all I wanted was to have the house to myself so I could put on a CD and lie flat on the floor to ease my aching back.

'You don't need to worry about what Susan'll think,' Colin added hastily. 'She won't worry if I don't come home tonight.'

'Why the hell should I care about Susan? Good God, I couldn't give a shit what your wife thinks!'

'Sorry, I thought perhaps . . .'

'Well you couldn't be more mistaken.' I studied his face, lined with fatigue and uncertainty. 'Okay then, you can sleep on the settee. Come on, I'll sort out some bedding.'

Next morning over breakfast Colin referred to the conversation which had taken place on Miss Walker's doorstep the previous afternoon.

'Funny old stick. All het up over some bills. Worried what'll happen if they don't get paid. She didn't say so in as many words, but implied something's wrong. Something to do with Namita and Jenny's cash flow. I told her there was no point telling me. Don't know why she doesn't talk to you directly.' After munching on his toast for a while he added, 'Well, actually, I do know. She's scared of you, you're such an ogre.'

Alarm bells rang. Could there be a connection between Miss Walker's comments to Colin and Jenny's letters? Or was Miss Walker just playing the interfering neighbour and spreading unfounded gossip? I would tackle her at the earliest opportunity and establish the facts.

As he was leaving to return to his loveless home Colin said, 'You will be all right won't you, Ann? I'd like to come down again to see how you're getting on, if that's okay with you.'

'Of course it's okay.' It would have been ungrateful to refuse. 'But you'll find I'm getting on just fine.'

I knew she couldn't keep away for long and, sure enough, Miss Walker popped in to check up on me the very first night I spent in Queen's Road. I confronted her immediately she came through the door.

'Colin tells me you were asking about bills, worrying who would pay them.'

'That's right,' she said. 'You know, the bills you picked out when you were sorting through their post. I saw you put them in your pocket and I was afraid you might forget. We don't want the electric disconnected, do we?' She smiled nervously.

'I'll take care of it. There's no need for you to worry. And I don't know why you mentioned them to Colin. He was only acting as removal man.'

'I asked him because you stayed in the van,' she said. 'I was going to come out and ask you myself but you beeped your horn. I thought you must be in a hurry and I didn't want to delay you.'

'I'll pay the bills and get Namita to reimburse me. It's not going to be a problem.'

'No?' Miss Walker gave me a meaningful look. 'I'm not so sure.'

'Why would it be? Namita's not short of money.' I felt grubby discussing their finances with a neighbour.

'Not yet maybe, but in the long term Jenny's going to find it difficult. What with Chandan's business failing. She won't get a penny after all his debts are paid off.' Miss Walker was observing me closely.

'Jenny's solicitor will do what he can.' I spoke evenly, determined to give nothing away.

This was the first I'd heard of financial difficulties. I'd taken it for granted Jenny stood to inherit a considerable sum from Chandan's business. Though come to think of it Jenny had hinted the branches weren't turning a profit as quickly as Chandan expected them to. What if Miss Walker was right and there were substantial debts to be repaid? Well then Jenny's position would be much less secure. And supposing Chandan had used his personal savings to prop up the failing business, then Jenny wouldn't have much to live on at all. Poor Jenny, she deserved better. She'd devoted her life to this family and this was her reward.

Hang on a minute, I didn't actually know anything was wrong. It was quite possible Miss Walker was exaggerating, jumping to conclusions. If Miss Walker knew Chandan's business was running into difficulties, then perhaps Mrs Hussain and the Nagras knew as well. It might be worth talking to them to check the accuracy of Miss Walker's account.

CHAPTER NINE

I WAS WOKEN DURING the night by a low persistent call
so faint and indistinct I couldn't immediately be sure if
it was animal or human. There it was again, a pitiful sound
accompanied by feeble tapping, repeated over and over,
pausing only briefly between each repetition. It ceased for a
spell then resumed with the same heartbreaking intonation
and I went to the window and pulled the curtain to one
side. The hunched shapes of parked cars lined the road on
both sides but nothing moved.

I heard the sound again and looking down I made out a
hooded figure in the shadow of the Nagras' porch but it was
too dark to distinguish any features. I watched as the figure
tottered out onto the pavement and stood under the harsh
street light. It began to circle the lamppost stepping heel to
toe, hands deep in pockets, head bowed concentrating on
its feet. After a few painstaking circuits the figure staggered
back towards the shadows. It stretched out a hand and
tapped weakly on the Nagras' door, emitting the same low
cry to accompany the tapping.

I opened the window and shouted into the night, 'Are you okay? Are you ill or something? Shall I get help?' The figure fell silent and shuffled out of sight. I waited a while but it didn't reappear so I went back to my bed.

When I drew the curtains next morning Mrs Hussain was standing in her doorway waving goodbye to her two sons as, dressed in new uniforms and weighed down by bulging sports bags, they climbed into the car. Just as Mr Hussain was ready to drive off one of the boys began urgently gesticulating to his mother through the car window. She stepped forward smiling indulgently then nodded and hurried back into the house to fetch whatever it was he'd forgotten. It annoyed me that she waited on them hand and foot like this.

I came downstairs a little later and caught Mrs Hussain struggling to keep her head covered in the autumn wind as she wheeled her bin out onto the pavement. I crossed the road and helped her manoeuvre the heavy bin into position.

'I thought I should say hello and explain I'll be staying in Mrs Das's house for a few weeks. Just in case you wondered what I was doing here.' I hugged myself as the razor sharp wind slapped my hair across my cheeks.

'I know. Miss Walker told me yesterday.' Mrs Hussain gave me a friendly smile and I wondered what else Miss Walker had told her.

'Two lovely boys you have there.' I nodded in the direction Mr Hussain's car had taken. 'Soon grow up don't they?'

'Don't they just! They're at big school now and getting so much homework. They're bright boys, both of them. Do well in exams. You don't have children do you?' She knew very well I didn't but posed the question from politeness.

'No children, no.' I allowed a respectable pause, implying acknowledgement of my failure in this area. 'I wanted to ask you something. Last night I was woken up by a voice calling out and someone knocking on the Nagras' door. I opened the window but whoever it was disappeared round the side. Did you hear anything?'

Mrs Hussain laughed and twisted her flying scarf more firmly round her neck. 'It happens at least twice a week. Mr Hussain and me, we don't notice any more. We're used to it, you know, been going on for years. Mr Nagra comes home late and his wife won't let him in. Punishment for his drinking. She makes him wait in the garden till he sobers up.'

'Funny, Jenny never mentioned it.' My eyes watered as I looked across at the spare room window out of which I'd observed the lonely figure, then at the Nagras' house and at the lamppost. 'Oh, of course! Jenny's bedroom's at the back. She wouldn't hear him from there would she?'

'Probably not. But Mrs Das can hear him. She complained to Mrs Nagra a few times.' Mrs Hussain hunched her shoulders against the cold and glanced longingly at her own front door but evidently decided it would be rude to end the conversation without inquiring after her neighbours. 'How are they, by the way, Jenny and Mrs Das?'

'Jenny's doing fine. Really enjoying herself by the sound of it. But Namita's not too well.' The wind stung my face and dropped icicles down my neck. I wished Mrs Hussain would invite me in.

'At least she was spared the embarrassment of seeing it in the Echo.' Mrs Hussain pouted as if to emphasise how awful that would have been.

'Has it been in the paper again?' I asked in surprise. 'I saw the original report of the accident, of course, and the notice they put in after the inquest.' Could it be that the editor, desperate to generate a few extra columns, had spotted the anniversary and decided to revisit the tragic tale? A plastic carrier bag scudded and swooped along the pavement before diving through a gateway and wrapping itself around a rose bush.

Mrs Hussain frowned at me. 'I don't mean the accident, I mean the End of Stock sale. You know, selling off all the stuff because of the bankruptcy.'

'Oh, that. Didn't catch it myself.' I shook my head and paused a moment to regain control of my voice. 'I've been away all summer staying with my parents. Do you still have the paper? I'd be interested to see what they were selling.'

'No, sorry. My sons make us take them to the paper bank. Mad about recycling,' she laughed. 'Those teachers don't realise what a lot of work they give us poor mums!' Still smiling she retreated with little skipping steps until she reached her front door. 'Sorry, I can't stand the cold. I'm going in now before I freeze to death!' She waved childishly and disappeared inside.

Back in the kitchen I sat cherishing a coffee. I cupped my hands around the scalding mug then pressed my palms to my cheeks, my nose, my forehead. Gradually the blood began to circulate and with it my brain resumed functioning. So Miss Walker was right, Chandan's business had gone into administration or liquidation or whatever the correct term was. Goodness knows where that left Jenny financially. But what I really couldn't understand, the thing that really hurt, was why Jenny had chosen not to confide in me. She trusted me entirely and, like an elder sister, I advised her from a position of greater knowledge and experience. This was the very basis of our relationship and her decision not to be open with me changed everything. Hadn't she told me Pradip's solicitor was dealing with Chandan's estate, no problem? Didn't that constitute an outright lie? I felt stupid and gross, a blundering giant beside fleet-footed Jenny who was dancing circles round me.

Who else had known? Presumably Chandan told Pradip and Namita that his business was in trouble. They would have found out soon enough anyway. Chandan ran the business from home, his parents would have overheard conversations, sensed the tension. But why hadn't they told Mohan, why didn't they involve him? He was round at Queen's Road often enough, they should have asked his advice. He would have been only too keen to help. How ironic! The demand for unquestioning loyalty to one's flesh and blood usually drove me mad yet now, when it applied to my husband, I resented the family's decision to exclude the eldest son. The only people who could throw any light on the subject were either dead or abroad. I would just have to wait for Jenny to come home and in the meantime rely on work to keep me sane.

That afternoon I went into college to attend a staff seminar designed to pump us full of enthusiasm for the coming academic year. I welcomed this return to a familiar environment with its particular demands and challenges. The main speaker was fairly upbeat with his obligatory lap top presentation but his colleague, an expert on loan from the university, was less inspiring. I could smell the academic mould on his breath and see clouds of scholarly dust rise from his clothing as he flung statistics at us. The faces of the assembled staff chanted 'boring, boring' in silent unison. Nothing daunted, he droned on and on.

One couple arrived late, a balmy tropical breeze wafting in with them. They glided into their seats glistening with suntan and joie de vive. The man's beard brushed his partner's smooth cheek as he whispered in her ear and she responded with a giggle. The audience shuffled and tittered, enjoying the interruption. I pushed aside the vivid memory of that other staff meeting when Mohan covertly declared his love for me.

I stayed on working in my office long after the seminar was over and came home computer crazed but satisfied at having organised my work load for the ensuing term. The answer machine was blinking, Colin wanted to know if he could come down for the weekend. His relationship with Susan was deteriorating, he said, and he needed to get away. So why not go to his parents, I wondered. But I wasn't complaining, the thought of Colin's company cheered me up. College kept me busy enough during the day but evenings and weekends there was only Miss Walker. And now this bankruptcy business, it would help to talk to Colin so I phoned him back immediately.

'I'll drive down after work on Friday, stop on the way to pick up a Chinese,' he said. 'Save you the bother.'

'Cheek! Be honest, you can't face the thought of my cooking. I'll order something from this end. You can supply the alcohol.'

We ate sheesh kebab from the Middle Eastern Diner and drank bottled beer. Colin moaned about Susan and the looming prospect of moving into separate establishments with all the inconvenience and discomfort that would bring. And when he failed to gain my sympathy he began to play the fool and fabricate outrageous slanders concerning his office colleagues. I was reduced to helpless giggles and Colin made the most of it, shamelessly keeping me in stitches. By the time we reached coffee we'd begun to sober up. He wanted to smoke so we put on our coats and went and stood together on the kitchen step. Above our heads torn shreds of netting dangled uselessly from the metal hoop which Pradip had, years ago, fixed to the wall for his sons to practise their basket ball.

'Did you ever find out what all the fuss was about? Miss Walker and those utility bills I mean.' He pulled out his pouch, pinched up some tobacco threads and proceeded to roll them round his palm with his thumb.

'She was right. I was talking to the neighbour opposite and Chandan's business—that's Jenny's husband—did go bankrupt. I don't think it'll stop them paying the bills though. Namita isn't short of cash.'

'I know a bit about bankruptcy, from work that is, not personally. Strictly speaking businesses go into liquidation, individuals go bankrupt. It's very stressful, especially if you're a small enterprise which I guess Chandan's was.' Colin packed the tobacco into the bowl, placed the stem between his teeth and summoned the pipe to life with a series of sharp intakes of breathe. 'Everything in the bank, everything you own, is put on the line. It would only apply to him though, the Trustees couldn't touch savings Jenny had in her own name. I'm not sure what happens to joint accounts.'

'Jenny can't have much money of her own. She never went back to work after the accident. She only earned a minimal wage in any case.'

'How come you didn't know? I thought Asian families stuck together.'

'Some do, some don't,' I said impatiently. 'There's no such thing as the Asian family. They're all different.'

'I'm not suggesting it's genetic. But you can't deny it's their tradition, a cultural thing.'

'That's true but the expectation itself causes bitter feuds. I know lots of divided families, brothers who don't speak, fathers against sons.' I rubbed my fingertips across my forehead. 'But I do wish Jenny had told me. She must have had an awful time. Namita was there to advise her at first but later, when Namita wasn't well, why didn't Jenny ask me? Perhaps she felt she had to keep it to herself because that's what Chandan wanted. Misplaced loyalty.' This was the best explanation I could come up with, at least the most palatable. I preferred not to face the thought Jenny would willingly deceive me.

'There could be other reasons. Like she wanted to try and manage on her own, without anyone's help.' He closed his eyes and puffed contentedly.

'It must be a complex process. All those legal terms. She wouldn't understand.'

'Depends when the order was made. If it was before her husband died then the Trustees would already be in charge of his estate. She wouldn't have to do much.'

'You haven't met Jenny,' I said. 'She doesn't do interaction with the outside world. I'm not saying she's stupid. Far from it. She's an expert in managing personal relationships, how else would she survive all those years living with Namita? But she's no experience of dealing with officials. It would be easy to take advantage of her.'

"That's rather patronising isn't it? Maybe she knew that's what you thought and wanted to prove you wrong, show you she could stand on her own feet.'

'I wouldn't have stopped her standing on her own feet,' I protested.

'Wouldn't you? You're very forceful, Ann.' Colin removed the pipe from his lips and regarded me thoughtfully.

'I only want to protect her.'

'Have you ever considered what she wants, I mean does she want to be protected?'

Did I know what Jenny wanted? Could you ever really know what someone else wanted? There was always going to be a subjective element, a degree of guesswork. Unless of course you asked them outright and even then there was no guarantee they'd tell you the truth. Anyway, who said Jenny knew better than I did what was good for her? Oh God! Now I sounded like my parents. It was all so complicated. Teaching, by comparison, was straightforward. I knew what was good for my students, what would gain them the best marks. So what in Jenny's life equated to a decent mark? Independence from Namita, definitely. Independence from me, well I wasn't so sure, which I had to admit rather confirmed Colin's point.

'Remember she was only a child when I first met her. She was so genuine. So naive. I had to keep an eye on her otherwise she would have been chewed up by the family.'

I pictured the eager eighteen year old stooping over her trousseau on the eve of her wedding. Her hands trembled as she folded the silky garments, smoothing out lace and frills before laying each one gently in the suitcase. As she straightened up I caught her eye in the mirror and she blushed, her quick smile conveying a mixture of nerves and excitement. At this point I abruptly closed the image down because Mohan came into view, ready to carry the bride's luggage to the car.

'When you talk about Jenny you do it tenderly, with real affection, not like you talk about other people. You must be very close.'

'I thought we were. Now I'm not so sure,' I said miserably.

'Look Ann, it happens. People change. Well not change necessarily, it's just that we can't ever know what people are capable of. Not until we see them in altered circumstances.' He tapped his pipe against the heel of his shoe. 'Take Susan for example. I'd never have guessed she could behave like this, but it must have been lying latent inside her all the time. You know what she said yesterday? She told me . . . .'

'It's freezing,' I said. 'I'm going back inside.'

I made us each a hot water bottle to slip between the cold sheets. I lay awake staring at the headlights travelling in succession up the walls and across the ceiling. Colin was right of course, Jenny mattered to me more than anyone else. Sometimes when I was with her, or even when I thought about her, my emotions weren't quite under control. Particularly since Mohan died. So was there a connection, had I transferred to Jenny some of the love due to my dead husband? Possibly. What else was I to do if Mohan, having taught me how to love and to be loved, deserted me. And was this fair to Jenny? I thought of Colin's comments and wondered if my feelings for Jenny were a burden to her. I curled into the foetal position and pulled the duvet over my face.

I was woken by the creak of footsteps crossing the landing then pausing outside my door. I fumbled for the alarm clock. It was 2am.

'Ann? Ann! Are you awake? There's someone out the front. I think he's in trouble. We ought to call the police.'

I half fell out of bed and clumsily pulled on my dressing gown. Colin stood in the middle of the landing in his buttoned up pyjamas. His ghostly limbs protruded too far from trouser legs and sleeves like a school boy who's outgrown his uniform.

'Okay, let's take a look,' I grunted, pushing past him on my way to Namita's bedroom. I drew back the curtain and together we peered out.

There stood Mr Nagra, a hooded figure under the harsh streetlight, hands in pockets, head bowed. I'd only been living in the house a few weeks but already I was immune to his night time antics. As we watched, he attempted his routine heel to toe circumambulation of the lamppost but was swaying too much to proceed. He grabbed the post with both hands to steady himself. Then he hooked one leg round it and rubbed his thigh up and down while pressing his lips coquettishly against the metal surface. Without letting go his grip, he turned and wriggled his bum suggestively.

'I don't believe it. He's pole dancing!' One glance at the expression of total disbelief on Colin's face and I was giggling helplessly. Mr Nagra must have noticed a movement at the window, he staggered away to hide in the shadows. I opened the window and we heard the sound of intoned phrases ending on a note of despair.

'What's he saying?' Colin asked.

'How should I know? According to Mrs Hussain he's pleading with his wife to let him in. She won't open the door till he's sober.' As if on cue a hand emerged from the darkness to tap weakly on the Nagras' front door.

'And how long does it take? Before he's sober, I mean.'

'I couldn't say. He's never there when I get up in the morning, that much I know.' I closed the window and drew the curtain again, eager to return to the warmth of my bed. But the sight of Colin standing bemused and sleepy in his under-sized nightwear brought a smile to my face.

'I know,' he said, stretching his pale arms in front of him so that the sleeves barely reached his elbows. 'First pair I ever bought by myself. Ma took care of pyjamas and underwear till I was married, then Susan took over. Pathetic, isn't it?'

Sleep eluded me. Something about Colin's appearance disturbed me but I couldn't pin it down. It wasn't the impropriety of the situation, Colin in pyjamas emerging from Namita's bedroom, Colin and me together at 2am without a chaperon. No, it was more visual than that. I pictured him again. His arms and legs were longer than Mohan's and much thinner, bony and hard where Mohan's were composed of soft flesh. But it wasn't their shape that troubled me, I realised, it was their colour. I was disturbed by the colour of Colin's limbs. Pale and insipid. Untouchable, unloved. I imagined my hand resting on his hand and recoiled from the image, not because it was Colin's hand instead of Mohan's but because it was the wrong colour. The discovery took me by surprise and I sat bolt upright. I was both shocked and intrigued. Naturally I'd wondered vaguely whether our friendship might develop into something more. Colin was good company and there were times when I needed companionship. He didn't attract me physically but who knows, with time his kindness and the thoughts we shared might transmute into the right chemistry.

Not that anything could replace what I had lost. Sex with Colin might provide comfort and reassurance but it could never match the passion of my intimacy with Mohan. Blood rushing to my cheeks and setting my palms on fire, climaxes unlocking every cell in my body and reaching to the very tip of each strand of hair. And now this revelation! It would never happen because Colin's skin was the wrong colour. Not only arms and legs, what of more intimate body parts? How could I kiss red lips and nipples and penis when what I loved was purplish brown? I was reminded of Henry VIII who'd grown so accustomed to Anne Boleyn's compact breasts and slender waist that when confronted by Anne of Cleve's full bosom and rounded belly he was rendered impotent.

I enjoyed living in Queen's Road. In the mornings children went by on their way to school, walking in a line behind their weary mothers who pushed babies and carried school bags stuffed with books. Miss Walker stood guard beside her gate watching them process down the road and pounced on any child who dropped a crisp bag or sweet wrapper. She scolded them and insisted they pick up their litter and because they were young and taken by surprise they usually complied. Their mothers looked on in disinterested silence and rarely came to their defence. Miss Walker scuttled down towards me as I loaded my car with bags for college.

'These Asian mothers make me so cross! Why do they walk in front of their children like that?'

'What would you like them to do?' I closed the boot and climbed into my car.

'Talk to them. They should walk beside their children and get them talking. Teach them the names of everything they see.' She gesticulated excitedly. 'Extend their vocabulary.'

'I expect they're too bloody exhausted.' I started the engine.

Most evenings, as I relaxed in the front room with a glass of wine, an elderly West Indian couple sauntered past on the other side of the road. With her stomach thrust proudly forward and a permanent scowl distorting her face, the woman directed a continuous flow of complaints at the diminutive husband who paced meekly at her side. He grinned up at her in placatory manner and sometimes dropped back a step or two and winked at me through the bay window before hurrying to catch up again. I raised my glass in appreciation of his resilience and humour.

Occasionally a group of leather jacketed young men with immaculate hair cuts sauntered by, laughing and joking and talking loudly on their mobile phones.

'Refugees,' said Miss Walker. 'From Albania and Kurdistan.'

'How d'you know that?' I demanded.

'I read the letters page in the Echo. They're on the look out for English girls to marry. The different factions fight each other with knives. You'll see, the Council will move them into our road as soon as a house falls empty,' she predicted knowingly.

At weekends children on bikes raced up and down the pavement and collected in huddles around gateways. I observed their antics and concluded they were harmless, more intent on looking cool than causing trouble. I recognised the lad who'd interrogated me the morning of Namita and Jenny's departure. Once or twice as he sped past he raised his brows, presumably in disbelief that I'd been sufficiently brave to move into this cursed place. The Hussain boys, sporting helmets, rode their bikes up and down the pavement in front of their house always keeping a safe distance from the other lads. Mrs Hussain popped out every now and again to check they hadn't strayed too far from her oversight.

But the red sisters were my favourites. You couldn't help noticing them. The majority of women whatever their ethnicity and age wore outer garments of black or grey, subdued colours at any rate, so these two stood out in their bright red winter coats. The saris hanging down below their coats were of gorgeous silk and on their feet they wore golden sandals. But their long thick plaits looked dry and ragged. The two women idled down the middle of the road ignoring the traffic until a driver hooted and they were forced to step grudgingly onto the pavement. The taller one walked in front, tight-lipped and stern, while her plumper sister followed behind, rolling a little and chattering away.

One day Miss Walker stopped the sisters and spoke to them. When they moved on again she hurried down to tell me what they'd said.

'I offered to buy them proper shoes,' she panted. 'I told them they'd surely get chilblains wearing only those skimpy sandals and no socks.'

'And what did they say?'

'Not interested,' said Miss Walker. 'They like their sandals. Poor things, they haven't a clue how to cope with the cold.'

Mrs Hussain saw us from her kitchen and came out to join in. 'They're bad news,' she warned. 'There's something funny about them. Maybe they're on drugs. Maybe they're up to something worse.' She mouthed the word prostitute as if saying it aloud would sully the air her boys breathed.

When I next saw them, the sisters were fading fast. Having suffered constant exposure to sun and rain, their coats were beginning to turn pink. Their hair was terribly tangled and the previously elegant saris now looked distinctly tatty. Each sister carried a red umbrella against the rain. On that occasion they were kicking beer cans along the gutter, carefree as children. They carried on a loud conversation as their saris trailed through the puddles. It was difficult to guess their ages, somewhere between twenty and thirty I supposed.

But I knew my stay in Queen's Road was temporary. I couldn't continue living there once Namita returned. One Sunday evening I decided I must think seriously about the future. Spending the summer with my parents had convinced me I wanted to try living in the countryside so the following day I made time to pop out in my lunch hour to pick up details of village properties from a number of estate agents and add my name to the mailing list of a couple more. As it turned out my timing was prophetic. The very next day Jenny phoned to tell me they were coming home and would arrive around midday on Friday.

CHAPTER TEN

A HARSH FROST CHASTISED the garden overnight. Earth's sleeping breath distilled to a white film which coated every surface and crystallised the spears of yellow broom and faded hydrangeas. Fortunately I'd stocked up on wild bird seed after my trip north. I saw the pleasure my parents derived from watching birds feeding in their garden and decided to follow their example. My parents welcomed a variety of visitors to their bird table; bustling long tailed tits, black and white with a hint of pink, and upside down nuthatches, sleek aristocrats of the avian world. Even pied woodpeckers with their crimson underpants and impressive beaks occasionally stopped by to snatch an easy meal. In Queen's Road we saw only homely sparrows, nothing else, but I liked their cheerful bossiness. They quickly chased away any blue tits which attempted to approach the bird table.

I ventured out to fetch a paper from the corner shop, treading carefully to avoid the frozen pools of curried vomit and canine diarrhoea. Children made their way to school wrapped in ridiculous scarves, their hands stuffed into oversized gloves hanging awkwardly at their sides. Babies in buggies were crowned with woolly hats then submerged beneath heaps of blankets. Mothers wound shawls round and round their heads until only their eyes were visible.

Inside the house again I wiped condensation from the windows and turned up the thermostats on the radiators. If this weather continued Jenny and Namita would suffer for the first few days until their bodies adjusted to the cold. I put fresh sheets on their beds and sprayed air freshener liberally around the kitchen door to mask the lingering odour of Colin's tobacco. I planned to fill the fridge but it occurred to me I wasn't really sure what I should buy, Namita had such set ideas about what you could and couldn't do with food. In the end I decided to buy the basics and do a proper shop later. Jenny could come with me and chose for herself. It would give us the opportunity to talk.

Jenny had sounded tired on the phone and kept our conversation brief. She gave me the number of their flight and asked if I could meet them at the airport.

'Of course! Don't worry, I'll be there.' I knew I'd get there well before their flight was due.

'Oh and one more thing. Bring a couple of coats will you, Ann?'

'You'll have to tell me which ones.'

'Doesn't matter. So long as they're warm.'

'Right, I'll do my best. See you Friday.'

'Can't wait to see you,' she said but I wasn't sure she meant it.

My excitement at the prospect of seeing Jenny was tempered by my knowledge of the bankruptcy, or more precisely by the knowledge Jenny had chosen not to tell me about the bankruptcy. My usual style would be to confront her the moment she arrived but, mindful of Colin's observations, I tried to consider how she would be feeling. I knew from her letters how much she'd enjoyed staying with Choto Uncle's family, the thought of life alone with Namita would seem pretty unattractive by comparison. On top of that was the certainty that everyone, including me, must by now have heard about the failure of Chandan's business. Overall I guessed Jenny was not looking forward one bit to coming back. She deserved a breathing space before I broached the bankruptcy question. Who knows, she might even raise it herself.

I picked her out immediately as she emerged from customs. Her hair was longer and she'd put on weight which suited her and gave her added gravitas. Typical Jenny, she was holding the hand of a frail looking woman in a sari and leading her towards the waiting group of relatives and friends. She returned my wave and I continued to scan the stream of passengers expecting to see Namita deep in conversation with someone she'd met on the journey, but there was no sign of her. Was it possible she'd changed her mind at the last minute and stayed on after all?

I saw Jenny settle the frail woman on a seat against the wall and hurry back to collect the luggage trolley then steer it carefully in my direction.

'Ann! It's great to see you.' She gave me a quick hug 'You're looking well.' She inclined her head and smiled and the skin around her eyes crinkled. The colour of her blouse, a delicate blue, brought out the colour of her eyes. Cornflowers in a meadow, bluebells in a wood.

'And you look wonderful.' I kissed her cheek. 'It's so good to have you back.'

'Just keep an eye on this for me, will you, while I go and get Mum? Back in a minute.' And off she went again to rescue the woman she'd been with earlier and I realised with a shock it was Namita. As Jenny propelled her forward, Namita glanced nervously about her. I said hello but she didn't answer and there was little sign of recognition in the eyes which momentarily met mine. It wasn't easy to make the connection between my proud mother-in-law and the pathetic figure in front of my eyes.

'What's up? Was she sick on the plane?'

'She's tired and weak, that's all. Can you manage the trolley? I need to hold onto Mum. Where are you parked?'

We made slow progress, persuading Namita to step into the lift was quite a challenge, but we eventually reached the correct level of the multi-storey and located my car. I handed over their coats and left Jenny struggling to get Namita into hers while I hauled their cases off the trolley and into the boot. Then between us we manoeuvred Namita into the front seat and Jenny settled herself in the back.

'Come on, let's get Mum home. She'll be okay when she's back in her own house.'

As she sat beside me Namita's fingers fussed incessantly, worrying at her nails and scratching back the cuticles over and over again. I tried a number of times to start a conversation but couldn't get any response. Jenny lent forward to offer intermittent words of comfort in a language I couldn't understand, Bengali I assumed.

As soon as we reached home I put the kettle on and tried to make them welcome. Jenny guided Namita through the front door but she came to a standstill in the hall. Her starched cotton sari, reduced to a grubby rag by hours of travelling, hung in trembling folds around her ankles. Her face wore a puzzled expression as her eyes took in the surroundings and it was obvious she didn't recognise her home of over thirty years. Jenny reached out to help her with her coat but Namita recoiled in alarm. Jenny waited patiently then tried again and this time Namita pushed her hand away.

'It's all right, Mum. No one's going to hurt you.'

'Come on,' I said. 'We don't need to stand over her.'

'D'you think she'll be alright?' Jenny followed me reluctantly into the kitchen.

'Of course she'll be alright!' I took mugs from the cupboard and opened a packet of ginger nuts. 'Humble supermarket tea bags I'm afraid, not up to your standard. What've you been drinking? Assam, Darjeeling?'

'Not sure but it was sweet and very milky. All boiled up together in the kettle. And they use tiny little cups. If they saw the size of these mugs they'd be totally amazed!' She went over to the fridge, checked the contents and frowned.

'I know,' I apologised. 'I didn't have a clue what to buy. We'll go out together later, after you've had a rest.'

'We can't leave Mum in the house by herself,' Jenny said firmly. 'You'll have to go alone. I'll make a list.'

'You can't watch her every minute of the day.'

'I have to,' Jenny said. 'You can't tell what she'll do next.'

We heard a thud. Jenny looked alarmed and hurried through to the front room while I followed more slowly. Namita was sitting on the edge of Pradip's chair closely examining some object in her hand. She hastily stuffed whatever it was back into her handbag and clutched the bag to her chest.

Jenny busied herself picking up the books which lay scattered on the floor. I'd left them balanced on the arm of the chair and Namita must have dislodged them when she sat down. I set the drinks on the coffee table and Jenny passed a mug to Namita who ignored it until Jenny gently curled her fingers round the handle for her. While we drank our tea and dunked our biscuits Jenny began a lively account of the flight, going over every trivial detail and throwing in the odd Bengali word or two. The performance was entirely for Namita's benefit, to engage and reassure her, and Jenny was rewarded by the occasional monosyllabic response.

As Jenny continued her empty chattering I was overwhelmed by a profound sense of disappointment. I longed for her to be still, to sit quietly and mingle her thoughts with mine. My eyes drifted out towards the garden where blustery rain had replaced yesterday's frost. The intense cold had killed off the few lingering autumn colours leaving only dismal greys and browns. Rain drenched leaves lay rotting on the sodden grass or mouldering in heaps along the boundary fence. At last the tinkling arpeggios of Jenny's narrative dribbled to a halt and my attention was recalled.

She turned to me. 'Where did you put my post, Ann?'

'In your room as you instructed,' I said curtly. 'In the top drawer of the dressing table.'

She stood up. 'Can you keep an eye on Mum while I pop upstairs?'

'Why should anyone need to keep an eye on her?'

'I just think it's better not to leave her alone,' Jenny whispered. 'Not yet anyway.'

'What on earth do you think is going to happen if she's left alone?'

'And then I'll put on a wash,' said Jenny brightly. 'We've got a whole suitcase of dirty clothes. Some of them won't ever get clean. I'd be ashamed to wear them here.'

Namita watched intently as Jenny left the room. Her lips moved without sound and she began to rock almost imperceptibly back and forth. I couldn't weigh her up. She was undoubtedly worse than when she went away but this was not a deepening of her former depression, heavy and dark. This was something different. Cocooned in her own world, she made barely any impression at all on ours.

'You don't need to be watched,' I told her. 'Jenny's making too much fuss.'

Namita looked at me warily for a moment then turned her head in the direction of the garden and the swirling wind. She stood up and went to press her face against the patio doors. Together we listened to the sound of water flung against glass.

Footsteps hurried down the stairs and Jenny crossed the room. She threw me a look which said, 'See what I mean?' and drew the heavy curtains to shut out the storm. Gently she guided Namita back to her seat.

'Did you find them?'

'Yes thanks. And thanks for tidying my things!' Jenny handed me a piece of paper. 'Look, I've made a shopping list. Can you go straight away? Please. So I can make us something hot for tea.' She gave me a conciliatory smile.

I struggled against the mesmerising beat of the windscreen wipers as they battled the lashing rain, and forced myself to concentrate. I was on a mission which must not fail. I marched along supermarket aisles and interrogated the shelves in a supreme effort to track down absolutely everything on the list. Usually I would have settled for an approximation, the nearest thing to hand, rather than waste time looking for the exact item requested. Today was different; I felt I needed to redeem myself in Jenny eyes for the way I'd behaved towards Namita. So I took the trouble to read labels carefully. I excavated the lowest levels of freezer cabinets. I even accosted a sales assistant to inquire whether they stocked a particular brand.

It was only when I reached the checkout that it occurred to me to wonder who would pay their bills. Did Jenny have access to any funds? Was Namita sufficiently sane to withdraw money from her account? I guided the disobedient trolley across the rain swept car park and hastily stuffed its cargo into the boot. The myriad headlamps and traffic lights reflecting off wet roads and pavements dazzled and confused me as I drove quickly home.

Jenny was delighted with my heap of slippery carrier bags and emptied the contents haphazardly onto the worktops.

'Hey, less of that!' I said. 'We have to preserve a semblance of order in this kitchen.'

'Okay,' she smiled and handed me tins and packets to put away in their proper places. When we'd finished she said, 'Ann, will you please go through and sit with Mum while I cook?' I threw a towel over my wet hair and did what she asked without protest.

Namita ate with her fingers, dividing her rice into sections which she mixed by turn with dal, vegetables and chutney. In the past she'd always used a fork, worried what the teachers would think when they noticed her turmeric stained fingers. Pradip, on the other hand, barely tolerated spoons and forks and when at home always ate with his hands. I supposed this was how Namita had eaten for the last few weeks so why go back to using cutlery?

We carried on a half-hearted conversation but Jenny's attention was monopolised by Namita who kept losing concentration and even tried a couple of times to leave the table. Jenny worked hard to sustain her interest offering a fresh dish of dal, a little more curry, another slice of lime. Namita only had to raise her eyes and Jenny was on her feet inquiring what she needed. I looked at my mother-in-law and thought, it's your destiny to come between me and the person I love.

Even before I'd cleared away the plates Namita's eyes were heavy and her head drooped forward onto her chest. I stayed in the kitchen to tackle the washing up and left Jenny to lead Namita upstairs and guide her through the bedtime routine. I told Jenny to shout if she needed me but, to be honest, I hoped she wouldn't. I plunged dirty dishes into foamy suds and reflected miserably on how completely Jenny had resumed the role of daughter-in-law. I found myself wondering how much Jenny really cared for Namita or whether she did it out of pity. Maybe she saw it as her duty to be loyal to the family, to Pradip and Chandan. Most probably she'd never asked herself why.

Saucepans, plates and utensils were washed, dried and returned to their proper places and still Jenny didn't reappear. On my way out of the kitchen I bumped into the suitcases which stood abandoned in the middle of the hall so one by one I carried them upstairs and reassembled them on the landing. I could hear shuffles and murmurs coming from Namita's room and I waited near the door a while, hoping Jenny would come out and speak to me but there was no sign she was aware of my presence. I decided against disturbing them and retreated downstairs. I wandered through to the front room and was deep into my book when at last Jenny came into the room.

'I think I've got her settled.' She yawned and stretched then lowered herself onto the sofa beside me. 'Actually

Mum wasn't too bad, did everything herself. Just needed reminding. We decided not to try the bath, she's much too tired.'

'So long as she can take herself to the loo,' I said.

'I wasn't sure how she'd get on with English loos again. She's got used to Indian ones. You know, the low down ones you crouch over.'

'All right, all right,' I said. 'No need for details.'

'Actually I prefer them. You get a better look at what you've done.'

'Jenny!'

'What?'

'You're disgusting!'

'No I'm not,' she said. 'It's you who's squeamish.' We giggled.

'Move along, Ann. You must have noticed I've put on a bit of weight.' She nudged me further into the corner.

'And it suits you,' I said happily. I made enough space for her to get comfortable. 'You look exhausted. I bet you didn't get any sleep on the plane. Let me bring you something to drink. Hot chocolate, glass of wine?'

'In a bit. I'll just sit here for now.' She closed her eyes and let her head roll onto my shoulder.

'It's good to have you back home.'

'I wondered if it would upset her,' Jenny said. 'You know, being in that bedroom. But she didn't seem to notice.'

'What's that thing she keeps in her handbag?' I asked.

'Her bati—a sweet little bowl made of bronze. Her Dad gave it to her when she was a baby, for her . . . . what's it called? You know this thing they do when a baby eats rice for the first time.'

'Annaprashan,' I said. We'd been invited to many such occasions but I'd always come up with an excuse and sent Mohan to represent us.

'Well Mum's name's carved, I mean engraved, on the side. She found it in one of Choto Aunty's trunks, now she keeps it with her all the time.'

'Namita talks to you in Bengali. I'm impressed you picked it up so quickly.'

'She doesn't really talk to me, more like mumbling to herself. Half the time I haven't a clue what she says. I just keep saying okay and that's right and it seems to work. I learnt the easy stuff, you know, the sort of things you say twenty times a day. Pradip and Mum used to talk to each other in Bengali sometimes so that helps.' Jenny removed her slippers, lifted her feet onto the table and yawned. 'I'm sooo tired.'

'I'll phone the surgery in the morning and get Namita an appointment,' I said. 'I'll say it's an emergency.'

'Will you? Mum doesn't like doctors. Perhaps we should ask her first.'

'She's seeing a doctor tomorrow whether she likes it or not.' No doubt Colin would accuse me of being bossy but in my opinion this was a time for firm leadership. 'You can't tell me in Kolkata people don't go to the doctor when they're ill.'

'Well no one went while I was there. Oh yes, of course! They did on television. The soaps are full of people having strokes and heart attacks and being taken to hospital and doctors saying there's no hope. They really love their soaps. You wouldn't believe the acting! Completely over the top. And the background music's so dramatic. The neighbours don't have their own television so they come round to watch. And you know what, some of them stand in the street and watch it through other people's windows!'

'Sounds chaotic to me.'

'But Ann, people are so happy.'

'And if they want to be alone? To read or really concentrate on something?'

'The children just get on and do their homework in the middle of everything. They read out loud from the text book. And if they get stuck one of the older ones goes through it with them.' Jenny looked at me thoughtfully. 'You know I don't think they'd understand wanting to be alone. It would be a bad thing for them.' Then to my dismay her eyes suddenly filled with tears.

'Jenny? What is it?'

'Oh Ann, I really loved it. I could have stayed forever. I only came back because Mum wasn't well.' She wiped her eyes on the back of her hand.

Then, suddenly frowning, she asked, 'Who is he, Ann?'

'What d'you mean?'

'There's a stink of tobacco near the back door.'

'Oh! Sorry. That's Colin, a friend of my brother's. He smokes a pipe. He helped me move my stuff and came down again the other weekend.'

'And?'

'And nothing.'

'Anyway, I'm pleased. I was worried you'd be lonely.'

She let her head roll back onto my shoulder again and I felt her breathing gradually deepen. The sofa gave no support to my back but I forced myself to keep quite still so as not to disturb her. I picked up my book and continued to read, being careful to turn the pages silently.

There was a sudden noise from upstairs. Jenny's muscles tensed and she sat up. We heard Namita's bedroom door open followed by the sound of footsteps crossing the landing and pausing at the top of the stairs.

'Better see what she's up to,' Jenny said.

'She'll be okay. She'll probably take herself back to bed in a minute. Wait and see.'

'I'll just pop up and check she's okay. Be back soon for that hot chocolate.' Jenny heaved herself off the sofa and ran upstairs.

I went through to the kitchen. Ignoring the instructions on the packet I poured milk into a mug, sprinkled powdered chocolate liberally over the surface and stuck it in the microwave. I carried the steaming drink back to the front room and waited but she didn't reappear so I left it on the table and crept upstairs. The door to Jenny's room was wide open but she wasn't in there. I peered into Namita's room and caught a glimpse of Jenny lying alongside Namita but on top of the duvet. I fetched a couple of blankets from my room, tiptoed in and spread them over her as she slept.

Floating on the intoxicating borders of sleep I recalled the weight of Jenny's head on my shoulder, the warmth of her body pressed against mine. I so much wanted her to be open with me, to tell me about Chandan's bankruptcy without me having to ask. There was no urgency after all, I could wait.

I phoned the surgery first thing and they agreed to give Namita an appointment the same day. I would have dropped everything, even if it meant cancelling classes and missing meetings, but Jenny insisted she could manage alone so I went into college as usual. Jenny waited till after our evening meal when Namita was upstairs before reporting back to me.

The doctor had listened to Jenny's account then asked Namita a number of questions, presumably to test her orientation to time and place. He spoke to her in English to begin with and only when Jenny suggested it did he call for someone to interpret. No-one in the surgery spoke Bengali but they discovered Namita could communicate quite effectively in Urdu. I remembered Pradip's impassioned accounts of riots, bloodshed and martyrdom when West Pakistan tried to impose Urdu as the official language on what was then East Pakistan. Namita must have grown up surrounded by the language.

'And did she get the answers right?'

Jenny shook her head. 'They didn't tell me.'

'You should have asked!'

Next the doctor examined Namita and pronounced her physically fit. He checked her records and was surprised to find how infrequently she'd consulted him over the thirty or more years since she and Pradip first registered with the practice. In spite of Jenny's attempts to persuade her, Namita had persistently refused to see anyone when her mood worsened following the inquest. In the doctor's opinion Namita's condition wasn't serious but she would benefit from a mental health assessment. He made the referral then passed her on to the practice nurse who, with some difficulty, took blood and urine samples. Now there was nothing to be done but wait for an appointment which could take weeks depending on the length of waiting lists.

When the hospital phoned a week later to say they were slotting Namita into a cancellation, Jenny was once more adamant she could manage by herself. I was hurt that she rejected my offer of a lift but I kept quiet and she set off with Namita by taxi. According to Jenny, the psychiatrist, a young Asian man who knew enough Urdu to get by, spent a considerable length of time with Namita.

'What's the diagnosis? Did he give it a name?'

'Not exactly. He said it's to do with the accident. Obviously. I told him Mum was okay at first, better than me, and she didn't get depressed till later. He said that can happen after someone very close to you dies. I think he called it delayed reaction.' Jenny drew her legs up under her and settled into the sofa. 'Mum doesn't know what's going on, that's what makes her frightened. She's forgotten stuff. Her mind can't cope with what happened so it's gone backwards. She thought going to India would make her feel better but it didn't because it's not her home any more.'

'And what's the treatment?'

'They'll see her every week, get her to talk about what happened, about the accident and everything. Only there's a long waiting list. She'll have to wait months before they start. But he thinks Mum might get better by herself, slowly, now she's back here. He says it's okay to talk about Pradip and Mohan and Chandan. It might even help, you know, jog her memory. Oh and I have to make sure she eats well and has enough exercise and no stress.'

'Common sense. You don't need a consultant's salary to know that.'

'He's going to send a letter to her doctor and let us have a copy.' Jenny looked pleased with herself.

The explanation sounded plausible. By mentally returning to the past Namita was blocking out everything to do with the accident, avoiding the truth as revealed by the coroner that ultimately her husband was responsible for his own death and that of his two sons. Her mind was shielding her from the chaos which threatened to engulf her, from the need to make sense of events which made no sense. Hadn't I done pretty much the same thing by going to my parents? Determined to graft my present and future self onto the child Ann, pruning away the bits in between, the bits containing Mohan.

We soon established a pattern of domesticity. Jenny cleaned the house and cooked, I shopped and washed up and did my own laundry, while Namita wandered from room to room somewhere beyond our reach. I was used to being alone in the house and found the adjustment difficult, two other people occupying my living space. Why did Jenny have to clutter up the bathroom window sill with half a dozen different brands of shampoo? Finish one then open another, that's what I would do. And I hated picking up the clothes Namita discarded on the bathroom floor, touching cloth which had absorbed sweat and odour from her body.

Mealtimes were a nightmare. I was sure my frequent bouts of indigestion were caused by the constant interruptions as Jenny sought to increase Namita's intake of calories, though I noticed Jenny wasn't eating much herself. I tried hard to be sensitive, to let Jenny do things her way without comment. I made no objection to the local radio station which formed the backdrop to her day, though it depressed me utterly, and I played my own music at low volume and only in my own room.

Of course Miss Walker was much in evidence. She was genuinely upset when she saw Namita's condition and insisted on carrying on long conversations with her undeterred by the lack of a response. And, to our surprise, she made some progress. Namita's wary watchfulness gradually gave way to tolerance until it almost seemed she welcomed visits from her long time neighbour. This meant Jenny could get away for an hour or two leaving Miss Walker in charge. I went to work each morning and left them to get on with it, Jenny, Miss Walker and Namita, a cosy trio who made me feel superfluous. When I came home I tried to join in but could contribute little to a discussion of the altered route of the number thirteen bus or the comparative price of mouthwash in high street shops.

Colin phoned from time to time and provided me with updates on the unravelling of his marriage. I filled whole sheets of lined A4 with doodles while he gave me the details; Susan was making lists of what needed to be done when, rather than if, they separated, and she'd started coming home late and leaving him to fend for himself foodwise. I phoned him from college at lunchtimes when I had the office to myself and told him honestly how things stood in the Queen's Road household. I always felt better after talking to Colin. He would listen patiently then invariably find a comic angle and make me laugh. He understood me well and let nothing I said go unchallenged.

'Well, have you asked her?'

'Asked who what?'

'Jenny. Have you asked her about her husband's business?'

'No. I haven't said anything yet.'

'Really? I'm surprised to hear that.'

'I told you. Namita's not well. Jenny's busy looking after her.'

'That doesn't seem to me like a good enough reason. Are you sure there's nothing else?'

I knew I could put it off no longer.

CHAPTER ELEVEN

'YOU WILL LET me know if you're short of money won't you? I expect things are a bit tight after the bankruptcy.' I stretched out my hand to take the notes Jenny was extracting from her purse. We had just finished packing away the weekly shop.

Jenny blushed and for a moment hid behind a curtain of hair. 'How did you find out?'

'Miss Walker hinted at it then Mrs Hussain confirmed it.' I struggled to keep my voice from shaking. 'Why didn't you tell me?'

'Because you'd have taken over! I wanted to see if I could do it by myself.' She counted the money into my palm and carefully put the purse back in her bag.

'Why do you say that?' I frowned. 'I'd have given you my opinion, of course, but I wouldn't have taken over.'

'Believe me Ann you would.' Jenny gave me a wry smile. 'You'd tell me what you thought and I'd end up doing what you said. Or have a battle not to. That's what always happens, you know it does! Only,' she added, 'you've been better recently, since we came back.'

'Colin said I should let you be more independent.'

'I'd like to meet Colin.'

'You could have told me before you went away at least. Imagine how humiliated I felt hearing about it from someone else.'

Jenny looked straight at me. 'I don't have to tell you everything.' This time there was no conciliatory smile, no comforting hand upon my arm. Of course she didn't have to tell me everything but in the past she wanted to and now she didn't. This was what I dreaded, this distancing, desertion.

'When did the trouble start?' I asked miserably.

'After Chandan opened the new shops. You know he was always on about expanding. But the new ones didn't do as well as he hoped. He bought loads of expensive mouldings and images. They sold okay in the main shop but in the branches no one liked them. But he couldn't close them down, something to do with leasing. And he had to keep up payments on the loan and paying our suppliers.'

'Did he ask Pradip for help?' I folded carrier bags and stuffed them into the gap beside the fridge.

'Pradip put in as much money as he could but it wasn't enough. Then one of our big customers, a hotel I think, got into trouble themselves and didn't pay us. We'd taken on new staff and we couldn't pay their wages.'

'Why on earth didn't Chandan tell Mohan? He would have helped.'

'Of course he told Mohan! Chandan never did anything without telling his big brother. You know that.' Jenny waited for me to indicate agreement but my face froze and shards of ice circulated my bloodstream. I recalled the pact we made the day before our wedding, Mohan's fingertips tracing the outline of my face. Everything out in the open. No secrets, no pretending. Right, Annie?

'Ann? Are you okay?'

I nodded. 'Did they tell Namita?'

'Mum knew something was wrong but she didn't know it was that bad. Pradip said she'd worry too much.'

Something moved and I looked up to find Namita standing silently in the doorway. The buttons of her cardigan were wrongly fastened and her hair formed a chaotic halo round her face. For a while her puzzled eyes held mine.

'What is it, Namita? Is there something you want?' She shook her head then disappeared without a sound. I turned back to Jenny. 'I don't understand why they didn't tell me. Was that Pradip's idea?'

'Chandan's problems were family stuff and you were never much interested in the family. Mohan said there was no point dragging you into it. I'm surprised you didn't guess though, that something was wrong.' Jenny rested her elbows on the worktop and cupped her chin in her hands.

How dare Mohan do this to me! How dare he leave me to find out in this way. He'd broken our agreement and I wanted to hear him explain why. Chandan was facing financial ruin, what made Mohan think I wouldn't want to know? I rapidly scanned the months prior to the accident searching for anything I'd missed. Once or twice I'd found him bent over his laptop in the early hours, working on a new idea he said. That wasn't unusual, he was often gripped by new ideas. How was I to know the family was in trouble if he didn't tell me?

But I should have known. Mohan would have. Had it been the other way round, if I was deeply worried and didn't tell him, he would have sensed it without me needing to say anything whereas I'd been too self absorbed to notice what was going on.

'Chandan said some people do it, go bankrupt I mean, to get themselves out of trouble but Pradip hated that idea. So Mohan gave us money but it wasn't enough to make a difference,' Jenny continued. 'Then one of the suppliers Chandan owed money to made a claim, a proper claim I mean, not just nasty phone calls. And that was it. The legal people took over. Chandan had to give them the keys to the shops. They took his credit cards and he couldn't get any money out of the bank. It was horrible, really horrible.' She shuddered. 'I'm sure that's why Pradip wasn't concentrating. He was worrying about everything, about Chandan, and he drove straight onto the roundabout. Didn't see the lorry.'

For a while we were silent

'Jenny, do you think Mohan and I were happy?' My voice sounded thin and dry.

'Of course you were happy! Anyone could see that. Mohan absolutely adored you.'

'And how well do you think I loved him?'

Jenny screwed up her eyes and put her head on one side. 'Why ask me, Ann? You know best.'

'But I don't know any more. That's why I'm asking you.'

'Okay, I'll tell you what I think. You loved Mohan, no question. But only so much.' She measured the extent of my love between her hands. 'You loved him but you thought a lot about yourself and did what you wanted as well. Like when you cancelled that week in Barcelona, remember?' Yes, I remembered. I had heaps of marking and a tight deadline so I cancelled and Mohan lost his deposit. I knew he really wanted to go but I cancelled all the same, to suit my convenience, without consulting him.

'And that time you promised to go to Kuldip's party then changed your mind,' Jenny went on. I remembered that too. I'd had a particularly fraught day and was too tired for parties but hadn't bothered telling Mohan. He waited ages for me at the station, wondering if I was all right and unable to contact me because I stubbornly refused to carry a mobile. A stubbornness in which I had persisted.

'And when you stopped Mohan playing football because . . . .' Seeing my expression Jenny paused. 'Oh Ann, I'm sorry. I wouldn't have said, only you did ask. None of it matters. Mohan adored you just the same.' She reached out and squeezed my hand.

Hell is truth seen too late. I'd failed to love Mohan as he deserved, I could see that now. Were things different at the start of our relationship? Probably, I wasn't sure. Maybe I'd always put myself first. But recently I'd taken him for granted, I knew that to be true. I was chronically self-centred and he'd let me get away with it. Why? Because it was easier to indulge me than to face my tantrums. In that case wasn't Mohan partly to blame? Not so, I should have loved him as he loved me.

I moved over to the table. 'Go on. What happened to the business after Chandan died? You must have been worried sick.'

Jenny sat down opposite. 'I got a letter saying the Trustees would be in charge of everything. I didn't have to do a lot really, just let them have whatever they asked for. Pradip's solicitor dealt with them mostly. He was brilliant.'

'And are you all right for money?'

'Chandan wasn't stupid! He'd been putting money into my account all along, just in case. Mum paid for most things anyway, out of Pradip's pension.' Jenny brought her lips neatly together in that special way of hers.

So that was it, Jenny had come of age. Colin had been right, she no longer needed me, not in the same way at least. Brilliant colours ran into the ground and the world turned drab and ordinary. So where did our relationship go from here? Towards a friendship of equals presumably but I had no template for that.

Namita was growing stronger and beginning to re-engage with her surroundings. She often came and hovered in the kitchen doorway, quietly watching as Jenny cooked. Then one day she moved closer, picked up a knife and started preparing vegetables, scraping potol, finely slicing karela, paring the tough skin off a pumpkin wedge. Another time she rolled up her sleeves and tackled the dishes piled in the sink. Her hands had lost none of their dexterity but her concentration was poor. One minute she was there working alongside you but when you looked again she'd disappeared leaving a trail of soapy suds across the vinyl floor.

One morning when no one was watching, Namita slipped out of the front door. A neighbour noticed her standing on the pavement opposite his house and went over to ask her about her recent trip. As he approached,

Namita began to scold him, looking about her as if searching for an escape route. He realised something was wrong and called his wife and together they guided Namita back home. She wouldn't let them touch her so they walked one either side like sheepdogs driving a ewe. Jenny was horrified. She pronounced that in future the front door would remain locked. I pointed out this amounted to imprisonment and, surprisingly, Miss Walker was on my side. It didn't matter what other people thought, she said, Mrs Das would only get better if she was given the freedom to experiment.

Nevertheless Jenny insisted that, for her own safety, Namita should only go out when someone could go with her but Namita was quick to take her chances and didn't always obey the rule. One day I came home to find her on the pavement in a huddle with the red sisters who had cropped their hair and put on weight. Their movements were slow and their speech slurred, possibly the side effects of medication. When I mentioned it to Jenny she hurried out and brought Namita back inside.

'I can't be on duty all day,' she complained.

'Don't worry. No harm done. They were chatting away quite happily in Bengali.'

'How would they know Bengali?' Jenny looked at me scornfully. 'Look at the way they wear their saris.'

'How do they wear their saris?'

'With the end piece hanging down in front. Most women have them the other way, hanging down the back. The sisters must be Gujarati.'

'You sound like a zoologist describing the distinctive markings of some exotic species!' I said but Jenny didn't smile.

I poured myself a drink. Jenny was often tired and occasionally irritable and when Miss Walker came round to keep an eye on Namita, Jenny frequently chose to rest in her bedroom rather than go out. I could see where the problem lay, she was exhausted by the effort of wrapping Namita in a protective covering but she ignored me when I advised letting Namita fend more for herself. In fact my comments only served to exacerbate the situation so I bit my tongue and tried to support Jenny in practical ways instead. I took over some of the housework and offered to cook at least one of the weekend meals. I even spent time with Namita, sitting silently at her side and watching as she ran her fingers round the curves of her treasured bowl until the patina was rubbed away and the surface polished to a yellow glow. Jenny appreciated my efforts and it seemed to me our relationship entered a new, more balanced phase.

As we sat comfortably together one evening over coffee Jenny announced she'd decided to go back to India. She would spend Christmas with us and leave for Kolkata a few days later. Her ticket was already paid for and it was no good me trying to persuade her to stay. She reminded me how, in the early days, I used to tell her she should put herself first. Well that's what she was doing, following my advice. She'd done her bit for Namita, now it was up to me. She had to go back because someone was waiting for her, the cousin she told me about in her letters, the one who played the harmonium and sang so beautifully. He was called Bhola. She hadn't expected anything like this to happen but it had happened and she couldn't miss this chance of happiness. She was only twenty six with her whole life ahead of her and she wanted to have children with Bhola and that's what he wanted too.

What could I say? There was a curious logic to it, a certain inevitability. She was right of course, to prioritise her own needs above those of her mother-in-law for once. Nevertheless I felt the pain of rejection, echoes of being jilted by an unfaithful boyfriend. I could have cautioned Jenny against making such a drastic move, warned her that holiday romances didn't last, but I could see from the determined set of her jaw that it would make no difference.

'I'll miss you.'

'I'll miss you too. And Mum. Promise you'll keep in touch? Bhola does email, that makes it easier.'

'Do you have to go so soon? Couldn't you wait till Namita recovers?' Unfair of me to sink this low, to resort to emotional blackmail.

Jenny shook her head. 'I need to go now. Sorry. Maybe you could come out and see us?'

'Maybe . . . .'

Christmas had never been much observed in the Das household. Namita joined in the festivities at school but decorations at home were limited to a string of fairy lights stretched across the bay window and a line of cards along the mantelpiece. Once Pradip brought back a real tree he'd picked up cheaply from a mate but Namita wouldn't have it in the house, partly because of the mess from falling needles. Chandan came out on his mother's side. We're Hindus, he said, leave Christians to celebrate their own festivals. In spite of Pradip's tirades Namita refused to cook turkey, domesticated vulture she called it, so he ate his Christmas dinner in the factory canteen. Jenny hadn't enjoyed a proper Christmas since her marriage and I was determined to make this one extra special. Who knew when she might be able to enjoy another?

We cut berries from the holly at the far end of the garden, tore ropes of ivy off the wall and fashioned a wreath for the front door. We covered every inch of ceiling with glossy, shimmery, twirling things and hung clusters of balloons in each corner, giggling like children as we puffed them up. I bought presents, sweet nothings most of them, wrapped them in pretty paper tied with lopsided bows and stacked them round the tree. I planned a traditional meal with sprouts, bread sauce and stuffing. Jenny warned me Namita wouldn't eat turkey or chipolatas wrapped in bacon. I wouldn't hear any objections and bought a whole bird plus all the extras, let Namita eat fish if she must. I chose expensive wine in the hope Jenny would appreciate it, though I knew my palette couldn't discern the quality. I was full of seasonal goodwill but drew the line at inviting Miss Walker to join us. It was only a matter of days until Jenny left the country, I wasn't going to share her with anyone.

Between us we produced a festive meal which seemed to last for hours. We pulled our crackers, donned our paper hats and groaned at the jokes. Infected by our mood, Namita consumed a large portion of salmon and even drank a glass of wine, though I noticed Jenny only sipped at hers. We poured gravy over glazed parsnips and crispy roast potatoes, stuffed home made rum butter under the lids of mince pies and smothered the plum pudding in thick cream. When we couldn't eat any more we washed up the china and adjourned to the front room leaving the roasting tin and saucepans to soak. Namita immediately fell asleep in Pradip's chair, a Belgium truffle melting between her fingers. Jenny and I snoozed in sympathy.

At supper time we dutifully cut into the Christmas cake, a luxury version containing dates, apricot and mango according to the label. At least Jenny and I did. Namita sniffed at her slice, pushed the plate away and took herself upstairs to bed.

'It's the marzipan,' Jenny laughed. 'Mum always thinks ground almonds smells like cockroaches!' She snuggled down amongst the cushions.

'You know, Ann, I've been thinking. Chandan and me weren't that happy really. We loved each other all right but we didn't do things together much. He'd go down the boys club and I'd stay in with Mum. When the business got into trouble, well then we started talking. I mean really talking, about what might happen and what we should do next. It made us closer. Chandan died just when we were getting to be a real couple. Sad, isn't it?'

'Yes, it's sad,' I said and wondered whether it was the nature of love never to be fully realised until it was too late.

'I'll make sure it's different this time, with Bhola.' She curled her arms round one of the plump cushions and clasped it to her breast.

Chapter Twelve

T HE DAYS RUNNING up to Jenny's departure were pretty hectic and my nerves were on edge the first night I spent alone in the house with Namita. I listened as she went upstairs, collected her night clothes from her room and took them into the bathroom. Then I heard her lock the door. Damn, supposing she couldn't operate the bolt and trapped herself inside? The sound of running water persisted for some time. Oh God, she was going to have a bath. Ten, fifteen, twenty minutes passed. I knew where the ladder was kept, if necessary I could climb in through the window. At last I heard the bolt being drawn. The door opened and footsteps padded across the landing. Later when I went to bed I discovered she'd put her clothes in the laundry basket herself (help! how did you wash and iron a sari?). I had expected to find them in a soggy heap in the middle of the floor.

I slept badly and dreamt Namita lay too long in her bath and when the sound of her snores eventually drove me to break down the door I found her flesh had dissolved entirely. Two eye balls and a set of teeth floated on the surface surrounded by a tangled mass of hair. When I pulled out the plug the water drained away to reveal an assortment of bones lying on the bottom of the tub.

Namita mostly communicated with me through silent gesture. It was strangely soothing to share a house with someone who listened but didn't answer back. All the same I kept up a continuous commentary on everything that happened, determined to expose her to as much spoken English as possible in the firm belief this would encourage her to use the language herself. When I came home from work I told Namita about the arrogant student who refused to vacate my office unless I revised the mark I'd given for his coursework. I told her how I hated the current jargon of higher education which was dry and weightless and felt like I was choking on a mouthful of polystyrene and I complained I spent half my working day clearing emails. And I asked her questions, had she been outside at all, had anyone visited, what had she eaten for lunch. She never replied but that didn't stop me asking.

I read all Jenny's emails out loud to Namita from the first one telling of her safe arrival . . . .

> *Bhola and me are sooo happy to be together*
> *again. I know I did the right thing coming*
> *back. And guess what, we're getting married in*

> *February!!!! They do it quickly here, it would take*
> *ages to arrange in England wouldn't it. I'm staying*
> *with Choto Uncle's family till the wedding which is*
> *GREAT. You and Mum are invited but everyone*
> *will understand if you don't come.*

. . . . to the one describing her wedding, which was a more modest and less traditional affair than her wedding to Chandan had been. She wore a simple cream coloured dress and Bhola a European suit and they only invited a hundred guests and that included the servants.

And I read out the email which contained her most exciting news.

> *We're expecting a baby! It's due sometime*
> *towards the end of June. Yes work it out I was*
> *already pregnant when we got back to England.*
> *Perhaps that's what made me so bad tempered, being*
> *pregnant makes you do things you wouldn't normally*
> *do, must be the hormones. Did you guess? I didn't*
> *find out till we'd been there a few weeks. After I*
> *missed two periods I bought one of those testing*
> *kits to make sure. So you see I had to come back to*
> *Bhola. His parents weren't too happy about it at first*
> *but they're very modern and open minded. It didn't*
> *take him long to talk them round.*

I felt a rush of love for Jenny and her unborn child. Red flowers sprouted at my feet and grew lusciously until they filled the room with their glorious perfume. Nevertheless, I was glad it was all happening thousands of miles away and I wouldn't be involved in feeding bottles and changing nappies.

One evening as I sat at the dining table hunched over a pile of assignments, despairing of the way they deviated from all conventional rules of spelling and grammar, I looked up to find Namita regarding me from the doorway.

'What is it? Is there something you want?'

She shook her head.

'I think you're trying to remember. It must be very frightening not to know.'

Namita came inside and sat down. Her eyes scanned the room before returning to fix themselves inquiringly on my face. So I began to tell her what I knew about the early times when she and Pradip, a newly married couple, arrived in Britain. She listened hungrily, though I had no way of telling how much she really understood. At any rate I continued the saga over successive evenings.

When she thought I'd worked long enough Namita would drift into the dining room and sit down opposite me. I put down my pen, closed my laptop and continued relating the story of her life. I told her about her sons when they were growing up, about Pradip and his garden, about her work in school, her colleagues and her friends, about her sons' jobs and their marriages. Then I told her about Pradip's retirement but I didn't mention the collapse of Chandan's business or the accident.

After that it seemed only natural I should share my memories of Mohan, saying the words out loud for the first time. I described his habits at once infuriating and lovable. The way he hummed incessantly, dragging me into the endlessly repeated tune until it drove me mad. The way his bouts of sneezing woke me each morning and how I lay there counting sneezes until the fit passed. How he left books open, face down, on every available surface and never finished reading anything. I told her he was gentle and that he removed thorns and splinters from my hands when we'd been gardening, using a razorblade to dig them out but so gently I didn't even flinch. I told her he loved cooking and everything he cooked tasted delicious to me because he'd cooked it. Especially when he used English vegetables in a Bengali way, parsnip bhaja, Brussels sprout chochchori and leek dal, for example. And how meticulous he was when making our sandwiches to take to work, spreading butter right to the very edge and distributing the filling evenly across each slice of bread.

Remembering was painful but the memories themselves were good. I began to see it was safe to bring them out in full daylight, I didn't have to avoid or bury them. After all, this is what Mohan had become, a beautiful and infinitely precious memory. Nothing could change that. I was alive and he was not so I must live for us both, live with twice the intensity.

I got into the car one morning, placed the usual stack of folders on the passenger seat, switched on the radio and drove off to the strains of Ravel's *Bolero*. The piece accompanied me all the way to work, amazingly well timed; the opening bars played as I left home and the final chords sounded as I arrived in the college car park. My car pirouetted round mini-islands, triple axelled over speed bumps, glided up to traffic lights and sashayed between lanes. The passionate music rendered me incredibly sensitive to the world around so that I perceived extraordinary layers of reality.

Exhaust fumes became the muck coughed up by cars as they cleared their lungs. Cavernous road works were evidence of major surgery, striped cones acted as clips holding the wound open while raw patches where the road surface had been scraped off waited for skin grafts of fresh tarmac. Rows of houses draped with telegraph wires and drainpipes became patients in hospital beds attached to drips and heart monitors. Cars hesitating as they emerged cautiously backward from private drives onto the main thoroughfare were constipated turds! When at last I arrived at my destination the tears were flowing so freely I had to sit a while before opening the door. I pulled out a tissue and wiped my face and when I looked in the mirror on the sun shade I realised they were tears of joy. I walked into college that day bright as a rainbow in wet sunshine.

I pursued my planned move into the countryside with renewed energy. I'd already viewed one property which more or less met my requirements so I invited Colin down to give me a second opinion. Although we kept in touch by phone we hadn't seen each other since Jenny and Namita's return, almost three months ago, and he accepted my invitation readily.

I couldn't settle to anything that morning. I was excited at the prospect of showing off my cottage but I was also eager to see Colin again and the minute his car came into sight I was there on the doorstep ready to greet him. He smiled self consciously and seemed a little awkward as he hauled his overnight bag out of the boot. I insisted on carrying it inside while he collected other bits and pieces and locked up. It hadn't occurred to me to wonder how Namita would react to having a man staying in the house but I needn't have worried. I introduced Colin as my brother's friend and she treated him with the same puzzled watchfulness with which she approached everyone else.

As Colin and I drove out of the city I put everything associated with Queen's Road firmly behind me. I wound the window down and air rushed in, bringing my hair to life.

'Goodbye graffiti, chewing gum and litter! Hello trees and tranquillity.'

'Hey, you've pinched my lines,' Colin laughed. 'You're supposed to say, goodbye culture and exotic restaurants. Hello peasants, bigotry and cow dung!'

The cottage was nothing spectacular but, as the leaflet claimed, it was deceptively spacious, enjoyed sweeping views and was conveniently located within striking distance of a major thoroughfare. Most importantly I could afford the asking price without stretching my finances too far. Colin took his consultant's role most seriously. He tapped partition walls to test their construction, inspected external walls for signs of damp, stuck his head into the loft space and crossed the road to stand well back and survey the line of the ridge tiles. Finally he pronounced the building sound and gave my plan to purchase it his seal of approval.

Together we walked into the village hoping to get a flavour of its character but the main street was deserted. Colin suggested we go into the Wheatsheaf where we would surely encounter the locals gossiping over a liquid lunch but again we were disappointed, though the landlord was friendly enough. Things were usually very quiet during the day, he said. They did their best trade serving meals of an evening when folk were too tired after a day's work to set to and cook for themselves. I was pleased to see how homely the cottage looked as we approached it on the way back.

'I'm going to put in an offer as soon as possible,' I announced as we drove off.

'Subject to survey,' Colin cautioned. 'Yes I agree, you could do far worse. But Ann, are you quite sure you want to move this far out into the sticks? It's a big decision. And what about Namita, what'll happen to her?'

'Namita's making progress. She's more aware of her surroundings now and I suspect her memory's coming back. I only wish she could talk to people, that would make all the difference. Miss Walker's indispensable, living on the doorstep as she does. Anyway, I won't move out until I'm satisfied she's ready. And I'll visit every week.

'You've got it all planned,' he said. 'I wish my future was as clear. We've had a good offer for our house which we'll probably accept. And once the house is sold there's nothing to stop us going our separate ways, so I need to start making plans too. Trouble is I don't know what I want.'

'That's a sign of immaturity isn't it, not knowing what you want?'

'I'm being less than honest. I do know what I want. Trouble is it involves another person and I haven't told her yet.' Colin turned towards me but I kept my eyes firmly on the road and wondered if I'd be able to handle what was coming next. We drove on in silence until we reached the outskirts of the city.

I brought the car to a halt in front of the garage and made to open the door. Colin reached out and stayed my hand, placing his hand firmly over mine. His touch was warm and it felt good and I was not revolted by the sight of his pale skin against mine.

'Hear me out, Ann,' he said. 'Please.'

'Okay. I'm listening.'

'Now's the right time for me to make some changes. I'm talking major changes. I've been looking around for another job. Imagine that, changing jobs for the first time in thirty years!' He waited for some expression of encouragement and I managed a smile. 'I've seen a few adverts that interest me, one's based round here. I wanted to check it out with you though before I applied. Find out how you'd feel about me working round the corner, so to speak.'

'Forget about me. Go ahead and apply if you think it's the right job for you.'

'That's exactly the problem, I can't forget about you.' He looked at me steadily.

I said, 'If you're asking whether you can move into my cottage with me, then the answer's no. If you're asking whether I'd like to see more of you, have you living closer, then yes that would be good. I can't say more than that.'

'That's enough for now. Thank you, Ann.' He clasped my hand more tightly.

'Elgar Cello concerto, first movement,' I said returning his smile. 'String section clambers desperately higher and higher up the scale before the tension resolves itself and the whole orchestra soars into the sublime central theme.'

'Not quite. I wouldn't say resolved. More like moving in the right direction.'

The following day, at Colin's suggestion, we took Namita to the park. He thought the exercise and a change of scenery would be good for her and she certainly seemed to come alive as we strolled along tarmac paths between rows of well behaved trees. The park was surprisingly full of folk who had ventured out to make the most of the winter sunshine. I wondered what they made of us, most likely speculating whether we were brother and sister or husband and wife taking an elderly Asian friend out for an airing.

A dutiful son pushing his father in a wheelchair nodded to Colin as if in recognition of a kindred spirit. An immaculately turned out woman in high heels and matching handbag tottered by with eyes averted. Namita watched everyone intently. She let go my arm and twisted round to follow the progress of an anxious father running behind his little girl who wobbled precariously on her bike. When an inquisitive dog came and sniffed the hem of Namita's sari, she lifted the cloth out of easy reach and tutted in disgust.

I pointed out the little brass plaques positioned at the base of each tree, detailing the names and dates of the individual member of the armed forces to whom the tree was dedicated. In some cases the expanding trunks had grown to encase the concrete marker posts, the flesh curling round until the plaques resembled toe nails in an elephant's foot.

We sat for a while on one of the numerous wooden benches and watched a group of footballers slithering around in the mud. A teenager wearing a turban stood near us, keeping guard over an assortment of sports bags. A couple totally engrossed in conversation passed by. The woman, wearing full burqa with state of the art trainers sticking out from underneath, gesticulated wildly as she walked and her companion responded with vigorous nods.

'Won't you miss all this?' Colin asked. 'The multicultural thing, I mean. Such an amazing variety of people in one place.'

'They're not the multicultural thing. They're parents and students and pensioners with the same preoccupations as everyone else.'

'Nevertheless, won't you miss them?'

'Perhaps I will, a little,' I conceded. 'But I'll be coming into college every day.'

I expected Namita would be too tired to help with the evening meal but she followed me into the kitchen as usual. She took the lead on rice and curry days while I was in charge when we ate European and, to my surprise, I was beginning to find the activity quite pleasurable. Perhaps after all there was a psychological element to my clumsiness. Afterwards Colin and I took our glasses and the remains of the wine and went and sat in the front room.

Colin looked about him. 'I like this room, the proportions are lovely. But it's not exactly cosy, is it? The colour of the walls doesn't help. Grey, for the lounge?' He frowned.

'They look dull in artificial light but they come alive when it's sunny.'

'It needs something brighter,' he insisted.

'Why don't you ask Namita?' Hearing her name, Namita looked up. 'Colin thinks the walls should be a different colour. What do you think?'

Namita looked at the walls and shrugged.

I turned back to Colin. 'So you're a homemaker at heart. Just wait till I move. There'll be plenty of opportunities to use the paintbrush on my cottage.'

'Why me?'

'Because I'm useless with a paintbrush. Mohan used to do it. Well he used to start then half way through he'd get distracted and begin something else so we'd end up paying for a decorator.' Colin studied my face. This was the first time I'd spoken to him about Mohan and we both knew it.

'Okay. I'll send you an estimate!' he said smiling.

I wanted to give Namita space to recover her former self-reliance so I asked Miss Walker not to call in too often which meant Namita spent the best part of each day alone and free to do as she pleased. There were dangers to the arrangement of course. One day Miss Walker found a smartly suited young man with ambitious sales targets and a large briefcase, sitting at the kitchen table. He was busy filling in forms while Namita watched him from the doorway. When Miss Walker arrived on the scene the salesman stood up nervously and began to explain that Mrs Das wanted to change her electricity supplier. Miss Walker assured him most emphatically that Mrs Das wanted to do no such thing and sent him packing. Later she contacted his employers, lodged a complaint and succeeded in getting him the sack.

Then there was Namita's relationship with Mr Nagra. Mrs Nagra would not entrust her husband with a key and he was often to be seen hanging around in front of their house waiting for her to come back and let him in. For some reason Namita took pity on Mr Nagra and invited him to wait in her hallway. Why the hall I couldn't fathom. Perhaps she felt it would be improper for him to proceed any further while she was unchaperoned, perhaps it was down to his own sensibilities. At any rate there he would sit in his duffle coat, perched on the telephone stool reading study guides to GCSE A level Physics and Chemistry of all things. His nicotine stained fingers protruded from holes in his fraying gloves and his spectacles were held together with strips of sticking plaster.

According to Mrs Hussain the Nagras were Punjabi but with Namita Mr Nagra spoke English in an accent which suggested he'd been educated privately. His vocabulary was spattered with colonial terms, for instance he called his watch a timepiece and the coat cupboard an almirah, and he addressed me as madam. Namita plied him with cups of sweet cardamom tea and bowls of Bombay Mix.

When the weather was fine I drove Namita to the park and it was here she started talking again. We had reached the little circular garden with its miniature box hedges smelling of cats' wee. Namita seemed a little tired so we rested for a while on a bench under a drooping willow and watched a group of magpies as they strutted over the damp grass.

'Cold.' Namita said and rubbed her gloved hands together.

'What did you say?' I looked at her in disbelief.

'Thanda lagchhe. I'm cold.' She stood up. 'Let's go back. Cholo.'

'At last! It won't be long before you're fluent again,' I said and wondered what else she would remember along with her English. When all the details of the accident came back to her would she experience the shock and devastation all over again? And would she recall the animosity which had existed between us since the day we met, and would she sense that I no longer felt it?

Colin came down when he could and our knowledge of each other deepened as did our commitment. But we were both cautious about moving the relationship onto another plane. Sometimes he put his arm around my shoulders and I might touch his hand affectionately but these gestures had no sexual content. It wasn't easy to negotiate the awkward physical distance between us, both of us reluctant to move beyond the only partners we'd ever known.

Once, as I stood washing dishes at the sink, Colin reached over to dip his fingers into the soapy water and his hand inadvertently brushed against my breast. He hastily apologised but when I turned my face towards him, he winked. I reached out to trace my wet finger along his frenzied eyebrows.

'Quite impressive!'

'My barber says I should have them trimmed but I prefer natural. They compensate for what's lacking elsewhere.' He patted the top of his head.

'A sign of virility?' I said, feeling vaguely embarrassed.

'Perhaps,' he said and turned his attention to the drying up.

The purchase of my cottage proceeded apace and I waited impatiently for the solicitors to finish their negotiations. My mother reproached me for not involving my father at an earlier stage so, to make amends, I invited him to come down and advise on what repairs and maintenance works were needed. I booked them into a local B & B and Colin joined us later the same day. When my parents offered to take us all out for a meal to celebrate my impending move, I took pity on Miss Walker and included her in the party.

I wiped condensation from the window before opening it to let in chilled air and the song of a solitary robin. A light fall of snow had transformed the drab garden, picking out the line of branches, defining the shape of shrubs and sketching round each pane of greenhouse glass. Similar to the way in which cosmetics highlight the eyes and lips of a plain face. Perched on the rusty fence, the robin welcomed the approaching spring with full throated enthusiasm. I stood for a moment listening to the silence behind the notes, grateful that on Sundays there was no rumble of traffic circling the inner ring road.

My father murmured his approval as we parked our cars beside the grand Georgian hotel standing in its own extensive grounds. I led the way across the chilly car park to the flat roofed extension at the back which housed the restaurant and my father snorted in disgust. It was steaming hot inside and full of noise and the smell of food. I wondered how Namita would cope but she seemed unfazed. She was wearing a pair of loose black trousers with a sparkly top and had gone to the trouble of colouring her hair and fashioning it into a large khopa. Miss Walker, wearing earrings and lipstick for the occasion, kept up a stream of banal remarks as the waitress showed us to our table and took our orders for drinks. My father, who was sitting next to her, responded politely while I struggled to conceal my irritation.

We studied the menus. What if Namita chose pork or beef, should I intervene or allow her to breech the restrictions of a lifetime? I needn't have worried. Namita watched closely as my mother selected the lamb then said she'd have the same. Our food arrived and I relaxed into conversation with my mother, trying to block out the sound of my father regaling a fresh audience with his oh so boring repertoire of jokes and stories. I smiled across at Colin who was listening courteously and responding as required. Miss Walker gasped and squealed her appreciation.

When my father paused for breath Miss Walker began a story of her own, about the City Council's treatment of Asian families living in Queen's Road. Everything was done for them and nothing for local people, she complained.

'They put a leaflet through my door, advertising computer lessons. So I phoned to find out more about it. They told me the classes were only open to speakers of other languages so I couldn't apply! Now is that fair?' My mother looked around uncomfortably to see if other diners were listening.

'And another thing,' Miss Walker continued. 'They build extensions without applying for planning permission and get away with it! The rest of us have to go through the proper channels. And you should see what they keep in their garages! Full of illegal goods. But they never get caught.'

'How many garages have you personally inspected?' I asked. 'And what exactly did you find?' Miss Walker took a deep breath but Colin hastily diverted our attention towards the fabulous dessert trolley, drowning in chocolate and whipped cream, before she could reply.

We had finished our main course some time ago and were waiting for the hassled waitress to clear the table. Namita eyed the piece of bone lying on her plate. Suddenly her hand went up to her head and deftly withdrew a silver hairpin. She proceeded to poke one end of the bone as she sucked marrow from the other with a juicy slurp. Then she dipped the hairpin in her glass of water, swished it around a bit, wiped it on her serviette and stuck it back into her elaborate coiffeur. Colin winked at me across the table. My mother glanced round self-consciously and my father kept his eyes firmly on his plate.

'That's right Mrs Das,' said Miss Walker approvingly. 'Don't let anything go to waste. Goodness knows, you must have seen enough people go hungry where you come from.'

We emerged into the cold afternoon, our breath hanging in the air like exhaust fumes. Namita linked her arm through Colin's and Miss Walker insinuated herself into the gap between my parents. We crunched across the car park and formed a huddle beside the cars while we debated our next move. My father said he'd like to inspect my cottage and Colin offered to take him there and talk him through the plans. Miss Walker begged to be allowed to go too and I gave my consent. Colin glared at me and I smiled sweetly back.

Namita climbed into the rear seat of my car and my mother, who decided she would view the cottage another time, sat beside me in the front. Her arthritic fingers struggled with the seat belt but she declined my offer of help. At last she succeeded in fastening it and we drove off.

'I met Colin's mother in town the other day. She said his marriage was coming unstuck.'

I nodded. 'So I believe. I think they're on the point of going their separate ways.'

'After all those years! Colin and Susan got married the minute they finished college. Too quickly maybe? I wonder what he'll do now.'

'He talks of starting a new life. New job, new place.'

'You two seem to get on very well.' She made the observation tentatively.

'We do. And Namita likes having him around, don't you Namita?'

'Yes, I like Colin.' I looked in the mirror and caught Namita's fleeting smile.

'She knows by instinct he's a good person. And kind.' My mother turned to me. 'You could do with a bit of kindness after all that's happened. In fact I think Colin's just what you need, Ann.'

'Yes, he's kind but he can also be pretty spineless,' I said. My mother looked offended. 'There's nothing wrong with that,' I laughed. 'Colin can be spineless and I can be pig-headed. It doesn't mean we don't get on. On the contrary, we get on very well. I like having him around and he must like spending time with us or he wouldn't keep coming down, would he?'

'Let me know of any developments.' Her profile expressed contentment, satisfaction that I was in good hands.

And it was true, I did feel cared for. Colin's frequent phone calls criss-crossed the week like wicker work, weaving a basket around me. But I was shit scared when it came to bodies. What if Colin's tobacco flavoured breath became Mohan's curry kisses and sex, the very act of intercourse, penetrated the membrane so that one of them leaked into the other? I had a sudden urge to seek reassurance but one glance at my mother's face told me this was a conversation, like so many other conversations, we could never have.

"There aren't going to be any developments," I said.

Later, when we were alone, my mother asked, 'Does Namita know Jenny has remarried? And about the baby?'

'I've told her but I don't know how much she takes in.'

'That's a shame. She could do with some good news. New life replacing old.'

'Ah but that involves remembering how old life, well not so old actually, was lost.'

Gradually Namita's shadowy form solidified and, instead of floating from room to room, she now placed her feet firmly on the ground. When the phone rang she answered it instead of waiting for me and if we ran short of anything she went round to the corner shop herself. She came with me on the weekly supermarket run and it was Namita who decided what meals we ate. In the kitchen she treated me as her assistant, complaining when I didn't slice the onions finely enough or wash the saucepans to her exacting standards.

She embarked on an energetic spring clean. Emptied her wardrobe and wiped the inside, moved the heavy furniture and got down on her hands and knees to brush the carpet underneath and ran her duster over every inch of skirting board in the entire house. Next she turned her attention to the greenhouse. She put on rubber gloves and carried bowls of hot soapy water out into the garden then proceeded to wash the glass, scrub the wooden staging and scour the many plastic pots. I took her to the garden centre to buy seeds, bags of compost and liquid fertiliser. Before long neat rows of seed trays adorned the benches, soon to be replaced by rows of plastic terracotta coloured pots each boasting an optimistic seedling complete with label.

Namita had her pensive moments too. She would pick up ornaments and trinkets and finger them as though trying to locate them in her past; the shell covered box Mohan brought back from a school trip to Blackpool with its jagged gap left where he'd prised off an especially pretty shell to keep for himself; the porcelain shepherdess Pradip gave Namita for her fortieth, claiming it reminded him of the way she cared for her own little flock. One day I came across her standing in front of the fireplace, her eyes travelling up and down the line of framed wedding photographs, her fingers moving over the glass as if to absorb the images more comprehensively. She turned to me, screwing up her eyes in the effort to understand.

'Tell me who they are.' She pointed at the bridegrooms.

'That's Pradip your husband. These two are Mohan and Chandan, your sons.'

She nodded then pointed at the brides. 'That's you and that's Jenny, right? And this one's me.'

'That's right.'

'Where's Jenny now? Why isn't she here? I've forgotten.'

'Jenny's married to Bhola. You know who I mean? Bhola, your cousin's son. She lives in Kolkata with him.'

'Why didn't you go away too?'

Why indeed? At first it had suited my convenience to use Queen's Road as a temporary base but when the two of them came back from India and things got crowded I could have rented a flat. Then again when Jenny left I had good reason to escape, let someone else take responsibility for Namita, but I stayed on. Perhaps I did feel I owed her something after all. Perhaps I was doing it for Mohan.

'I'm moving to my own house soon. Remember, I told you?'

She studied Jenny's photo. 'I wish I could see her.'

'Jenny's expecting a baby. She can't travel right now.'

Namita went over to the glass-fronted bookcase and took out an album. She flipped through the pages till she found what she was looking for and extracted two photographs. I recognised Mohan and Chandan aged a wobbly six months, snapped during their annaprashan ceremonies. Their surprised chubby faces, topped by paper crowns, were caught in the flash light. Kajol was liberally smeared around their eyes and a black smudge placed off centre on their foreheads to ward off jealous spirits. Namita propped the photos up on the mantelpiece next to the wedding pictures.

'My boys. My lovely boys. Two angels.' She remained in front of the fireplace for some time every so often picking up one of the photographs and pressing it against her cheek.

That night I dreamt of Mohan. He was disguised as a fresh faced child but I knew by the eyes it was him. He was building sand castles on the beach, patting them down with his spade then running off with his bucket to gather shells and strips of seaweed. Seagulls circled high above and on the horizon I saw a huge wave forming, darkening the sky as it approached. I tried to warn the little boy but he continued to press shells into the turrets of his castle, humming happily to himself. The wave swelled higher until it blocked out the sun. I tried to run and sweep Mohan up out of its path but my feet sank deep into the sand.

Chapter Thirteen

THE COMPLETION DATE arrived and contracts were duly exchanged. I wanted to redecorate before having carpets fitted and Colin nobly offered to take charge of the painting. Our choice of colours coincided, no battles there, but his pace was painfully slow and I quickly grew impatient.

'I won't be in till Easter at this rate!' I'd just come in from tidying up the garden to find Colin crouched over the same stretch of skirting board as when I went out.

'Perfection takes time,' he said without looking up from his work.

'I'll settle for nearly perfect if it'll speed things up.'

'Sorry, I only do perfect.'

Later, as we perched on packing boxes chewing cheese and pickle sandwiches and drinking fizzy lemon, Colin told me of another baby which was on the way.

'My daughter came round earlier in the week to tell us she's pregnant. Our first grandchild! Should be delighted, shouldn't we? And so we are but it's going to be tough for

Laura. Her boyfriend's decided not to stick around, says he's not ready for fatherhood and family life.'

'At least she'll have a devoted grandmother on hand to help,' I said. Then, suddenly doubtful, 'Susan will want to help out, won't she?'

'Very much so, in fact she's taken it on as her next big project.' Colin grimaced. 'Laura's determined not to let this baby interrupt her career so Susan's suggesting we both reduce our hours. That way there'll always be someone on hand to baby sit. There's no way Susan's going to have strangers bringing up her grandchild.'

'I thought Susan was ambitious?'

'She was. Trampled all over our marriage in her rush to get to the top. But a three month foetus has changed all that.' Colin put his glass down on the floor and pulled a pipe from his pocket.

'Then there's no chance you'll be changing jobs and moving south to live near me. You'll be ferrying the baby between your place and Susan's. This baby's going to have three homes!' I was trying to conceal my sense of dislocation. Only a few moments ago I'd been standing in a sunlit meadow, now I could feel brackish water rising as my feet sank into the marsh.

'Well actually Susan's changed her mind on that score too. When she heard about the baby she immediately called off the sale. Told the agents we'd changed our minds about moving. She thinks we two grandparents should stay together for the sake of the baby.' His grey eyes transparent, reasonable, met mine.

For a while I stared at him in disbelief. 'I told my mother you were spineless. She said you were kind and I said, yes, Colin's kind but he has no backbone.'

'Meaning?' He was wounded.

'For months you moan on and on about your wife, say your marriage is dead and she wants out. Now, suddenly, because there's a grandchild on the horizon everything changes. You're going back on your word, betraying yourself.' And me, I thought. And me.

'That would only be true if I wanted to do something but hadn't the courage to make it happen.' Colin ran his fingers back and forth along the stem of his unlit pipe. 'I've weighed this carefully. Fact is I don't want to live alone. I don't enjoy being by myself. It wasn't me who wanted to end our marriage, I was happy to continue as we were. Routine and boring maybe but comfortable. I always thought we'd turn the corner if we just kept plodding on.'

'And now I suppose she'll let you back into her bed!'

Colin winced. 'It's possible, but unlikely. Be honest, Ann, you would never have let me share your home would you? Let alone your bed.' His eyes begged me to play the adult, to take his question seriously.

'We'll never know now, will we?'

'Look, this is how I see it. We met at a particular time. We were both in need of friendship and we found each other and it's been good. These past six months have been very good. I've no regrets.' He regarded me earnestly from under his brows. 'But things move on. You've got this cottage and you'll make friends round here. I have a grandchild on the way and a wife who thinks it's worth trying to save our marriage. I don't see this as the end for you and me, just another stage in our friendship. We can talk on the phone and I'll visit when I can. We'll ....'

'Bullshit! Now who's being dishonest? You know damn well our relationship went beyond friendship.'

'From my side maybe, not from yours.' Keeping his eyes on the leather pouch, he extracted a pinch of tobacco. The pale skin of his scalp streaked with strands of grey was helpless, unprotected.

'You're pathetic!' As I left the house I slammed the door so violently it set the windows rattling.

Outside in the dense fog I could barely see far enough along the narrow lane to be sure where I was going. I set off at a brisk pace, head up and arms swinging, converting my anger into speed. I breathed the moist air deep into my lungs, tiny water droplets settled on my face and hair and clung to my sweater. Ghostly hedges shut me in on either side and the rhythmic drip drip pursued me like the restless tapping of a disembodied soul.

One by one they had deserted me. Mohan went unwillingly and I had grieved for him. I was reconciled to Jenny leaving in search of happiness because I wanted her to be happy, but I saw Colin as an essential part of my future and had counted on him being around for years. I wanted everything to remain exactly the way it was and I certainly wasn't prepared to share him with his wife and daughter. A car approached cautiously. The thick air muffled the sound of its engine and dulled the beam of headlights as it crept past forcing me onto the muddy verge. Undeterred I kept on walking until at last the dampness chilled my passion and I slowed to a halt.

Had I learnt nothing? Had I for even one moment considered this from Colin's perspective? He'd made no explicit promises to me and I'd given him only limited encouragement. His first duty was to his family, that was obvious. He was bound to give his marriage one more try. Over the next few months he was going to need someone to confide in and, if this experiment with Susan and Laura came unstuck, well then he would need me around to help pick up the pieces. There was nothing to be gained by losing my temper and risk driving him away. Why on earth would I want to do that? It made no sense.

Colin had finished glossing the skirting board and progressed to the architraves by the time I returned. Without looking up he said, 'I deserve an apology.'

'Okay, I'm sorry. It was childish of me to storm out like that.'

'So why did you?'

'Because I've had your full attention for six months and now suddenly you've looked away.' Perched on the window sill I watched as he continued to apply paint evenly.

'Don't be silly.' He paused mid-stroke and waved the brush at me. 'Look what I'm doing! And you've booked me next weekend as well. You can hardly claim you've been abandoned.'

'I know. It's fine. I understand.' Through the window giant beeches loomed motionless out of the grey fog.

'I think I understand too.' He unscrewed a bottle of white spirit, poured some into a plastic dish and began methodically cleaning his brush. 'First Jenny goes off to find herself a husband. Then I tell you Susan and me are going to give it another go. Feels like everyone's deserting you.'

'Mohan was the first to leave. Don't forget that.' He looked up form his brush cleaning and our eyes met.

'By the way,' I added mischievously. 'You're right about the sex. If I had made love to you it would have been for the wrong reasons.'

He looked alarmed. 'What are the wrong reasons?'

'Out of kindness or pity. As a form of bribery even. I should thank you for saving me from that.'

'Such excoriating honesty!' We both laughed.

Colin came down to help me move and we repeated the process of six months earlier when we'd transported my furniture to Queen's Road, only this time Namita was there to keep an eye on proceedings and provide us with regular refreshments. While we were loading up Mrs Husain crossed the road to find out what was going on. She hung around for a while, watching us manoeuvre my grandmother's oak wardrobe into the van, and apologised for not giving us a hand. She'd just had her nails done, a present from her sister. She displayed them, magenta with silver twirls, for us to admire. Then Mr Hussain called her from the doorway saying it was time she got the boys ready for their maths tuition and she skipped back up the path to her house.

It was late when we finished unloading so Colin stayed with me in the cottage over night. I came downstairs next day to find him on his hands and knees already busy under the worktop.

'Just connecting the washing machine.' He crawled out backwards and began packing spanners into his tool box. 'Will you be okay, Ann?'

'I'll be fine,' I said. 'You get on back to Susan and Laura.'

'You'll phone?' His face wore the familiar peevish expression.

'Try stopping me!'

Suddenly he reached out and gathered me in his arms. I buried my face in his sweater and for a moment we held each other tight. Then I pulled away and studied him at arm's length.

'You made the right decision.'

'I know I did.' He took his pipe and penknife from his pocket and began scraping burnt tobacco into the bin.

'What does Laura say about you smoking?'

He grimaced. 'I've promised her I'll quit before it's born.' He drove off as soon as we'd finished breakfast.

Alone at last I experienced the delicious taste of freedom. I unpacked boxes, arranged and rearranged the furniture, experimented with different combinations of pictures on the walls, tried ornaments in various positions and debated how to order my kitchen drawers and cupboards. At intervals I went outside to feast my eyes on the distant view and breathe the smell of open fields and mud. I stood under the trees, gazed up through their branches and rubbed my palms across their bark. After lunch I strolled into the village to buy stamps. The postmistress was cheerful and inquisitive but mostly the place was deserted, except for a group of children trying to make the most of their half term.

I even enjoyed the daily trek into college and back, a journey which lasted just long enough to act as buffer between work and home. I drove down the dual carriageway isolated in my car yet belonging to the community of commuters. We never spoke but communicated effectively via our vehicles, winking and flashing of lights, increase and decrease in speed, occasional blasts of the horn. We travelled side by side but never met, sharing adversity as we bunched up nose to tail approaching road works or caught up in rush hour traffic, and sharing the relief as blockages cleared and our cars were free to stretch out again in long parallel lines.

Colin visited at intervals and Susan didn't object, in fact she thought the occasional break from each other might prove beneficial to their relationship. Colin told me they coexisted peacefully now there was a common focus but continued to occupy separate bedrooms. People must think he was getting double helpings, he joked, when in fact he wasn't getting any at all! I was relieved to find we were still relaxed and comfortable in each other's company, in spite of the change in his situation.

We walked for miles when he visited, often in drizzling rain, listened to and argued over our favourite CDs and compared notes on our respective pregnancies. Colin described Laura's elaborate preparations for motherhood and boasted he'd been given the honour of decorating the nursery. In return I shared Jenny's news. She and Bhola were living with his parents, which suited Jenny who had no wish to spend all day alone and pregnant in a rented flat.

The weather's getting hotter and my bump's getting bigger. They booked me into a very good nursing home, I like the doctor she's a family friend. I told Bhola in England dad's stay and watch the baby being born but he doesn't like the idea!!!

His mother won't let me buy baby thing's, she says if something goes wrong I'll see them and cry even worse. She wants to do this thing where a woman feeds her pregnant daughter-in-law whatever she fancies. Trouble is most of the things I'm dying to eat you can't get here.

I want a girl and I'm sure it is a girl but I won't mind if it's a boy. Everyone else really wants a boy but they don't say it. Bhola says baby is sure to have brown eye's and dark hair but you never know do you? I can imagine this lovely shade of olive for her skin.

I keep touching my bump and telling myself I'm going to be a mother but I can hardly believe it!! Hope I'll be a good one. I want a Moses basket and a buggy but Bhola couldn't get them in New Market, never mind. We'll love her and that's what matters.

I had no particular interest in babies, not till they were old enough to hold a conversation anyway, then they could be quite engaging. But I did know bringing up a child was no easy matter at the best of times and doing it cross-culturally while living with your in-laws was not going to make it any easier.

Soon I was ready to share my house with other guests and began by inviting Namita and Miss Walker over for the afternoon. It was the first time Namita had visited the cottage and she seemed to think it her duty to inspect it thoroughly. She ran her finger over every surface within reach checking for dust and examined the kitchen to see if it contained adequate supplies of food. Eventually she pronounced herself satisfied and sat down to enjoy the plate of hot cross buns and simnel cake I'd bought at the village Spring Fayre. Miss Walker sat primly on the edge of her chair and generally behaved as if she was visiting a member of the aristocracy.

'Just look at that view!' she exclaimed. 'But as Mother used to say, you can't eat the view.' I sent them away with pots of homemade jam and local honey.

I progressed to having my parents to stay for a couple of nights. My father busied himself tidying up the garden and was no trouble but my mother required more entertaining. And of course she subjected me to the usual inquisition, wanting to know if I'd joined anything and how many new friends I'd made, meaning eligible men.

'I hate to think of you alone, Ann.' She frowned.

'Then don't think of me! Alone is how I like to be, you know that. By the way, Jenny's invited me to go out to Kolkata after the baby arrives. She wants me to meet her new family. I think I might go.'

As spring warmed the earth, greys and browns turned green and I was woken much too early by a deafening dawn chorus. Large dollops of whipped cream melted on the branches of the mountain ash behind the cottage and the lilac tree hung its luscious purple cones over the front wall. Weeds overran the garden threatening, if I didn't cut them back, to suffocate the palace while the princess and her courtiers slept. When I drove over to Queen's Road, Namita led me through the kitchen out into the garden and pointed proudly to neat rows of antirrhinums, pansies and calendulas in immaculately weeded borders.

If people in the village asked about Mohan, I told them as much or as little as they wanted to know. I could talk about him because he no longer filled the space between one breath and the next, the gap between my heartbeats. We were separate entities. Days passed without me thinking of Mohan then, suddenly, I heard someone humming in the corridor and there he was beside me. Afterwards I was left with a gnawing loneliness, an ache which could never be filled.

I craved expression beyond words. Having spent my life dissecting texts I found language a troublesome companion. You could always argue with words. I joined an art class for beginners and elected to work in oils, against the advice of the tutor who thought me too ambitious. Oils belonged to the intermediate class, he said, and recommended I try charcoal and pastels. I stuck with my first choice. I loved the paraphernalia, the messy business of linseed oil and turpentine and palette knife. And I didn't do still life as instructed, preferring instead to sculpt abstract shapes from the thick layers of paint.

In the summer I received an email from Jenny, proudly announcing the birth of her son and providing a host of unsavoury detail about the actual process.

> *Ann you MUST come and see baby. Every bit*
> *of him is perfect. He's got black hair sticking up in a*
> *Mohican and his eyes are sort of purple so I suppose*
> *they'll end up being brown. His skin's almost the*
> *same colour as mine but they say babies are mostly*
> *fair to start with and get darker when they get older.*
> *They call him Buro (old man) cos he hasn't got any*
> *teeth!!!*

I want you to see him NOW while he's still new. It's your summer holiday isn't it so you could come but I suppose Christmas is better for you, it's not so hot then. You can bring cracker's and mince pies and Christmas cake and we can have a proper Christmas!!

I'm sending some photo's. Please show them to Mum and let her keep a few. How is she getting on?

Lots and lots of love. See you in December!

Jenny X X X

P.S. I've never been this happy in my whole life.

A package arrived a few days later, post-marked Kolkata and containing a bundle of photographs. One photo showed Jenny smiling delightedly at the tiny baby cradled in her arms, his eyes tightly shut against an alien world. Her husband, Bhola, appeared in the background, his hand resting on Jenny's shoulder in a gesture of adoration rather then possessiveness. He gazed down at the newcomer in surprise, proud but a little over-awed by his responsibilities and looking far too young to be a father.

I took the photos to Queen's Road on my next visit. I wanted to provide Jenny with an accurate report so I watched closely as Namita studied them one by one.

'Buchu, buchu,' she murmured fondly. Then on seeing my expression explained, 'Baby talk.' She selected a photo.

'Come on Buro, I've been waiting a long time for you,' and took it over to the fireplace where she propped it up between Mohan and Chandan.

'But my sons didn't have any children. Whose baby is this?' The face she turned towards me bore such a weight of bewildered pain I found it hard to meet her gaze.

For some time it had been clear Namita remembered she had a husband and two sons, now she'd worked out they were dead and not just temporarily absent from home. How painful it must have been, that lonely journey from first vague inkling to desolate certainty.

'That's right. Mohan and Chandan didn't have children. This is Jenny's baby. Jenny and Bhola. I'll bring you more photos of him when I go out at Christmas.'

'Did I hear you say you're going out to see Jenny?' Miss Walker appeared in the doorway. Catching sight of the packet in my hand she hurriedly put down the tray she was carrying and began studying the photos.

'Oh how sweet! Jenny's looking well, motherhood suits her. So that's her husband. My goodness, he's a handsome fellow! But very young.' She went over to the fireplace. 'Can I have a look?'

'Don't touch,' Namita warned and Miss Walker stopped where she was.

'I wonder if she's feeding him breast or bottle?' Miss Walker mused. 'And do you suppose she can get hold of disposable nappies or do they use terry cotton out there? A lot of work but much better for the environment.' She handed round the cups. She always dug out Namita's best china, according to Mother mugs heralded a drop in standards.

'I expect she has servants to do the washing,' I said.

'I'm going with you.' Namita announced, hands on hips and pouting like a petulant child.

'What, to Kolkata?' Miss Walker looked at her doubtfully. 'I don't think so, Mrs Das. You're not well enough.'

'I want to see Jenny. I have to talk to her. Ann, please take me with you.' Namita's eyes dared me to refuse.

As I told Colin later, it wasn't so much a question of me taking Namita as Namita taking me. In other words I saw her as an asset rather than a liability. He agreed up to a point but wondered if it might be too much for her. She was still vulnerable, he warned, and could easily tip back into psychosis.

CHAPTER FOURTEEN

THE SECOND ANNIVERSARY came and went and I was only temporarily destabilised. Autumn, and I drove to work through billows of honey-comb toffee trees interspersed with splashes of copper and peach. Once in the city my car crawled along suburban streets lined with parchment yellow leaves and I glimpsed the milky green of ancient firs through park railings. I took these colours with me to my art class and tried to capture them on canvas.

Colin's granddaughter arrived. He was utterly besotted and talked of little else. He emailed a constant stream of photos which clogged up my Inbox until eventually IT services added his name to their blocked sender list. Laura reacted badly to the birth and couldn't be left with her daughter so Colin and Susan were permanently on call. It sounded to me as if they were playing out their marital tensions via the baby, competing to be the one who cared the most, and I told him so. He claimed their motives were pure and wouldn't speak to me for days. I apologised and he admitted I might have a point.

I was equally preoccupied with making arrangements for our Kolkata trip. I took the precautionary injections and insisted Namita do likewise. She raised no objection though I guessed she thought them unnecessary. Having consulted with the pharmacist I stocked up on water purifiers and three types of mosquito repellent. Then I amassed a pile of festive bits and pieces, the components of Jenny's English Christmas; a box of crackers top quality, light but squashable when it came to packing, silver tinsel extra long and thick, angel chimes to remind me of my childhood, a miniature fibre optic tree with an ever changing sequence of colours pulsing through its branches. Would the electrics raise suspicion when they showed up on the security scanner and would the voltage be compatible?

Namita bought clothes for Jenny, good quality clothes which wouldn't lose their colour or fall apart in the wash. She claimed to know what styles Jenny liked and what shades suited her. And for the baby she bought toys, carefully selected to stimulate manual dexterity and imagination because she wasn't sure how much Jenny knew about child development. Miss Walker bought children's books, painstakingly vetted for grammatical errors because she wanted him to grow up speaking perfect English.

I spent the night before our departure at Queen's Road so we could make an early start. After breakfast Namita went down the garden and returned with a handful of twigs she'd cut from the holly tree, intending to pack them in her hand luggage. I advised against it citing import regulations.

'Do you think Jenny really wants to see me?' Namita, suddenly doubtful, stood in the middle of the hall with secateurs clasped in one hand and in the other sprays of red berries held cautiously to avoid the prickles.

'Of course she wants to see you! Why do you think she wouldn't?' I looked up from the luggage labels I was writing. Here and there her face was marked by little patches of darker pigmentation and the bags under her eyes looked as if they were full of blood.

'Because of the way I treated her when she lived here. Was I very unkind?'

'Not at all! You and Jenny got along very well. I never heard her complain.' This was not the time to probe her memory and fill in the gaps.

'She was a good daughter-in-law. I couldn't have wished for a better bauma.' And she went outside to throw the holly out with the garden rubbish.

We boarded the aircraft and found ourselves packed in like battery hens with hardly any room to stretch our legs let alone do the exercises recommended to prevent deep vein thrombosis. The confined space gave me an attack of claustrophobia and I had to resort to deep breathing. We observed the safety demonstration and Namita passed me

a handful of barley sugar twists and butter mints to see me
through take off. Once airborne I did my best to forget we
were thousands of feet up in a 50 degree sub zero sky. We
ate the paltry plastic coated meals served up by the cabin
crew on flimsy trays, to be accurate I ate mine plus half of
Namita's because she found the food tasteless. Afterwards
Namita struck up a conversation with the young Bengali
couple sitting next to her and I wondered how she would
field the inevitable questions. Conversations had nowhere
else to go once you'd disclosed the fact your husband and
both sons were dead.

They dimmed the cabin lights to replicate night and
encourage us to sleep. Namita inclined her chair into the
resting position, spread the coarse airline blanket over her
knees and tucked her shawl around her upper body right up
to her chin, but every time I looked up from my book her
eyes were open. After a while the steward came and asked
me to switch off my reading light for the benefit of fellow
passengers. I grumbled but complied.

A man in the seat behind us began snoring. Every so
often the rhythm of his snores was interrupted when a
passenger squeezed past him in the darkness on the way to
the cramped toilets. A baby screamed from the far end of
the cabin and I caught a glimpse of the exhausted parents
walking up and down the aisle in a vain attempt to pacify
it. One woman at the end of our row spent the entire

journey swaddled in her blanket, not emerging even for refreshments. I noticed her reappear fresh faced and perky when we finally touched down in Kolkata and resolved to follow her example on the return flight.

Feeling dishevelled and unrested I followed Namita down the steps from the plane to the tarmac from where we scrambled into a bus, Namita pushing ahead to grab seats for both of us. Kolkata airport had nothing to commend it. Scruffily dressed officials stood around aimlessly and there was a general absence of authority. At Immigration Control we joined the patient queue of British Bengalis who were behaving like tourists in their own land. Most of the computers were either on a go slow or not working at all so we made little progress and Namita added her comments to the many muttered complaints. I had plenty of time to read the notices stencilled on the walls and was appalled by the obscure English and poor spelling.

After an interminable wait we emerged to form yet another queue at the one and only currency exchange counter. When our turn came Namita checked and rechecked their calculations. At last, our transactions complete, we emerged into the airport proper where we were met by an official from the hotel. Jenny would have preferred us to stay with her in-laws but I thought we were better off in a hotel, somewhere to retreat to in case either of us felt we needed to escape. A jostling group of coolies hemmed us in, competing for the right to carry our luggage to the waiting taxi.

'Don't let them. They charge too much.' Namita shielded our suitcases from their eager hands.

'I don't mind paying. They look like they could use some cash.'

'They'll run off with our cases.' She was adamant. 'We'll carry them ourselves.' Reluctantly the hotel courier took charge of the largest suitcase.

The taxi pulled away and Namita sat back and pressed a handkerchief to her nose while I peered out of the window. Dawn was struggling to penetrate the heavy smog and illuminate a ghost world where nothing seemed to be in working order. The hunched lorries and blue and yellow buses parked in lines at the side of the road were covered by a layer of dust. Dust coated the buildings and roadside stalls and obscured the greenery of the occasional shrub and tree and even the aimlessly wandering cows were coloured a dusty grey. A few people were on the move, coughing and spitting, smothered in mufflers and shawls against the surprising cold. We passed huge advertising boards depicting wealthy, well dressed families who sported brilliant smiles. I shivered as we bumped and jolted along the broken roads but in spite of my protests, relayed by Namita, the driver insisted on keeping his window open.

It was a relief to reach the hotel. The grit and dirt had mostly been banished from our rooms, there was drinking water in the fridge and a generous pile of clean towels in the bathroom. We unpacked and managed a couple of hours sleep then made use of the washing facilities. Namita emerged wearing a 'synthetic' sari, more practical than cotton which she preferred but had rejected on the grounds it needed to be starched and ironed.

The flight had left us both with queasy stomachs so we avoided the array of tempting but greasy dishes displayed in the restaurant and ordered a continental breakfast. Namita scooped up the last of the jam and licked the leftover crumbs from her finger tip.

'I'll go to Reception and order a taxi. Then I'll phone Jenny's house to let them know we'll be leaving in ten minutes,' she said.

'I can do it if you like,' I offered.

Namita stood up. 'They wouldn't understand your accent. Your mouth's too soft. They speak Indian English here.'

Kolkata in full daylight was a different story. A chaotic tangle of trams, buses, taxis, tempos, rickshaws and private cars, with pedestrians risking life and limb as they wove their way in and out between the vehicles. Blaring horns seemed to be the principal road safety mechanism. Conductors with hands stuffed full of carefully folded tickets hung out of buses, banging the sides and shouting at whoever was listening to clear the way. Far from being poverty stricken and down trodden, people appeared confident and cheerful, except for the well dressed individuals who sat in the back seats of their chauffeur driven cars looking superior and immensely bored.

On the pavements crows gobbled up phlegm and pecked at discarded food packets made from stitched together leaves. Office workers hurried past carrying briefcases or shoulder bags and schoolchildren with well oiled hair and starched uniforms dawdled to their lessons. Stallholders sold green coconuts for their milk, slicing off the tops with a machete, and cans of Pepsi. The air was choked with fumes and within a very short time I developed a sore throat.

At last our taxi turned into a narrow street and the driver indicated we had arrived. While Namita was busy haggling over the fare I took in the row of slowly decaying mansions, the pot-holes and the verges littered with discarded plastic bags and other household debris. Then suddenly there she was, hurrying towards us, her hair wound up in a knot and her face an all-consuming smile. She'd thrown a shawl over her long house coat but I could see her figure bore the signs of motherhood. I returned Jenny's smile in double measure.

'Jenny!' We held each other close, my cheek pressed into her warm hair. 'You look wonderful.'

'And you look like the typical tourist!' She pulled away laughing and pointed at the bulky rucksack hanging from my shoulder. 'Oh, Ann, it is good to see you.' She turned to Namita who stood to one side watching us.

'Mum! I'm so pleased you came. How are you? How was the journey?'

'Everything's fine now I've seen you.' Namita stepped forward and took Jenny's face between her hands, kissed her on both cheeks then embraced her so fiercely they almost lost their balance. When they parted I saw the tears tremble in Namita's eyes. 'Cholo. Let's go inside,' she said, keeping hold of Jenny's hand.

Jenny led us through large wooden double doors in the outer wall and into a paved area in front of a building of colonial proportions. The lintels were crumbling and plants sprouted from crevices and plateaus in the outer walls. We ascended the steps and on Jenny's instructions removed our shoes before entering the house. She supplied us each with a much used pair of indoor-wearing sandals, men's for me as none of the women's ones came near the breadth of my feet.

'Everyone's out at work,' Jenny explained. 'You'll meet them later. Except Baba, Bhola's father. The company he works for is owned by Arabs. He goes away a lot, to the Middle East. Come on, I'll show you our room.'

We passed through a dingy vestibule packed full of chairs like a waiting room and continued along a dim passageway with a cobweb festooned ceiling. Paint was flaking off the walls, the concrete floor was laced with cracks and everything looked grubby. I wondered what had happened to Jenny's intolerance of dirt. Half way along Jenny popped her head through a doorway, a kitchen possibly, and spoke to someone inside.

At last we reached a large, well lit room the chief feature of which was a truly enormous bed. In contrast to the rest of the house this room sparkled. The floor was tiled in shiny marble while lacquered cupboards and glass fronted showcases glistened against the freshly painted walls.

Jenny pointed proudly to the corner of the room. On a thick cloth spread out on the floor lay a tiny figure, motionless. We went over for a better look. The baby was protected from above by a small framed tent of fine netting. Through the mesh I made out a shock of dark hair, the curve of a chubby cheek and a miniature clenched fist and I noted the rhythm of his sleeping breath as his brand new lungs filled and emptied. So this was what all the fuss was about. Well yes, I did feel a certain fascination, a sense of wonder at the sight of this living being who, only a few months ago, had no independent existence.

'He is rather wonderful,' I conceded. But I was quite content to let him lie there. I had no desire to scoop him up and cradle him in my arms.

'He's absolutely gorgeous,' Jenny sighed.

Namita crouched down. 'He's beautiful. Beautiful and a blessing,' she murmured. Jenny fetched a stool, only a few inches high, so Namita could continue her adoring vigil more comfortably and I wondered if her thoughts were with the grandchildren she would never have. As there were no chairs in the room I joined Jenny on the bed though I didn't even attempt the cross-legged position she adopted with such ease.

'Now tell me about the journey. Did you get a good seat? Did they open your suitcase? Have you brought the things I asked for?'

'Is there such a thing as a good seat?' I said wryly. 'And no they didn't touch our cases.'

I opened my rucksack and handed over the Christmassy bits and pieces. Jenny examined each package with childlike excitement. Miss Walker had sent chocolates which I thought would melt. 'They'll be fine in the fridge,' Jenny said. And a bottle of apricot brandy which I wasn't sure would be permitted in this household. 'No problem,' Jenny said. 'We often have a nightcap.'

A woman wearing a brightly coloured sari and carrying three little dishes came softly into the room on bare feet. Jenny looked up momentarily from her unwrapping.

'Mishti! Remember I told you the shondesh here is much, much nicer than the stuff you get there?'

Namita enquired where the sweets came from and, when Jenny gave her the name of the well known shop, expressed her approval. This led to a discussion of their favourite varieties of mishti, during which Namita came over and joined us on the bed. She tucked her legs under her, twenty years older but far more supple than I was in spite of having spent most of her adult life in England. It felt vaguely embarrassing the three of us sharing a bed in such close proximity, sitting beside someone on a sofa was somehow less intimate, but both Jenny and Namita seemed totally relaxed. The brightly coloured woman handed us each a dish of sweets and returned a few minutes later with glasses of boiled water. She finished serving but remained standing in the doorway, staring directly at me for so long I began to feel uncomfortable.

Jenny looked up again. 'Ann, this is Masi. She works in the kitchen.' I smiled at Masi who pulled her sari more tightly round her shoulders and giggled self-consciously. She disappeared once more and this time came back with miniature cups of tea which Jenny indicated she should place on a little table. This done Masi leant over and whispered something to Jenny.

'She's asking about your hair. She thought all English people had fair hair like mine,' Jenny explained.

'Tell her English people come in all shades of hair and skin colour because our island has been invaded by, and provided refuge to, people from across the globe.' Jenny grimaced and Namita supplied Masi with a simplified version of what I'd said.

We ate balls of soft, uncooked shondesh and shondesh made with fresh date palm molasses and set in pretty moulds, both as good as Jenny said they would be. And we drank sweet milky tea. Namita went to wash the stickiness from her fingers and change into the house-wearing sari Jenny supplied so she could relax more comfortably. I refused the churidar Jenny offered me. Let my clothes get crumpled, I wasn't interested in wearing someone else's things. Later I realised the custom had as much to do with separating outside from inside, preventing contamination of the living space, as with comfort.

Namita lay down saying she was tired so Jenny brought a lep, a thin quilt stuffed with kapok, and spread it over her. I wondered why Namita didn't lie down somewhere more private. Was the whole of life lived out here on the bed? Then Jenny instructed Masi to bring the albums one of which contained photos of her wedding, the other recorded every hour of her son's life or so it seemed as she leafed through it page by page. Then she asked me to describe my cottage and I in turn brought out a stack of photographs taken by my father.

'But what's it like actually living there? I mean, don't you get lonely? Aren't you frightened all by yourself at night?'

'Frightened of what? Burglars or ghosts! The crime rate's much lower than in the city and my cottage isn't haunted.'

'That wouldn't stop me being scared.' When she had finished looking at my photos Jenny sat back. 'Now then tell me all about Colin. I like the sound of him.'

'Colin's a nice man,' Namita said from under her lep.

Before I could respond, the baby woke up and assumed his rightful position at the centre of the universe so that all other activity ceased. Jenny leapt off the bed and Masi hurried in shortly afterwards. The baby arched his back and thrashed his limbs and yelled. Jenny picked him up and emitted a long stream of meaningless babble. Namita sat up and added her equally unintelligible version.

Together we climbed the stairs onto a flat roof edged with flowering plants in fluted clay pots and surrounded by graceful coconut palms. I caught a glimpse of women on neighbouring roofs chatting idly as the warmth of the morning sun dried their long hair. Jenny stripped off the baby's clothes, rubbed his skin with olive oil and placed him in the winter sunshine. He chortled juicily as he kicked his banana legs and grabbed his own feet, pulling them effortlessly up towards his mouth. He strained to roll over onto his front and when he couldn't quite make it his face turned red with frustration.

Jenny said, 'We keep him out of the sun most of the year. But in winter it's good for you. Something to do with vitamins.'

A young boy, goodness knows where he came from, carried up a large tub of warm water. We stood round making amused and admiring noises as baby splashed and gurgled and the boy stood and stared open mouthed at me. After his bath was over Jenny insisted on me holding her son but I found the sensation of his compact little body squirming in my arms quite unpleasant. This confirmed what I had suspected, I was devoid of maternal instinct. I wondered what Mohan would have made of him. I couldn't remember ever seeing Mohan hold a baby but I had seen him keep the children entertained at weddings once or twice and he was good at it. Would Mohan have liked a family? I realised I had never asked. From the start I'd made it clear I did not want children and we'd left it at that.

We went back to Jenny's room and she put the baby to her breast, draping a modest chiffon scarf over the proceedings. I could hear the snuffles and panting as he gulped down the sweet milk. When he resurfaced, Jenny rested him over her shoulder and patted his back. He screamed and went rigid and Jenny began to look as distressed as he sounded. She passed him to Namita who patted more vigorously and he screamed even louder so Masi had a go. Two more women (friends, neighbours, hangers on?) hurried into the room to find out why the precious son and heir was making so much noise.

'Colic,' Jenny informed me. 'He should have grown out of it by now but he's so greedy.'

Masi fetched a baby bottle full of water in which she'd dissolved a special crystal traditionally used to relieve colic. The baby's little stomach grew taut enough to burst but at last his screams turned into exhausted sobs and his eyes closed. With an air of reverence Jenny laid him on the floor again under his miniature mosquito net.

'Isn't he gorgeous?' she beamed.

At midday Bhola's mother came back from the college where she taught history. Her appearance was immaculate, not at all as my colleagues looked after a morning in the classroom. Her perfectly pleated sari was pinned at the shoulder, her dark hair framed her face in smooth layers and she wore crimson lipstick. She greeted Namita with the respect due to one's husband's widowed older cousin and welcomed me warmly before going to check on the baby and exchange a quick word with Jenny. I liked her immediately and, because we were members of the same profession, found her easy to talk to. We swapped accounts of our respective jobs and discovered we shared many opinions but when she disagreed she didn't hesitate to say so.

Lunchtime arrived and we were summoned to sit at a large table in an adjacent high-ceilinged room. Masi brought in a succession of dishes and Bhola's mother spooned the food onto our plates, coaxing and teasing and cajoling us into eating more than we required. Not knowing how many courses were on their way made it hard to judge how much food to accept. Every time I paused for breath there was Bhlola's mother at my elbow urging me to have just one more creamy slice of fried aubergine, another piece of fish smeared in mustard seeds, a ladle of jhol to moisten the rice, a fresh bowl of coriander dal, a taste of last year's pickle, until I no longer knew if this meal was mine or hers. She laughed when I suggested she put all the dishes on the table and let us help ourselves. Eventually, taking my cue from Namita, I formed my hands into a physical barrier against anything more being deposited on my plate. Conversation round the table was limited and confined to food related topics. Evidently eating was a serious business.

When we were able to move, Namita and I resumed our stations on the universal bed while Jenny and her mother-in-law had their meal. Custom dictated the women of the house should only eat once their guests were satisfied. I noticed the baby safely asleep in his corner and prayed he wouldn't wake up. Bhola's mother popped in to say goodbye before disappearing back to college. Jenny brought a couple more leps and settled down next to Namita.

'Aren't you going to sleep?' Namita, cosy under her covering, lifted her head to look at me.

'Come on. It'll help your digestion.' Jenny patted the space beside her then laughed on seeing my frown.

'What, all of us on the same bed?' I said doubtfully though my stomach felt heavy and my back longed to stretch out flat. I lay down near the edge of the bed but I couldn't relax.

'Is she good to you?' Namita's question was directed at Jenny.

'Who? Bhola's mother? Yes she's good to me. She loves having us here, specially baby. One of Bhola's cousins has a mother-in-law from hell. Makes her do all the work around the house. Before she got married her in-laws promised to let her finish college but now they've changed their minds.'

'Does she want to finish college?' I asked.

'Everyone wants to get more qualifications. Bhola wants me to study some more but now I have baby it would be difficult.'

'In England I wasn't very nice to you was I? You know, after they died.' Namita's muffled voice came from the depths of her cocoon.

Jenny jerked the lep clear of her face and shot me a questioning look. I nodded reassurance.

'You were ill, Mum. You couldn't help it.' Jenny continued to look at me as she spoke.

'I wanted to say sorry. I was so miserable and bad tempered and you were so kind. Though you were suffering too.'

'Jenny is kind,' I said. 'She's kind to everyone.'

'Hang on!' Jenny protested. 'It's me that left Mum and came back here. It's me that didn't tell Ann about Chandan's business going bankrupt.'

I opened my mouth to reply but Jenny put her finger to her lips and pointed with her eyes in Namita's direction from where came the sound of slow, deep breathing.

'Hope she doesn't snore.' I whispered. Then as an afterthought, 'Do you?'

Jenny giggled. 'Ask my husband. You'll meet him later.'

I must have drifted off. I was woken by the sound of subdued voices and when I opened my eyes I saw two figures standing not far from where I lay. The woman, her folded arms resting on her stomach, was talking quietly to Namita while the man kept his hands sheepishly in his pockets and all three were looking in my direction. I sat up, bleary eyed and crumpled, and swung my legs over the side of Jenny's bed while Namita introduced me to the couple and their daughter. It was only then I noticed the little girl who every so often peeped out from behind her mother's sari to stare at me for as long as she dared. I managed a few minutes of polite conversation with the husband, who was keen to hear my opinion of the current England cricket team, before I excused myself and made my way to the bathroom which, thank goodness, had been modernised for Jenny's benefit. There at least my privacy was guaranteed.

Bhola didn't come home until evening, just as we were preparing to return to our hotel. He was good looking in a boyish sort of way with his toothpaste advert smile, shiny round cheeks and well oiled curls. He kissed Jenny full on the lips and sat listening to her account of their baby's day while his mother brought him tea and extracted the tiffin box from his bag to be washed ready for when he next needed it. Namita watched Bhola closely and asked for details of his work and friends and hobbies but when she progressed to questions relating to his finances, Jenny intervened.

It was dark by then and Bhola insisted on accompanying us in the taxi back to the hotel. I thought this unnecessary but hadn't the energy to argue. Bhola sat in the front beside the driver and, stretching his arm along the back of the seat, he turned his head towards us so as to make the most of his captive audience.

'Kolkata used to be the capital of India so it's got history but it's a modern city too. There's lots to see. We'll start tomorrow. I'll take you to Victoria Memorial, the museum, Botanical Gardens, 'Splanade, New Market . . . .'

'I hate shopping,' I said. Having been exposed to public scrutiny all day my stock of good manners, meagre at the best of times, was exhausted.

'Did you know,' he went on, 'we're going to run out of water in a few years? It's the biggest problem facing our country at the present time. In Delhi people have to buy water for cooking. How will poor people afford it? There's going to be riots. Kolkata's underground water levels are dangerously low. Plenty of water falls in the rainy season of course, but the city authorities don't have a system for storing it. It's getting worse in the districts as well. My uncle lives in Nadia and he says it used to take twenty minutes to fill his water tank. Now he has to leave the pump running for over an hour.'

Too tired to take any real interest in what he was saying, I looked out of the window and was alarmed by what I saw. Our vehicle was weaving through lines of trucks, overtaking on the left or right whichever had most room, once even going the wrong way up a dual carriageway when our side was blocked. A scooter suddenly appeared out of the gloom a few feet in front of us, close enough for me to look into the frightened eyes of the woman sitting on the back. Our taxi swerved sharply throwing us to one side. Namita screamed. Bhola shouted at our driver.

'Tension korben na! Don't worry,' the driver said with a placatory grin. He continued to drive just as recklessly so I was relieved when we finally arrived at the hotel, said goodbye to Bhola and went inside.

Namita paused outside her room. 'That's how they died isn't it?'

'What do you mean?' I frowned, not understanding.

'Pradip Kumar and the boys. They died in an accident.'

'That's right. They died in a road traffic accident.' I tried to keep my voice even, create a sense of calm. Namita opened the door and I followed her inside. We sat together on the bed, legs hanging over the side, while I reiterated what was known about the accident and the circumstances surrounding it.

'He said the cause of the accident lay in the hands of the driver of the car, I remember now.' Namita's expression was one of painful concentration and she pressed clenched fists into her thighs. 'My husband was driving but that's not to say it was his fault.'

'It was an accident,' I repeated.

'You know, Ann, I still wake up in the night and think I can't go on. Can't go on living without my sons. They were my blessing, the beating of my heart. But then it's morning and I know there isn't any other way. The daylight traps me and I have to keep going.'

'I know,' I said. 'But I think it will get easier, in time.'

Namita's hands relaxed. She kicked off her sandals and drew her feet up under her. 'Tell me what you think of Bhola.'

'He seems okay.' I shrugged. 'Jenny likes him. That's enough.'

'He's a good man. She'll be all right with him.' Namita fixed stern eyes on me. 'And what about you, Ann? Will you be all right?'

I nodded. 'Of course I will.'

I looked at my watch and did the calculation, Colin should still be at his desk. I left Namita to catch up on lost sleep and ran downstairs to arrange an international call through Reception. With Colin as audience I trawled through the day's experiences. I told him my general impression was of a warm and contented household, of course there was a lack of privacy and surely they must fall out sometimes, but I could understand why Jenny relished this model of family life. I complained of exhaustion and Colin pointed out Bengal and babies were both alien territory for me, naturally I was tired.

Then he told me Laura had made up with her baby's father who had moved back in which meant Laura didn't want her parents coming round so often. Somewhat perversely, Susan saw this as a reason to be even more vigilant. She said they needed to be permanently available as baby sitters so Laura could spend time building a sound relationship with her man.

The next day Bhola took Namita and me to New Market. We paced through endless aisles between shops selling the usual handicrafts, carved elephants and mother of pearl inlay boxes, sandalwood Hindu gods, paper knives and key rings, silverware and painted leatherwork, embroidered shawls and cushion covers from Kashmir. I bought two Moghul miniatures, intricate designs painted on silk with brushes made from a single strand of human hair if the sales assistant was to be believed. Local stalls sold mirror-encrusted skirts and tops, fancy churidar, cheap jewellery, hair pieces, nuts and dried fruit, CDs and pirate DVDs. We even saw a shop displaying cakes, beautifully iced but not in the least bit appetising. Namita bought two large blocks of pressed mango, made by mashing the flesh of overripe fruits and spreading the resulting pulp layer upon layer in the sun to dry.

The aisles were arranged like spokes of a wheel and, as many of the stalls were selling the same goods, it was easy to lose your bearings. I was continuously assaulted by men who thrust their grinning faces close to mine, offering to conduct me to their preferred retail outlets or wanting to buy pounds sterling from me at black market rates. More than once I lost my temper and shouted at them to go away but it made no difference. They dispersed briefly only to re-group a few minutes later.

We made the trip in the morning so the place was almost empty, only a few young Indian women with well-groomed hair and heavy make up buying stick-on bindis and perfume. And a few foreigners. I noticed two broad shouldered men in tight suits engaged in serious negotiation over the many purchases piled up on the counter, the whole operation being closely observed by their minder. The stall holder, who didn't know whether to feel honoured or intimidated, had sent out for tea and the best quality biscuits to please his customers.

We kept bumping into one bad tempered woman in baggy shorts and skimpy top whose tattered rucksack looked as though it had traversed the globe. We came across her again in a jewellery shop, fingering a double headed dragon bangle. When Bhola heard the asking price, he stepped forward to warn her she was being grossly overcharged. The ungrateful woman glared at him and announced she was quite happy to pay what the sales assistant asked. Bhola shrivelled with embarrassment. He was keen to show us the meat and fish markets but I said I'd seen enough.

Jenny begged me to go with her to church on Christmas Day. She never went to church in England but this year, finding herself in a place where few people celebrated Christmas, she was determined to go. Bhola approved the plan saying he thought it was important for Jenny to keep up her own cultural traditions. So we left the baby with Masi and Bhola's mother and went off to a church where the congregation was English speaking and everyone was dressed up in bright new clothes. Men fished out their handkerchiefs to wipe sweat from their foreheads and upper lips and women tugged the ends of their saris reverentially over their heads and trapped the cloth between their teeth to keep it in place. We sang English carols at a gradually reducing tempo which drove me mad, listened to the Christmas story in a Mickey Mouse translation and sat through a long and tedious but impassioned sermon. Later, when I phoned him, Colin asked what the minister had said and I couldn't remember a single word.

The young couple sitting on the row in front spent the entire service attempting to hold hands without their respective families noticing. They dropped their arms down the back of their seats and moved them inch by inch, hands flapping hopefully, until they almost touched only to be thwarted by the minister's summons to stand for the next hymn or bend forward in prayer. Every so often one of their relatives, turning to whisper to their neighbour, noticed what was going on and delivered a disapproving nudge. We slipped out before the final hymn because dark patches appeared on Jenny's blouse where milk was starting to leak from her overfull breasts.

So the fortnight rushed by in a blur of baby worship, sightseeing and being stared at, paying attention while children danced and sang for us, smiling more than was customary for me, consuming all kinds of fish while avoiding choking on the bones, sleeping during the day, fielding questions about my future, removing and replacing my shoes, outlining the English system of further education, watching Bhola's mother cook but not being allowed to help and chatting endlessly, some of it trivia though State politics did feature significantly. And it was time for us to leave.

We spent the last day as we had spent much of the holiday, engaged in activities converging on Jenny's bed (by then I was used to sharing the space with anyone who happened to be around). And at Namita's insistence we ate only bland food. That was fine by me, my stomach was still recovering from the farewell feast Bhola's mother had served up the previous night; pulao and luchis fried in the best ghee, moog dal roasted and cooked with fish heads, lobster jhal with coconut pieces, and as much doi (sweet curd firm enough to cut) as I could swallow.

'Look at him!,' Jenny knelt beside her son, hands at the ready. 'He's sitting up by himself.'

'Let me hold him.' Namita reached out and slid the infant closer. He smiled up at her, stretched out a wobbly hand and entwined his fingers in her hair. His little body smelt of warm olive oil and his head of coconut, rubbed into his scalp to make his hair grow thick.

'Bhola sat up at four months. This one's a bit slow.' Bhola's mother was folding laundry, cracking the air with each garment then smoothing out the creases. When it came to bed sheets and cotton saris she and Masi took opposite ends and pulled the cloth taut, corner to corner diagonally, one way then the other before folding it.

Namita said, 'Chandan was walking at nine months. Mohan took longer. He was so fat.' Jenny and I exchanged looks. This was progress, she never referred to them by name. Namita scooped up the baby and settled him on her hip.

'I'm taking him onto the roof.'

'I'll come up with you. Masi can finish this.' Bhola's mother threw down the full length petticoat she was about to fold and followed Namita upstairs. I guessed she wanted to keep an eye on her grandson.

Once Jenny and I were alone I said, 'Namita remembers the accident. She doesn't blame Pradip any more.'

'She's so much better. Did going to the hospital, you know seeing the psychologist, help?'

'She never saw the psychologist. When her appointment came through she said she didn't want to go. She asked me to phone up and cancel it. I suggested she went at least once, to see how she got on, but she refused.'

Jenny looked at me thoughtfully. 'Ann, you've changed.'

'In what way changed?'

'Less angry, quieter. And the way you are with Mum. It's different. I think you're a happier person.' She shook her hair free then deftly twisted it back up into a tighter knot.

'Not sure happy is the right word to describe it,' I said. Contented, yes, living in the village was mostly responsible for that. But happiness implied something more than just the absence of misery, something positive, dynamic. Something to be worked at and maintained.

'What about you?' I looked at Jenny, hemmed in by the demands of those she loved.

'Oh! I'm soooo happy! Can't you tell?' She hugged her knees and shivered to illustrate how happy she was.

Bhola wandered into the room wearing lungi and an old vest which he'd yanked up round his armpits to make it easier for him to scratch his belly.

'Jenny! I've been calling you. Didn't you hear? Have you seen last Friday's paper? I put it on the bureau and someone's moved it. There's an article in there I wanted to cut out.'

'Men!' Jenny shuffled to the edge of the bed and hurried off in search of the missing newspaper.

Chapter Fifteen

I ARRIVED HOME FEELING pretty rough what with jet lag, persistent diarrhoea and a troublesome cough. I must have picked up a stomach bug at the airport along with a chest infection. My parents phoned to check I'd arrived safely and, when they heard I was unwell, threatened to come down to look after me. I succeeded in putting them off by pointing out whatever it was I had must be contagious. Colin was terrified he might carry germs back to Laura's baby so postponed visiting for a week or two. I rarely took sick leave but on this occasion I stayed away from college until I'd fully recovered. Apart from anything else there was a cold snap to contend with.

Being alone in my cottage after two weeks of intense socialising felt like removing corsets, my diaphragm expanded as I breathed in broad and deep. Yet at the same time I was conscious of a vague melancholy, the feeling you get on finishing a good novel or watching the final episode of a classic serial. I spent hours scanning through my photos, reliving the scenes they portrayed and trying to decide which ones to print; Jenny on the roof cuddling the freshly bathed baby in her lap, Bhola and Jenny standing proudly side by side in front of their house, Namita and Bhola's mother on the roof briefly interrupting their conversation to look at the camera. It struck me the photos concealed as much as they revealed. Without the accompanying smells, noise, heat and dust, the bright and sanitised pictures distorted the truth. Everyone smiled for the camera and of course, with the audience I had in mind, there were no snapshots of Masi in the chilly yard at 6 am scrubbing pots and pans with cold water or of the foul open drains choked with sludge that ran beside the street.

Colin finally decided it was safe to visit and I couldn't wait to show him my photographs. He made a satisfying audience, listened attentively to my commentary and asked lots of questions some of which I could answer others which I couldn't. I supplied details of the baby's routine and reported on the state of the roads, for example, but couldn't shed any light on the construction of the Metro or tell him how much Bhola earned. Then Colin talked about his granddaughter, how she mimicked the sounds he made and would stop crying if he played Vivaldi. He took out photos of a chubby little girl, beautifully dressed in designer outfits and grinning in open-mouthed, shiny-eyed delight at the photographer. I mentally filled in Laura's broken nights, frayed temper and readjusting hormones.

I'd been cooped up since returning from Kolkata and was desperate for fresh air so, in spite of the cold drizzle, we put on our walking gear and tramped down the muddy lanes. We walked in silence listening to the steady drip of rain through saturated leaves and the rush of water in a stream swollen by melted snow. Every so often Colin wiped his nose on the back of his glove to remove the drop which kept forming there.

We reached a little bridge and I drew his attention to the metal plaque in the middle, marking the boundary between two parishes, and he drew mine to the row of metal strips riveted to the bevelled coping stones to prevent them moving apart. He insisted we scramble down the slippery bank to inspect the construction of the main arch with its central keystone and edging of narrow slabs sitting proud of the surface.

Then it was my turn to show Colin how to play Pooh Sticks, a lesson he took very seriously. We dropped our twigs into the water at precisely the same moment then waited, impatient and eagle-eyed, for them to reappear on the other side of the bridge. It wasn't easy to tell which stick belonged to whom so Colin suggested we chose distinctive shapes to avoid disputes. Sometimes the twigs didn't come through at all so we tried to work out which was the best spot to drop them from, where they wouldn't get caught in vegetation or drift towards the bank. Then Colin experimented with sticks of different thickness and length, timing each one to a fraction of a second. I stood and watched and felt an unexpected rush of tenderness.

I wanted to replicate for Colin some of the dishes Bhola's mother had cooked so we drove into town to buy the ingredients from the Asian grocers. It was my first visit to the area, I'd left all that to Mohan and more recently to Jenny. I always bought my spices from supermarkets not caring that the range was limited and the prices high. We parked in a narrow lane lined with terraced houses and made our way towards the main road where colourful displays of fruit and vegetables under striped awnings encroached onto the pavement. We chose the busiest shop where women were picking through the boxes, smelling and pressing fruit to test for ripeness, inspecting each individual okra, chilli, bundle of sak before slipping it into their wire basket.

Inside we encountered shelves stacked high with numerous varieties of dal, packets of whole and powdered spices most of which I'd never heard of, at least two dozen different kinds of savoury nibbles, and everything available in enormous quantities if that's what you wanted. There was also a section devoted to hair oil (coconut, almond, jasmine-scented) and cosmetics designed to suit Asian complexions. On the floor, lined up on palettes down the middle of the aisles, lay sacks of chapatti flour and American long grain, premium basmati and Thai fragrant, rice.

At one side there was a halal meat counter and freezers full of unfamiliar fish and convenience foods for busy families, little frozen cubes of ground ginger, garlic, green chilli, and packets of samosas ready for frying. Colin looked around bewildered while I was transported back to Kolkata. We added urid dal, asafoetida, dried tamarind and rose water to the vegetables already in our basket. I even picked up a little round wooden board, rolling pin and wire net for making ruti. When it came to paying I couldn't believe how little all that cost.

'Here, you peel these and I'll cut the onions.' I passed Colin a piece of stem ginger and some garlic cloves.

'This seems rather a lot for the two of us. What does the recipe say?'

'No recipe. Women learn to cook by watching. No measuring or weighing.' I pushed a chopping board and knife towards him.

'Who do they watch?'

'Their mothers until they marry. Then they have to cook the way their mother-in-law does.' I heated oil and tipped in the onion slices.

'And if they don't like the way she cooks?' He was cutting the ginger painstakingly into paper thin strips.

'Tough. They have to please their husbands. Colin! Get a move on!' The onions were turning brown and still the spice mixture wasn't ready. 'Look, I'll finish that. You can entertain me.' I added some chillis to the other spices and switched on the blender.

Colin picked up some potatoes and began juggling them. He added an onion and looked at me for applause. As his concentration wavered the onion landed in the bowl beside me, sending up a spurt of chapatti flour.

'Sorry!' Having fished the onion out and wiped the worktop clean, he picked up the rolling pin and pretended to smoke it like a giant cigar.

'Looks as if Laura's boyfriend will stay around. They're talking of getting married.'

'That's good, isn't it?' I poured the contents of the blender into the pan, mixed in some powdered spices and stirred. 'Shows commitment.'

'Possibly, but Susan doesn't approve. Doesn't think he'll make a good dad.' Colin reached for the bottle and held it up enquiringly. I shook my head and he emptied the remaining liquid into his glass.

'But he's the baby's father!' I added vegetables and sprinkled a little water, trying hard to conjure up a picture of Bhola's mother at her stove and wishing I'd taken notes.

'Biological father, yes. Doesn't mean he'll make a good parent.' Colin peered dubiously into the pan. 'Is it supposed to look like that?'

'No one vetted our fathers. They just got on with it.' None too well in my case, I thought as I mixed water with the flour and began kneading.

'I know just what Susan will be like with this wedding. She'll go to town on it. Laura wants something small scale but that's not going to happen. It's so depressing.'

I was busy rolling rutis and transferring them one by one to the frying pan, the nearest thing in my kitchen to a tawa. My rutis weren't perfect circles like Masi's but when I suspended them on the net above the flame they puffed up just as they were supposed to. It was my turn to seek applause.

'Laura's like me. Avoids trouble, lets her mother have her own way. Her boyfriend won't. He's keeping his head down at the moment but he's a match for Susan. Once they're married there'll be fireworks.'

'If things are that bad,' I heard myself say, 'you'd better get a divorce and marry me.' We looked at each other in stunned silence.

I said, 'I've no idea where that came from,' and resumed rolling balls of dough. Colin said, 'I thought you were supposed to go down on one knee,' and went into the other room to check the latest scores.

We'd finished eating and the table resembled the palette on which I mixed my oil paints, raw sienna and burnt umber, yellow ochre and cadmium red, sap green and viridian smeared over plates and empty serving dishes.

'That was truly amazing! I can't believe you made it.' Colin sat back and patted his stomach.

I surveyed the table. 'And I can't believe we've eaten all of it. I'm pleased with how it turned out, though I'm sure a more discerning tongue would find lots of faults.'

He made a face. 'Hope there are no adverse consequences in the morning.' Then looking at me steadily, grey eyes puzzled, cautious. 'Ann, what you said earlier, about getting married. Have you worked out where that came from?'

'While we were in Kolkata, that's when I realised.' I rested my elbows either side of my plate. 'I was thousands of miles away but you were there with me, quietly in the background. Whenever something interesting happened my first thought was to tell you. Like a child needs to tell its parents, but more than that because I cared about how you were getting on as well. I really missed you, Colin.'

'And I missed you. Spent a lot of time wondering how you were, hoping you and Jenny were enjoying your time together, that it wouldn't all be too much for Namita. Yes, I missed you but that doesn't mean we have to change anything. Our current arrangement works well enough, doesn't it?' I recognised the cat all curled up and cosy in front of the fire, not wanting to be disturbed.

'But now I'm back home I want things to be different.' I looked at him earnestly. 'I don't want to live by myself any more. Being there with Jenny's family made me realise what's missing. Do you understand? I want you around all of the time not just now and then.'

'I'm flattered. But it's a big decision, involving other people. Remember, I'm a granddad.' He glanced instinctively at the packet of photographs lying on the sideboard. 'Divided loyalties.'

I nodded. 'I know. I've thought about that. Laura's welcome to come here. She can bring her family down to stay whenever you like. Actually I think I'd quite enjoy being an honorary grandmother. So long as it's only part-time.'

'But why marriage? Why not just ask me to move in with you?' His voice was slipping into the familiar whine.

'For God's sake, Colin! Why are you making this so difficult?' I stood up, intent on escape, but he reached out and caught my wrist.

'No, don't go storming off. Please. We need to discuss this.' I hesitated for a moment then sat down.

'I said marriage because I want things to be different. Not just more of the same.' I forced myself to speak slowly, patiently.

'In what way different? I don't understand.' He frowned.

'Sex,' I said. His eyebrows shot up in mock horror and I smiled. 'I'm serious. I want our relationship to include the physical. Of course I know we can do that just as well without getting married, and I won't insist on marriage. But symbolically it feels right.'

'The whole thing's got to feel right for me too. You can't just announce we are going to become lovers, or husband and wife, and expect me to fall in line!' He was smiling now.

'Are you saying you don't fancy me?' My eyes challenged him to deny it. 'Can you honestly say you've never imagined the two of us making love?'

'I'm a bloke, of course I've imagined making love to you. Not recently though. I've got used to thinking of you as my closest friend.' He shrugged and spread his hands.

What else was there to say? I sat there gazing helplessly at the colours on the table turning a few shades darker as the food residues dried out.

'However, I think I could be persuaded.' He took my hand and pressed it gently to his lips. 'I need time to think it through. My job, I could probably do more from home . . . .'

'If you need too much persuasion then it's not going to work.' I put my arm around his shoulders and pulled him towards me. He turned and we kissed lightly on the mouth.

'I think I've just been persuaded,' he said. We kissed more deeply this time. I flushed with the flow of emotion between our bodies. And I was relieved to find it had nothing to do with Mohan. I did not feel I was betraying him.

We agreed to take it slowly, let things develop at their own pace. But while I was watching the late news Colin said he was popping out for a minute and I thought, well, not that slowly then! We went upstairs together and took our clothes off. Once we were in bed we kept our eyes shut and didn't inspect each other's nakedness. I had to guide his hands, inviting them to touch my breasts and reach down between my legs. When I lagged behind he was considerate and, moving slowly, waited for me to catch up. The climax when it came was more complete and satisfying than I could achieve by myself, though not so exquisite. Afterwards I heard Colin come out of the bathroom and go back to his own bed as though he thought waking up together would be too much intimacy all at once.

We were a little shy at breakfast but the awkwardness had evaporated by the time we poured our second coffees. Colin went out to buy a selection of Sunday papers and we spent the morning sprawled together on the sofa exchanging supplements and crossword clues. When we became bored Colin suggested we go to bed again and this time we explored each other's bodies in the daylight. We compared the tautness of Colin's paunch, which he attributed to quitting nicotine, to the soft layers encircling my waist. I finger combed the grey fuzz covering his chest, as thick and tangled as his eyebrows. He was surprised by the dark hair on my legs and I explained I hadn't shaved them since Mohan died but might start again if he wanted me to. He said he wasn't bothered either way so long as I didn't take to wearing mini-skirts. This time when we made love I came first and it was Colin who hurried to catch up.

Namita phoned and invited us over for tea. I would much rather have spent the afternoon at home but Colin insisted we accept her invitation. Namita opened the door and scanned us intently for a few moments, then broke into a wide smile and congratulated us.

'How did you know?' I asked.

'Just look in the mirror!' She leaned forward to kiss my cheek and I let her. 'You have my blessing.'

Once inside, Namita gestured towards the furniture which she'd pushed towards the middle of the room and covered with old sheets.

'Excuse the mess. I'm having the decorators in.'

'What colour have you chosen?' Colin inclined his head thoughtfully.

Namita produced a chart and pointed to one of the little squares. I peered at the label.

'Cornflower. The exact shade of Jenny's eyes,' I said and looked at Namita who nodded.

'Yes, that's why I chose it.'

'But it's not that different from what you've got already! Why not go for one of these?' Colin took the chart and stabbed his finger at the reds and pinks.

'Colin!' I grabbed the chart from him.

'I don't want to change it that much,' Namita laughed. 'Just make it a bit more cheerful.' She lowered herself into the high-backed chair and we occupied the sofa.

'No sign of Miss Walker?' I glanced at my watch. 'She must have noticed the car by now.'

'Oh, I meant to tell you.' Namita looked concerned. 'Miss Walker's in hospital. She was going out of her back door and tripped over the step. Fractured her hip. They won't let her come home till she can manage everything herself again. She'd be better in a bungalow but who's going to organise it? Poor thing, she's got no family.'

Colin picked up the local paper lying on the coffee table and turned to the property pages. 'What about you, Namita, do you fancy living in something smaller, more manageable?'

'I'll never move from here. Never. This is where I find them, in every corner of the house.' She looked at Colin sharply to check he'd understood. 'I mean Pradip and the boys. I hear him singing in the kitchen when he comes in from the garden and I hear them bouncing their basketball at the back. Once I heard them talking, all three of them, but I couldn't hear what they said.'

It was getting late by the time we left. I noticed Mr Nagra's hooded figure disappearing down the road in the direction of his favourite watering hole. The air was frosty and the sky already full of crystal stars, it would be cold under the lamppost tonight. Colin strained against his seat belt as he rummaged in the CD compartment.

I said, 'She kissed me! Did you notice? Namita kissed my cheek.'

Colin found what he was looking for and we drove off to the strains of Brandenburg 4, played in this version on treble recorders (whatever Bach meant by *flauti d'echo*), with Oistrakh junior as conductor and soloist. I loved the opening movement, so clean, so pure. Sometimes the violin danced with the two recorders hand in hand, sometimes it chased them in and out or spun them round until they were dizzy, and sometimes it wove an elaborate filigree of notes around the recorders in a dazzling display of virtuosity. But the innocent pair were not intimidated. Each time the violin paused for breath they stepped forward and sang their simple motif in unison.

We drove on down well lit city streets, past bright shop fronts and lines of curtained windows then out onto the dual carriageway where an eerie light shone remotely from on high. Eventually the lampposts petered out altogether and there was nothing to guide us but the beam of our own headlights.

ABOUT THE AUTHOR

THE AUTHOR GREW up in small towns and villages across Britain. After graduating, she went to India as a volunteer intending to return and work in the field of Community Relations. This plan was thwarted when a Bengali colleague introduced her an older brother to the author—within a few months the couple were married and setting up home in Kolkata! They eventually settled in Britain for the sake of their disabled daughter, initially in rural areas of the north and later in the multi-cultural environment of a Midlands city.

Alison Mukherjee's working life has been divided between social work and teaching in schools and college. In 2001 she gained a PhD for her work on the Bengali translations of the Hebrew psalms and the following year her first novel, Nirmal Babu's Bride, was published by Indialog Publications.

The author has two daughters and a son and lives with her husband in the Midlands.

Lightning Source UK Ltd.
Milton Keynes UK
UKOW04f1945061013

218584UK00001B/3/P